COMING HOME

"Why are you still trying to make it work with Arthur?" he asked, turning to face her as they got into the living room.

"Because I always knew we were meant to be together. You said it yourself. Your first love is special. You never forget it."

"He was an idiot to let you go. And from what I've seen, he hasn't improved with age."

"He's trying."

"Great, give him an A for effort and tell him he's too late."

"Why? Because I let you kiss me?"

"Yes, and because you enjoyed it."

"I've been kissed before. That doesn't prove anything."

His thumb brushed across her lips and she gasped at the subtle intimacy. "Does he make you feel like this?"

"No, but . . . I—" She stepped back and his hand fell away, but he stepped toward her and reached for her again, and Charlie found herself retreating, with him slowly following—until her back hit the wall. "He loves me," she said desperately.

"You care about me, too," he said definitely, as he closed the small remaining space between them until he was only inches away. "Isn't it obvious to you that we could have something amazing together?"

"No, that's not obvious to me," she denied. "Not at all. There's never been anything but friendship between us."

"I think that's changing," he said, lowering his head slowly. Charlie waited, holding her breath, unable to protest or to look away from the glint in his coffee-colored eyes. His hands came up to her waist and he held her, gently, as his lips met hers.

BOOK YOUR PLACE ON OUR WEBSITE AND MAKE THE ARABESQUE ROMANCE CONNECTION!

We've created a customized website just for our very special Arabesque readers, where you can get the inside scoop on everything that's going on with Arabesque romance novels.

When you come online, you'll have the exciting opportunity to:

- View covers of upcoming books

- Learn about our future publishing schedule (listed by publication month and author)

- Find out when your favorite authors will be visiting a city near you

- Search for and order backlist books

- Check out author bios and background information

- Send e-mail to your favorite authors

- Join us in weekly chats with authors, readers and other guests

- Get writing guidelines

- AND MUCH MORE!

Visit our website at
http://www.arabesquebooks.com

COMING HOME

Roberta Gayle

BET Publications, LLC
http://www.bet.com
http://www.arabesquebooks.com

ARABESQUE BOOKS are published by

BET Publications, LLC
c/o BET BOOKS
One BET Plaza
1900 W Place NE
Washington, DC 20018-1211

All Kensington Titles, Imprints, and Distributed Lines are available at special quantity discounts for bulk purchases for sales promotions, premiums, fund-raising, and educational or institutional use. Special book excerpts or customized printings can also be created to fit specific needs. For details, write or phone the office of the Kensington special sales manager: Kensington Publishing Corp., 850 Third Avenue, New York, NY 10022, attn: Special Sales Department, Phone: 1-800-221-2647.

BET Books is a trademark of Black Entertainment Television, Inc. ARABESQUE, the ARABESQUE logo, and the BET BOOKS logo are trademarks and registered trademarks.

First Printing: August 2002
10 9 8 7 6 5 4 3 2

Printed in the United States of America

I'd like to dedicate COMING HOME to my old friend, Kathy Bowers Comfort, and my new friend, Richard Comfort. Thank you for sharing your little farm with me. I'd also like to acknowledge John Brummer, D.P.F., for the information about what a country doctor might have in his bag of tricks, and Laura Modlin, researcher extraordinaire.

Part One

One

The lunchroom at the Darby school was a large rectangular room, thirty feet deep and forty feet long, located in the basement of the sturdy old brick building. At the end of the school day, for events such as PTA meetings, the tables were collapsed and pushed up against the walls, and folding chairs were arranged in rows up to the wooden podium that was wheeled from the storage closet to the front of the room. That was how Charlotte Ann Brown was used to seeing it. But today, as the lunchroom monitor, she was seeing this room as it was intended to function—as a cafeteria for 150 students aged four to ten.

The kindergarteners ate before the other classes, filling only one of the long standard-issue tables with their built-in benches. The children's voices bounced off of the tiled floors to the twenty-foot ceiling and were barely dampened by whitewashed brick walls.

Leanna Holmes threw a grape in Ben Wrigley's mouth

and started to giggle hysterically. "I did it, I did it!" she yelled. Charlie, volunteer monitor, was the only one who was watching. Leanna's classmates paid no attention to her. They were busy examining the contents of their lunch boxes.

"So what? I'm the one who caught it," Ben claimed. "Now it's my turn." He grabbed her lunch bag out of her hand. Leanna's triumphant expression melted away as she tried to snatch it back, but he pivoted away, digging inside for more grapes. With no other recourse available, the little girl promptly dissolved into tears. Charlie started toward the combatants, but she stopped when Emma Jamison, the biggest girl in the class, stepped between the two children.

"Give her her lunch back," Emma said menacingly. Ben reluctantly obeyed. Emma was six inches taller than Ben, and everyone else in the class, and when she gave a command, they paid attention. It was a good thing she was a nice girl, Charlie thought. That much power was dangerous.

"Okay, guys, I'll be back after lunch," Mrs. Baum sing-songed. The five-year-olds barely noticed her departure, but Charlie watched the retreating figure until she disappeared from view, feeling abandoned. The kindergarten teacher had spotted Charlie that morning when she dropped her son, Deon, off, and had begged her to supervise the class during lunch because she needed an hour to prepare for a conference. She knew Charlie quite well, and knew as well as anyone that she would not be able to say no. That had always been a problem of hers. She was much too accommodating.

Not, Charlie rationalized, that she didn't owe it to Gretchen Baum to help her out after all the times that Charlie had roped her into monitoring bake sales and hosting parent-teacher breakfast discussions. Besides, she hadn't ever done any lunchroom duty for her son's class because her work had made it impossible to come to school in the middle of the day when her son was in this woman's kindergarten class five years earlier, so . . . it was only fair that she put in an hour or two now. Right?

Although she always tried to help out with anything that was needed when she was in the school in the early morning and in the evenings, before and after work, there was always so much more that needed to be done. As the secretary of the PTA, Charlie tried to do her part for the Darby school, but that was mostly paperwork and was generally pretty boring. This, on the other hand, seemed like it might be fun and that was why, Charlie told herself, she agreed to be responsible for the entire kindergarten for the next half hour or so. It wasn't because she'd been played by a woman who looked like Della Reese and sounded like Shari Lewis. True, there were other things she should have been doing on this one, oh so rare weekday off, but she looked around at the kids with their big, round eyes, and gap-toothed smiles, and she honestly couldn't think of anywhere else she'd rather be.

Charlie felt nostalgic for the days when her son had been this small and cute. Deon was ten, and had always been big for his age, right from the start, but he *was* under three feet tall once. Back then he had the same minuscule hands and size-one feet these munchkins had, and that curious, open expression that made them look more like little baby birds than tiny humans. She missed that stage sometimes. He had hugged her a lot then.

A good mother wanted her child to grow, of course, and become more and more independent, until he was a strong, self-reliant man. And Charlie wanted that. It was her top priority, her primary goal in life. But—and it was a big but—there was a part of Charlie that wished her baby would stay her baby forever. The problem with being a mom was that the desire to care for her child, to protect him, never left her, not for a minute, while the child himself disappeared before her eyes.

She knew she wasn't unique in this feeling. Shrinks made millions on it. Writers had been exploring the paradox since . . . well, probably since the first person put paint to papyrus. What else, after all, was the story of the return of the prodigal? Even before the Bible, in the great myths of all cultures, stories had focused on birds who spread their wings and flew away, out of their parents' control. Fifty thousand years ago, cave men and women probably watched their baby's first steps with the same strange mix of joy and fear.

Every generation went through it, and she guessed it would continue on forever—the eternal struggle. Kids would always want their parents to let them go their own way. Parents didn't know how to let go, despite having been young once themselves and having felt exactly the same way. She didn't want to be one of those mothers who smothered her child. She tried to give Deon room to grow, but he was only ten years old, and that was too soon for a formal declaration of independence in her opinion.

Since she never knew her mother and father, she never had the opportunity to wish they would leave her alone to live her life. Dad left before she was born, probably because he was already married to someone other than Mom. Mom left for reasons Charlie never clearly understood. Nana had been a great substitute parent, but she wasn't Charlie's mother and she didn't pretend she was. Charlie missed the mother she never knew. She dreamed of meeting the woman she'd seen in the photographs in her grandmother's album.

She was probably wrong, but she would have sworn on a stack of Bibles that if her mother walked back into her life today, she'd be grateful for anything the woman had to offer. She wouldn't resent any maternal advice. On the contrary, she'd welcome any chance to talk to Clarice

Brown, any token of affection from the woman. If her mother walked up to her right now and gave her a hat or something to keep her warm on this nippy fall day, she would be careful to hold on to it. If Clarice spent precious time and money buying some item she thought her daughter needed and would really like, Charlie would definitely not turn snide or sarcastic or tell her that the loss of a hat bought at the bargain bin at the 99-Cent Store was not worth making a fuss over. Charlie spent six dollars on that stupid Redskins hat. Deon had no right to lose it the minute he walked out of her house.

It was not, actually, the five-year age difference that separated these adorable little tykes from the prepubescent youngsters in her son's fifth grade class—it was the lack of cynicism. The boys—including her son—who invaded her house regularly searching for sustenance and guzzling down whole cartons of milk in one sitting were too cool to ever again appear that vulnerable. As much as they needed her, as much as she knew Deon needed her, none of them would ever admit it. These little creatures were so sweet and innocent, so obviously defenseless, they just screamed need.

Charlie looked around at the pure, unsullied faces of Mrs. Baum's kindergarten class and blessed the babbling five-year-olds for reminding her of the sweet, innocent baby her own son had been. On days like this one, it was hard to remember why she had taken on the impossible task of raising her son by herself. She was grateful for the reminder.

She noticed the commotion at the opposite end of the table just before a little girl's piercing scream split the air. The high-pitched shriek of a child could split an eardrum, Charlie had read once, and she believed it. It was probably one of those survival things. Kids didn't have a lot of strength, or wisdom, so their strong little lungs were their primary weapon. She was separating the combatants and checking for injuries before she was even conscious that she'd traveled the length of the Formica table.

Trina Mitchell sobbed wetly and raised her tawny arm for Charlie's inspection. A perfect impression of a five-year-old's baby teeth was imprinted on the soft underside of her skinny forearm. The skin hadn't been broken. Charlie waved away the student teacher who started toward her. She had enough to do just trying to maintain order at the other end of the table.

"Sit down!" Charlie commanded. The children who had gathered around scrambled back into their seats. All except for Trina, of course, who was still quietly blubbering. "You'll be okay, honey," Charlie reassured her. "No blood, no boo-boo. See?"

"B-but I b-banged my elbow on the table and it still hurts," the little girl whimpered.

Charlie couldn't find a mark on the child, but if she hit her funny bone it could be a while before the sensation faded. "It'll be all right." She spoke soothingly while wiping away Trina's tears. "You'll be fine. See, it's already fading."

The tears had already ebbed and the only sound that was audible as Charlie turned to face the boy sitting next to her was Trina's sniffling.

"Danny Underhill, did you bite her?"

The boy was shaking his head in denial before she'd finished asking the question. "I didn't do it. We were just playing dinosaur."

"So who's the T-rex?" Charlie asked in her best no-nonsense voice, her hands on her hips.

"There wasn't any. I was a leaf eater," Danny proclaimed. "A duckbill."

Young voices rang out in a chorus. "Me, too. Me, too."

"I'm a triceratops," Lesley Barnes volunteered.

"Brontosaurus," someone else chimed in.

"Pterodactyl."

Charlie noticed that only a few children remained silent, those closest to her, including Trina and the two little girls sitting on either side of her. All three looked away guiltily when she asked, "Who were the meat eaters?"

All eyes turned to that section of the table. "We're a raptor family," Trina said softly. "We were just showing those guys that getting eaten wouldn't hurt." The other two girls held up their arms and Charlie saw the identical faint impression on all three.

"You bit each other?" she asked, astounded.

"It didn't hurt," said the biggest of the three, Kathy Turner.

The fracas over and the matter resolved, the children got back to the all-important business of eating their lunches. They chattered about the game of dinosaur they were going to play at recess.

"They've been in school six weeks," Charlie muttered to herself. "We've got almost the whole school year left." She didn't know how the teachers managed to keep their energy up through the entire year. She would be ready to collapse after spending an hour with these little monsters.

On her way out of the school, Charlie stopped in the teachers' lounge to pick up a permission form for Deon's next school trip. Steven Parker was sitting on the couch, apparently doing some paperwork. He had come to teach physical education at the Darby school the same year that her son had started kindergarten, and they had become good friends. Their children were in the same class, and they baby-sat for each other, played bridge with two of the other moms, and often worked on PTA events and functions together.

"What are you writing?" she asked, nosily.

"Stats for the b'ball team," he answered, without looking up. "They might as well learn a little math while we play."

She nodded. "Sounds like a good idea to me," she said approvingly.

"What are you doing here in the middle of the day? Is Deon okay?" he asked, still immersed in his work.

"Yeah, he's fine. Roger gave me the day off," she announced. "He suddenly realized that I haven't taken sick leave or a personal day in six months and so he told me to take a day this week, and two more before the end of the month."

"Wow! How did you manage that?" Steve asked, so surprised that he actually paused in his calculations to look at her.

"I didn't do anything, I swear. He came up with this all by himself." Her anal-retentive boss had completely surprised her, too, with the suggestion, though once he explained his reasoning, she understood completely "He doesn't want me to accumulate any more days off. He's afraid I'm going to take a week-long holiday."

"Only Roger could manage to do something so nice and insult you at the same time," Steve commented, shaking his head.

Roger Wheeler was a pain, but this small new twist to his quirky personality was one that Charlie could definitely live with. She planned to do a couple of chores: maybe shop, plant some iris bulbs, and then relax until Deon came home from school that evening. It was a rare treat, and Charlie had every intention of enjoying it thoroughly.

"Why are you wasting your day hanging around here?" Steve asked. "Go have some fun!"

"I'm planning to, believe me," Charlie answered.

But he had already gone back to his paperwork. "Uh-huh."

"See you Sunday," she called as she left.

"Sure. See ya," he muttered. They had a standing date for brunch every Sunday in the spring, summer, and fall, because Sunday was the one day of the week when the store where she worked didn't open by eight A.M. and neither she nor Steve had to get their sons to school, or peewee baseball, soccer, or basketball practice. Her son, Deon, was the light of her life, but there was only so much time you could spend talking to a ten-year-old, even if he were interested, which, these days, Deon was not.

Charlie enjoyed socializing with the other mothers in the PTA, and discussing parenting, and venting about men and work and life in general, but her friendship with Steve was unique. He hadn't grown up in Frementon and so, unlike most of her friends and neighbors, he hadn't known her when she was seventeen and pregnant.

They had met on Deon's first day of nursery school. She hadn't seen Steve at the parents' orientation the previous week so, when they ended up sitting next to each other while the teacher introduced himself to the class, she whispered, "Which one is yours?"

He nodded toward a pint-sized version of himself. "The short one, over there. You?"

She pointed to her son with her chin. "His name is Deon."

"Mine is Mike. And I'm Steven Parker."

"Charlotte Brown," she introduced herself, as she always did. Calling herself Charlie Brown invited silly responses and even the occasional raised eyebrow.

Steve was busy watching his son. The children had been told to sit at small tables decorated with animal decals and other colorful items. The parents, for the most part, hovered near the doorway. One or two nervous mothers sat next to their little ones as the class got under way.

"Do you know how long we're allowed to stay here?" Steve asked, sotto voce.

"At the orientation the teacher said we could stay as long as we wanted. Some kids take longer to adjust than others and if your child is crying and clinging, it may mean he or she needs you here."

Steve looked toward his son and shook his head. Charlie followed his gaze. Mike was completely absorbed in what his teacher, David, was saying. "I don't think I'm going to have a problem. He's already forgotten all about me," Steve said, smiling wryly.

Charlie could sympathize. "Deon started in preschool when he was three. The minute we got there, he walked away without a backward glance. A week or so later, right around the time that I started adjusting to his being someone else's responsibility for a few hours a day, he started throwing a fit every morning when it was time for me to leave him there."

"Oh, God, I don't think I could take that," Steve said. "Let's see if we can sneak out."

"I don't like to do that," Charlie told him. "I always say good-bye. Wait a minute." Deon glanced her way and she gave him a little wave. He waved back, distractedly, then turned back to the girl sitting next to him. "Okay," she said to Steve. "I'm ready."

"Whew!" Steve said, as they walked away. "That was weird." They ended up having coffee together.

He never asked who, or where, Deon's father was. Strangely enough, Charlie told him anyway. Usually she avoided the topic of her short-lived marriage to her high school sweetheart, but with Steve Parker she felt comfortable talking about it. Married and pregnant at sixteen, divorced and a mother at seventeen, she hadn't had much time in the intervening years to make new friends. It was fun talking with someone who hadn't met Arthur Ross, and hadn't been a witness to her ill-fated romance with the boy. At twenty-one, she didn't know a lot of people from outside the small town she grew up in and they had opinions of their own about the relationship, then and now, that they didn't hesitate to make known. Steve hadn't attended school with Arthur and her from grades one through twelve. She told him her life story, and he listened without commenting. Then he told her about himself.

She and Steve, as it turned out, had a lot in common. He, too, was raising a son alone. His wife had died in a car crash when Michael was an infant. After that first day at the grammar school, they just seemed to gravitate toward each other. As the boys grew older, over the years, they fell into a simple routine. They met every Sunday morning for brunch. They relaxed, ate, drank coffee, and commiserated about the difficulties of raising strong-willed, intelligent, delightful sons whom they loved beyond measure and whom they feared they would ruin forever with their parental short-comings. "Poor man's therapy," her friend Brenda Tremaine called their weekly sessions, and it seemed an apt description. They certainly felt therapeutic. Steve made her feel better about her life, if only by comparison. She had lost her man years ago, had no career, and had the love life of a nun, but at least she was at peace. Steve, on the other hand, had a great job, women who were falling all over themselves to be with him, and a fantastic kid, but he had an obsession—finding the perfect woman to be a mother for his son. He was on a quest, and had been for a couple of years now. But at the rate he was going, it was a hopeless venture. No woman would ever measure up to his exacting standards. Charlie smiled as she walked out the front door of the school, remembering that Steve had another blind date tonight. She couldn't wait to hear about it on Sunday.

Charlie strode out of the old brick building into the cool fall air, and breathed deeply. This time of year was really something to see in the Blue Ridge Mountains of Virginia. It was mid-October, and the leaves on the deciduous trees had just begun to turn. Flashes of golden color shone against the dark pines that dominated the landscape. This mountain range had been worn down, through the millennia, into a series of rippling hills that stood less than a mile above sea level. They were hundreds of centuries older than the sharp, impressive peaks out West, and though Charlie longed to see those awe-inspiring mountains someday, the gentle slopes of the Shenandoah Trails were her home. They enfolded her little house within their long blue shadows, and made her feel peaceful and protected. She loved living here.

The sweltering heat of the past summer was an unpleasant memory, fading slowly as the temperature dropped with every passing autumn day. When winter's unrelenting chill lodged itself in her bones and fingertips, she knew she would remember the summer's warmth fondly, but at the moment she could feel only intense appreciation for the refreshing breeze that wafted lightly over her skin. She felt wonderful. Charlie had an entire afternoon ahead to do whatever she liked. She could do anything, or nothing. It was incredible.

After stopping at the grocery and the hardware store, Charlie headed home. Her farm lay nestled in a valley formed by two nameless, blue-shadowed hills that embraced her eighty-year-old clapboard house, her mishmash of a vegetable garden, the pastureland she rented out in the summers whenever she could find someone to lease it, the sad little orchard that her grandfather had cultivated during his short-lived marriage to Nana (before he went off and got himself killed in the Second World War), and the wooded acreage beyond that extended back up the lower slopes of Hill One and Hill Two as she had affectionately dubbed her mountains.

She brought the groceries inside and put them away, then sank into one of the smooth wooden seats at the kitchen table and breathed a sigh of relief. Her chores were done, and now she had only to please herself. She chose to putter about the farm that generations of Browns had tenanted since before the Civil War. The property had been passed from one woman to another, though never, by same strange twist of fate, from father to son. The first woman to own it was a slave named Sophia Yates, who had accepted ten acres of land from her mistress, along with her freedom, after the war. The name of the mistress was long forgotten, but every Brown remembered the name of her son, Tom Yates, who had tried to reclaim the land after his mother's death and lost it to Sophia in court. That was when she rechristened herself, and her progeny, Brown. And while the descendants of that first owner hadn't all fought for the farm as she had, they had managed to keep most of it in the family.

Bits and pieces of the original acreage had been sold off over time, but the title to the remaining five acres was Charlie's. The farm belonged to her, and she belonged to it. She felt rooted here, connected, but she rarely had the time to sit back, breathe deep, and enjoy the natural beauty around her. Today she did, and it felt good. She was happy.

Charlie was planting iris bulbs by the fence out front when the phone rang. She had brought the portable phone out into the garden, so she dusted the soil off of her hands and picked it up. "Hello?"

"You're home!" Gandy Ross was her ex-husband's grandfather, which made him her son's great-grandfather. The old gentleman had also been her grandmother's lifelong friend, so even after Arthur's defection he'd been a fixture in their house. He had spent long hours with Nana after her stroke, and he and Deon were very close. Charlie loved him, too.

"I got the day off," she explained.

"I'm glad you're there. I didn't know what I was going to say to your answering machine. I hate talking to those things, but I have some big news. I had to call right away!"

"Good news, I hope," she prompted him.

"Great," he answered. "Arthur's coming home. He's taken a position at the hospital at U.V.A. and he'll be living there in Charlottesville. Can you believe it? Our boy is coming home."

Two

Sunday mornings were sacred to Charlie—not because it was the Lord's day, but because it was the one day of the week when she gave herself permission to lie in bed— reading, thinking, or just zoning out—sometimes for as long as an hour after her internal alarm went off at about six. She no longer attended the little A.M.E. church where she'd been a member since childhood. She'd stopped going ten years earlier when Deon was born, unable to handle either the mean-spirited gossip of her high school rivals or the good wishes of well-intentioned friends and supporters. It wasn't that Charlie lacked interest in her neighbors, but in the small rural town everyone knew everyone's business and it was too taxing to face all of Frementon every week, knowing they were judging every move that she made.

For the next nine years—until she died—Nana had spent the better part of her "day of rest" filling Charlie in on everything she'd heard about that day in church—which included the comings and goings of most of the folks in the county. The old woman meant no harm. She prayed for those in trouble, and celebrated the good fortune of the others, and she shared her concern, and her joy, with her granddaughter because she was a caring soul. If all the talk generated by the membership of the A.M.E. congregation was as charitable as Nana's had always been, Charlie might have found her way back to worship.

Unfortunately, most people weren't as kind as her grand-mother, so she had never been back, except for Ruby Brown's laying out. She had been surprised at how comfort-able she felt at that funeral. It was as if she never left. Over the years, Nana had kept her so well informed about the membership that Charlie still felt connected to the commu-nity she had grown up in. The threads of her life were inextricably intertwined with her neighbors. Old Mrs. John-son still smelled like Ben-Gay, Edith Braverman was ex-pecting again, and the Miller twins, whom Charlie had baby-sat for every Saturday night since she was thirteen, had graduated from high school. The new preacher wasn't nearly as fiery as Mr. Shawnel had been, but the small wooden church felt exactly like it had when she was a small girl, sliding back and forth across the worn, wooden pews, or skipping around in her shiny patent-leather shoes. It had been a comfort to celebrate her grandmother's life in the church she loved, but Charlie hadn't been back since, except to visit the graveyard out back every month or so to tend to her grandmother's grave.

She did not feel the slightest inclination to roust Deon out of his warm bed on the one morning of the week when she didn't have to rush off to fulfill her responsibilities—just to dress up for the benefit of Frementon's matrons and present herself at church for their approval. Since she couldn't seem to sleep past seven A.M. no matter how hard she tried, Sunday morning was the perfect time to catch up with her best friend, Steve, who did attend church, and who also had to work the other six days of the week.

This week, Charlie had a real bombshell for Steve. There was no way he could have seen this one coming. She certainly hadn't.

She looked in on her son before she left. Deon always slept like a rock and this morning was no exception. He lay curled up on his side, his shoulders and feet uncovered. No matter how often she came in during the night to tuck him back in, he always ended up the same way. He looked chilly to her, but she knew he wasn't. His internal thermostat was set a lot lower than hers. He slept peacefully. His thick black eyelashes curled up away from his cheek, and his closed eyelids hid the mischievous twinkle that set his face alight during the day.

Charlie often left him sleeping in on Sundays, but today she felt a little strange leaving him alone. She felt awful . . . as if she were sneaking out. Charlie knew perfectly well why she felt so guilty. She was going to tell Steve the big news before she told her son, and that went against her instincts. Deon was the one who would be the most affected by the news of his father's return to Virginia. He would have to be told, and soon. Charlie told herself that she just needed to talk this over with her best buddy first. She needed a plan of action before she spoke to her son.

Steve was waiting at the diner when she walked in. He smiled and waved when he saw her. He was wearing a dark blue suit over a crisp white shirt, and he looked so solid and good and respectable sitting there. She was sure he would be able to tell her just what she should do about the terrible predicament she suddenly found herself in. He was a rock: reliable, protective, sensitive. He might be a little confused about his own life, but he was sure he could help her with hers. And he would, too. That was why he was her best friend.

"So what's this big news you couldn't tell me over the phone?" he asked.

"Give me a minute. I need tea first," she told him as she sat down.

He waved the waitress over. "Talk to me, Charlie. We're not on the telephone now."

"Let me just get settled first," she said, stalling. To the waitress she said, "I really need a cup of tea, right away. It's an emergency."

"No problem, be right back," the young woman responded, and hurried away.

"Tell me about the date last night," she told Steve.

He grimaced. "There's not much to tell. I'd rather hear your news."

"I need a shot of caffeine first. Now, report," she ordered.

The waitress came back to the table with her tea and Charlie ordered her breakfast: eggs, bacon, and toast. "What was this one's name again?" she inquired of Steve, before he could change the subject.

"Serena," he answered, reluctantly. "Serena Wilson."

"And?" she prompted him. "What's up, bud? What aren't you telling me?"

"Charlie," he said sadly, shaking his head. "There's not much else to say. It was just a date." He sighed, defeated. "She was . . . nice," he said, smiling halfheartedly.

"You know I do all my dating vicariously—through you. How am I supposed to do that if you don't give me the details? What did you do? Where did you go?"

"I took her to Jake's Place for dinner and we talked, but we didn't really click."

"Again? What was wrong with this one?" She had been

vetting his dates for over two years now, as Steve searched for the perfect mom. This was all a part of the ritual.

"I don't know. We didn't have a lot to talk about, I guess. She didn't seem to have much to say. About *anything*." He looked at her ruefully. "I tried to draw her out, I really did, Charlie," he said sincerely. Then he went on. "But she didn't have an opinion on any of the subjects I brought up: books, films, politics . . ."

Sometimes his dates were so disastrous that Charlie could only be grateful that her own social life was so uneventful. Other times, though, it was clearly Steve's own reluctance to get involved that made it impossible for him to pursue a real relationship with any of the women he dated. She suspected the latter was true in this case. When he couldn't find anything wrong with a woman, he had a tendency to invent character flaws for her.

Charlie understood why he held back. He was still in love with his late wife. She could understand that. Some small part of her still loved Arthur Ross. The big jerk.

This woman didn't sound that bad. A little boring, perhaps. Steve concluded his litany. "She doesn't have time to read. She doesn't like movies because there are no good women's roles. She's been to D.C. twice in her life and doesn't feel the need to go back there. Or anywhere else. She likes it just fine, right here in Charlottesville."

Without movies, books, and her dreams of adventure in faraway places, Charlie couldn't imagine getting through the week. But that didn't make this woman, Serena, any less marriageable. "Some people are happiest just puttering around their houses, going to work every day, and coming home to their families," she commented.

Steve shook his head. "I don't think so. She hates her job. Which is understandable, since it's at the Department of Motor Vehicles." He made a wry face at Charlie, who laughed out loud.

"All right, so she has a boring job. Not everyone gets to do something they like for a living the way you do. For example, I don't exactly love my work."

"I know, but you have a life," he said.

"I'm sure she does, too."

"I wouldn't be so sure. She says she lives in an apartment in town, but she wants to buy a house in the country. But she's worried that she'll feel too isolated out there."

"Okay," Charlie said. "So what *does* she like to do?"

"I can't quite figure that out. By the way, what's a spin class? She did mention that she liked her spin class."

"It's an exercise class. Stationary bicycling. You know. The wheels spin."

"Yeah," he said, nodding. "She did mention her gym a couple of times."

"Oh, God," Charlie said. "She's one of *them*."

"Them?" He raised an eyebrow.

"Fitness nuts! They're addicted to exercise. A couple of my friends have joined the craze. They work out for hours every day. Perfectly normal women suddenly exhibit this obsessive compulsive behavior."

"At least it's healthy," he remarked.

"It doesn't seem very healthy to me. I don't know if it's the endorphins or what, but it's a really annoying obsession."

"There are worse habits."

"But people don't talk and talk and talk about them. Why anyone thinks anyone else will be interested in their step class, their ab class, or their spinning, is beyond me."

"I get it, I get it," he said, laughing. "So you won't mind if I don't ask this one out again?"

"I would never interfere in your love life, you know that," Charlie informed him.

"Yeah, right," he said sarcastically. "And I suppose it's someone else that always tells me I'm too picky when it comes to women."

"I just think your standards may be a tad high. Just a little," she clarified. "Like this much." She held her thumb and forefinger about an inch apart.

"Okay, it's your turn." Steve changed the subject. "I've told you everything, so tell me. What's up?"

"Well—" Charlie gulped down another mouthful of tea before she told him. "Arthur's coming home."

He reacted with exactly the right degree of shock. "What!" he exclaimed. "Home, here?"

"Yeah, here. He's taken a position at the teaching hospital at U.V.A. He's going to do his residency right here, less than half an hour away."

"Holy Mary, Mother of God!"

Charlie had felt the same way herself when she first heard the news. Two days later, all she could say was, "Wild, huh?"

"Did he call you?"

"No, of course not." She hadn't spoken to Arthur since the previous Christmas when she'd heard his voice on the telephone and told him to hold on while she called Deon. The lines of communication between her ex-husband and herself had been severed about three years before when Deon was old enough to dial his dad's phone number by himself.

"How do you know?" he asked as she shook her head.

"Gandy told me," she explained to him. Arthur's grandfather, Gandy, was an old friend of the family and a very regular visitor in her household. If he wasn't actually sitting in her kitchen, he was on the telephone with his great-grandson. When Charlie first became friendly with Steve, Gandy had gone out of his way to warn her new, very male friend that she was off-limits. She tried to tell the old man that she wouldn't take his grandson back if he came crawling to her on his hands and knees, but he just turned a deaf ear to her protestations, and she gave up. Eventually, he came to accept Steve and his son as part of her extended family, and she just let the subject drop.

"Gandy must be happy," Steve commented. He knew that the elderly man had never given up on his dream that Charlie and Arthur would end up together after all.

"Thrilled," she said with a wry smile.

"And Deon?" he asked.

"I haven't told him yet," she admitted, embarrassed. "I don't know what to say," she offered wanly.

She had hated that Arthur had barely been involved in his son's life all these years but, in a way, it had made things easier. Gandy and Deon—once he was old enough—accepted Arthur's excuses for neglecting to visit over the years. They believed Arthur when he said he couldn't get away from school and, later, the hospital. It didn't seem to faze them that he had only seen his son three times in the past ten years. In fact, they felt *she* was to blame—for refusing to let Deon go to Chicago to visit him. But Charlie had given up on Arthur long ago.

Steve had never shared his thoughts on the subject—not even when she drank too much on New Year's Eve four years ago and cried all over him because he was such a wonderful daddy to his little boy. He let her vent, then and since, without ever commenting one way or the other. She found it comforting, and freeing, to tell him what an idiot she had married. Talking to Steve was safer than talking to anyone else she knew. Not only did she trust him, but he seemed less judgmental than her female friends. Women, when Charlie told them about her situation, always jumped in with war stories of their own about the jerks they had known. Steve didn't do anything like that. He just listened. Now Charlie waited nervously for his opinion.

"Are you sure Gandy hasn't told him already?" he asked skeptically.

"I asked him not to," she explained. "So I don't think he will."

"You're going to have to figure out what you want to do," he said gently.

"I know, I know," Charlie answered, relieved that he didn't seem to disapprove. "I don't want to get Deon's hopes up," she said lamely. She knew she was being a coward, but it made her feel a little better to see that Steve didn't seem totally disgusted with her. "Gandy thinks we're going to be one big happy family now. You should have seen him. He could barely contain himself. But I'm not too sure. Arthur has never been interested in being a real dad. He could have come to see us, or at least his son, but he never did. I did try to get him to come, you know, in the beginning, for Christmas and birthdays and stuff, but he always had to work. What if he still can't find the time? Deon will be crushed."

"You'll work it out," Steve said soothingly. "You have never let that boy down and if his father does, you'll be there for him. He'll know he has you."

Just hearing the words made Charlie feel better. She thought she was a pretty good mother, but ... she could never be absolutely sure. Lots of horrible parents thought they were good mothers and fathers. Her ex probably didn't realize what a truly terrible dad he was. "If he hurts Deon, I'll kill him," she vowed.

"What about you? You have a lot of unfinished business with this guy," Steve pointed out.

"Me I'm not worried about. I'm fine. Arthur can't hurt me anymore." He looked like he might want to argue the point, but Charlie continued before he could say anything. "All I really care about is making sure Deon's okay."

Steve didn't look convinced, but he nodded. "You'll deal, Charlie. You've handled worse."

"He's coming to dinner," she announced.

"Your ex?" he blurted out.

Charlie almost laughed at his startled expression. "Arthur? Heck, no. Gandy."

"Oh."

"Yeah. Oh." She took a deep breath. "I've got to tell Deon before then. Otherwise it'll be too strange. Like a lie. I've never kept any secrets from my son."

"Until now."

"I haven't—" She started to protest, shaking her head.

He stopped her with a simple question. "How long have you known?"

"A day and a half. But I was in denial," she said, excusing herself.

"Uh-huh," he muttered.

"I could just let Gandy tell him tonight," she said doubtfully.

"You could," Steve agreed.

"But it wouldn't feel right."

"Okay."

"Okay what? What's okay? Help me," she pleaded. "What should I say?"

"Why are you asking me? I'm no expert at this kind of thing," Steve exclaimed.

"But, but," Charlie spluttered. "You're a man. And a father!"

"I'm even a son," he added. "What difference does that make?"

"Well, you know." She was grasping at straws and she knew it. Then, inspiration struck. "You're a coach. Aren't coaches supposed to advise other people about how to do things?"

"You want my help with your hook shot, let me know," he answered. "Meanwhile, I've never been in a situation remotely like yours, and I don't have a clue what to tell you."

"Great," Charlie said, ungraciously. "Thanks a lot."

"Sorry," he said, but his tone was unapologetic.

"You're supposed to be my buddy, my pal," she groused. "You're no help at all."

"Tell you what," he offered. "You can practice on me."

"It's better than nothing," she said, then added under her breath, "I guess."

"I heard that. But I'm going to ignore it because I know you're under a lot of pressure at the moment."

"Yes, I am," she said, pouting. "And I was counting on you to make it go away."

"I'm not really into the damsel-in-distress thing. If you wanted a knight on a white steed, you called the wrong guy."

"That has become clear to me," she said, unhappily.

"Haven't you figured out yet that you have the worst judgment when it comes to men?" he said, only half joking.

Three

Charlotte Ann Brown was not what she would call smart. Sure, she read a lot of books, and taught herself to use the computer, but she made some rather stupid choices. She couldn't help thinking about some of the mistakes she had made as she planted fresh flowers by her grandmother's grave.

"Getting married at sixteen was not a brilliant move," she finally said aloud. "Just because you and Gandy thought that it was a match made in heaven did not mean it was a good idea." She didn't voice the thought that getting pregnant was a pretty big mistake, too. She figured her dead grandmother could probably hear what she was thinking, though, so she quickly proclaimed, "I love Deon more than anything, and I wouldn't change it, even if I could ... but if I'd been smart, I would have waited until I was older." Of course, sometimes she felt as if she were a hundred years old. Then again, at moments like this, she felt like a seventeen-year-old girl again, staring at the unmistakably positive pregnancy test, uncertain whether this was the beginning, or the end. "Nana, just give me a hint. What should I do?" She stood silently, waiting, but there was no response from the mums. Nana loved the large football chrysanthemums, so she always tried to buy some as Nana's birthday grew nearer. Luckily, they were fall flowers, and they would last outdoors at this time of year.

Charlie spoke with her grandmother every month or so, and always went home with renewed energy, as if she'd actually gotten a pep talk from the woman who had raised her and nurtured her and pushed her to follow her dreams. This was different, though. Usually, she talked about little things she'd done around the house, and bragged about how well Deon was doing in school, and complained about her idiotic boss. Usually, Charlie led a very ordinary, uneventful life—the most exciting thing that ever happened to her was discovering a wonderful new author among the books that she brought home from the library every week. Usually, her long-lost love stayed lost.

She sighed. Stupid or not, the choices she had made— including her divorce—had shaped her life. She loved her home and the tight-knit little family she'd created, and that was enough. Her grandmother's death left a gaping hole in her heart and in her life, it was true, but her friends tried hard to fill the gap. She was lucky that she had so many people who were there for her. She knew that, and she was thankful.

There was nothing Steve, or her friend Brenda, or anyone else could do to help her at the moment, though. It was all up to her. Things were about to change, and Charlie didn't know if she was equipped to handle that. Every time she thought about the conversation she had to have with her son, about his father's impending arrival, one petty thought kept intruding. How on earth could she compete with the man who had been the love of her life?

She knew what her grandmother would say. Ruby Brown always believed Charlie would make it back to school, though in the last few years before she died the subject was treated with delicacy. "Eventually" was the word that hovered in the air between them whenever they talked about it. Maybe after Deon finished school, Charlie had thought, but she didn't even fantasize about getting her college degree anymore. Not since Nana died. There was nothing like being confronted by your misspent past to inspire the most fool-hardy behavior, though. "I'm not dead yet," she said, glancing around guiltily at the silent headstones. "Maybe I should start now," she said tentatively.

"Arthur got his degree, and he has his residency, and he can just step in any time and have his son, too. It's not fair." She had worked hard at being a good parent. Arthur had not. "I did all the work, and paid the bills, and what have I got to show for it? I mean, I'm proud of Deon and every-thing, but . . ." Her son was growing up fast. And she was stuck in the same old groove, with her dead-end job, and her unpaid work for the school, and the hundreds of thankless tasks that went into making a home for her son.

"Deon doesn't really need me in the evenings. He'd be thrilled if I wasn't around to bug him about doing his home-work and eating his vegetables." Even if he hated it, Charlie knew Deon would support her decision if she decided to go back to school. He was a great kid. "We did a good job with him, Nana." She stood up, looking down the row at the Brown family's history. Most of the nearby headstones marked the resting places of blood relatives. One of her great-great-grandfathers had been the first pastor at the A.M.E. church when it was first built, 120 years after the black members of a Philadelphia Methodist congregation followed John Allen out of their church in 1787 in protest against their segregation and formed the African Methodist Episcopalian church.

As she drove home, Charlie decided it was time she made her own stand against injustice. Why shouldn't she have it all? she asked herself. Other people did. Love, family, education, career—it was all just waiting for her. She just had to get organized. When she arrived home she started making lists. She made to-do lists for fixing up the house, for PTA fund-raising, for long-term goals such as putting in a new shed in the garden when she saved a little money, and exercising daily, and for going back to college. When she was done, she still wasn't sure what to tell Deon about his father. It was a complicated situation and he was only a little boy.

Charlie took a deep breath, squared her shoulders, gathered her thoughts, and went to his room. She knocked on the door before she could lose her nerve.

"Who is it?" he called. He was as fresh as a teenager, but she couldn't help smiling.

"Your mother," she answered dryly. She couldn't resist his goofy sense of humor. He probably got it from her. His dad had always been so serious, so intense. Charlie felt her smile falter, then fade, as she thought about Arthur as he had been when she had walked away from him ten years earlier.

"Enter," Deon called. Charlie went in. She sat on the side of his bed and waited while he finished up with what looked like a homework assignment Then he turned to her, looking up inquisitively into her face.

"Deon," she started slowly. "I know you and Gandy talk about your dad when I'm not around." He looked away, and she hastened to reassure him. "I don't mind. It's okay. Gandy is Arthur's—your Dad's—grandfather, and your great-grandfather, and it's only natural that he . . . well, you two guys . . . umm . . . talk. So . . ." Charlie blurted, then hesitated, unsure of what else to say.

"What?" he asked, looking at her as if she'd grown a second head.

"Well, it's also perfectly natural for him to hope that everything will . . . sort of change now because . . ." She took a deep breath. "Because your father is moving back here, to Charlottesville."

"Really?"

"Really," she confirmed. "He got a job at the medical center." His wide smile left her in no doubt as to his reaction to the news. She struggled on. "Gandy thinks . . . he thinks this means your dad and I are getting back together again, but, you know, just because he thinks it doesn't make it true."

"I know that," Deon said, rolling his eyes. "I'm ten, Mom. I'm not an idiot."

"Okay." She considered backing off, but she couldn't just drop it—not now that she'd finally gotten up the nerve to tell Deon about his father's move to their area. "Your dad is a good man, and I want you to get to know him, but I don't know what's going to happen. All that has really happened so far is that he's got a new job and so he's here in our part of the country. Gandy might think he took the position at the university to be nearer to us, but that doesn't mean he's suddenly going to, I don't know, become super-dad."

"Mom," Deon whined.

"I just don't want you to get your hopes up. No one knows what will happen. Not Gandy, and not me either. We'll just have to wait and see what happens. Okay?"

"Okay," he grudgingly agreed. "But you are still going to see him, right?" The expression in his big brown eyes made it clear that she hadn't made a dent in his hopeful heart.

"Yeah," she said, defeated. "I'm still going to see him." It was pointless to try to reason with him. He was going to wish for what all kids wished for—a mother and father who loved each other and lived together and created the perfect family. Nothing she could say was going to change that.

Now that Deon had been told, the really difficult part of her week was coming up. She had to arrange a meeting with his father. Worse than that, pretty soon she was going to have to face the man. Deon's question, "You are going to see him, aren't you?" echoed in her mind as she prepared dinner for her son, herself, and Gandy Ross, Arthur's grandfather.

The old man arrived in high spirits—which was no big surprise to Charlie. She imagined he'd been walking on air for the past few days. He looked at her questioningly as he entered the kitchen where she was just setting the table.

She nodded. "I told him," she said, answering his silent query.

"About Dad?" Deon asked, careening toward the old man, his skinny arms and legs flying as always, his slim, healthy young body skimming over the tiled floor as if he were jet propelled. Deon sprang into every room; every movement he made was a graceful, sprawling flight from one place to another. His energetic presence in the kitchen always made Charlie feel slightly uneasy, and never more so than when his great-grandfather was around. As he neared Gandy, she sucked in her cheeks and held her breath. She released it with a small hiss as he slid to a stop just two inches from the old man.

Charlie didn't know why she worried. Deon would never hurt Gandy, even if he could, which was doubtful. The gentleman was not particularly fragile. In fact, he was very sturdy, for a great-grandfather. Though his knees had bowed a bit with age, he always stood with his back straight and shoulders squared, like the soldier he had been fifty years ago. He may have thinned down some since that time, but he remained tall, long limbed, and wiry. His slender nut-brown cheeks were still smooth, and the wrinkles worn into his forehead did not detract from the lively twinkle in his round dark eyes. He looked a lot like Deon when he smiled, which was frequently, as evidenced by the deep grooves carved into the skin at the corners of his mouth. Tonight his grin was wide, and very infectious. Charlie could see that her son's happiness at the prospect of seeing Arthur again was increased exponentially by having someone to share it with. She might not feel the same way, but she could still celebrate the event that brought so much joy to the two people who were closer to her heart than anyone else in the world.

"I've got his number," Gandy announced, over dessert.

"Really? Here?" Deon squeaked. At his great-grandfather's nod of confirmation, he looked at Charlie. "Can we call him?"

"He might not be there," she warned.

"He's got an answering machine," Gandy countered.

"Well, then," Charlie said, staring into two identical pairs of round, imploring eyes and knowing she'd been doomed from the start. "We might as well give it a try."

"Yeah!" Deon said, punching the air triumphantly with his fist. Gandy took out his wallet and removed a piece of paper that he slowly unfolded and then carefully smoothed out on the table while Deon got the portable phone. He hesitated, then held it out to her. "Mom?"

Charlie realized this was why she'd been so filled with foreboding all evening. She'd been dreading this moment. She had known it was coming, but hoped it wouldn't happen quite so soon. Part of her, though, had known that these two wouldn't be able to wait. And she didn't have the faintest idea what she would say to her ex-husband. The man had been her life—the sum total of her existence throughout junior high and high school—but he had also been the worst thing that ever happened to her. She had definitely not had enough time to reconcile the contradictory feelings she had for him.

"Let me finish clearing the table first," she said, stalling.

"*Moom,*" her son whined, impatiently.

She quickly stacked the dessert dishes and went to the sink, where she could keep her back to Deon and Gandy while she tried to think.

Charlie always assumed she would get over Arthur Ross in time. She planned to sit next to him with perfect equanimity when Deon graduated from high school. That was what she hoped, anyway. But that was still a long way off. She hadn't had anywhere near enough time to forget, let alone forgive, the boy who had broken her heart, and the man who had never even tried to apologize for deserting his family when she needed him the most. Arthur Ross had caused irreparable harm to her and, she was afraid, to Deon. How could she trust him?

Probably her stupidest move *ever,* she realized with the benefit of hindsight, had been putting her future in the hands of her young husband after Nana had her stroke. Arthur was, like her, only seventeen at the time. Also, like her, he was worried about leaving home and going away to college, and everything else that had seemed to happen to them so suddenly that spring.

Charlie remembered the night that had signaled the beginning of the end. She had been standing at this very sink, helping to prepare dinner, just as she and Nana had on almost every night of Charlie's life, when her grandmother suddenly

slumped over the table, motionless. Charlie had been terrified. Nana was the only family she had ever known, her
new marriage notwithstanding, and she hadn't ever pictured
a world in which the strong, spirited woman hadn't been
there for her. In fact, her grandmother had only just finished
lecturing her on how she had to be unselfish if she wanted
her marriage to work, and told her she had to make up her
mind to take care of Arthur and herself while he went to
college so that they could build a life together. Seconds
before her collapse, Charlie would have sworn that Arthur
was the center of her universe, but by the next day, everything had changed.

Charlie hadn't realized how much she had counted on
Nana to advise and take care of her and her new husband.
Ruby Brown was a sharp-tongued, difficult, affectionate old
woman who guided her granddaughter through every shoal
that life presented to her. She was a constant, guiding star.
Looking at her sixty-eight-year-old body lying so frail and
tiny against the white hospital sheets, Charlie began to grasp
the enormity of how her life was about to change.

Nana's sandalwood skin was so pale. This sickly, weak
shell of a woman couldn't possibly be the grandmother
whose thin arms had carried her until Charlie learned to
walk, and had embraced her so tenderly, yet firmly, on her
wedding night. Those small, feeble, calloused hands couldn't
be the ones that had washed their clothes, made their beds,
mopped this kitchen floor, and fed and clothed them throughout her whole life. This frail creature couldn't be the wise,
wonderful, spiritual old woman who was teaching her to
cook the old family recipes, and telling her the story of the
Brown family so that some day she could write the Brown
family history in the form of short stories or even a novel.

The doctors didn't know, at first, how badly the stroke
would affect her. The first night they could only hope she

would live. By the end of the first week, they were suggesting that Charlie might need to put her grandmother in a nursing home because she would need constant attention, and would barely be able to walk or talk normally again.

Luckily, they were wrong. Nana never recovered the full use of her arms or legs, but she learned to speak pretty clearly and her mind stayed as sharp as a tack. And that left Charlie with an invalid to care for twenty-four hours a day. Arthur didn't know what to do about the mess they had gotten themselves into any more than she did. When Charlie realized that it fell to her to take care of the elderly woman, they talked endlessly about whether it was sensible to stay married or not. Arthur had a full scholarship at Boston College, and Charlie had arranged to graduate early so she could go with him. Since they couldn't figure out what to do, they decided—in the time-honored tradition of teenagers the world over—to wait and see what happened. They were counting on a miracle to rescue them from their predicament. What they got was an unplanned pregnancy.

Charlie waited for Arthur to come home from college and promise he'd take care of everything, but he didn't do that. She was alone and scared, so what else could she do but buy the do-it-yourself divorce kit her favorite librarian recommended? She filled out all the paperwork, hoping the shock and finality of an actual divorce would motivate Arthur to come home and rip up the forms, but that didn't happen either. When he finally showed up, he left it to her to decide. She decided on divorce, for reasons that had more to do with pride than practicality. She didn't want him to be saddled with a sick old woman and a new baby out of obligation. She only wanted him if he wanted her. So she let him go. To her surprise, he went.

The dishes washed, Charlie turned back to the table, to face Gandy's and Deon's anxious brown eyes—eyes that reminded her so forcefully of Arthur Ross that it was almost as if he were there in the room. She couldn't delay any longer.

Charlie nodded at them, and Deon quickly dialed the number, then held the headset out to her. Keeping her expression neutral, she took the telephone from her son and put it to her ear. "Hello, Arthur."

"Char! Hi!" he exclaimed, sounding surprised and genuinely pleased to be speaking with her. "I've been looking forward to seeing you."

Charlie definitely didn't share the sentiment and she couldn't bring herself to say she did. "I've—" She paused, looking into two pairs of expectant brown eyes. "I figured you'd call one of these days." Miraculously, she managed to keep her voice free of recrimination. She could have been speaking to a casual acquaintance—except for the bile she felt rising up at the back of her throat. She forced herself to smile at Deon and Gramps while Arthur spoke into her ear.

"We should probably get together sometime soon."

"Yes," she agreed. She had a few important things to explain to him, namely the guidelines for any relationship he planned to start with his son.

"How about dinner Tuesday?"

"*This* Tuesday? The day after tomorrow?" Charlie asked, completely unprepared. She couldn't face him so soon. She needed time to get ready for this.

"Sure," he said, as if getting together with her were the most natural thing in the world for him. "Are you free?"

"Ummm, I'll have to check my calendar," she spluttered.

"Check your calendar?" Deon repeated surprised. "What for?"

Charlie glared at him. It was true that she didn't go out much, especially on school nights, but her son didn't have to sound quite so incredulous. She did occasionally spend her evenings doing something besides making him dinner. "I'll get back to you, okay?" she said into the phone.

Deon's scornful expression changed abruptly. "No! Wait! I'll get it!" he offered eagerly and ran out of the kitchen before she could stop him.

"Hold on, Arthur," Charlie said reluctantly. Deon was back with her daytimer almost before she finished speaking. He held it out to her, so she took it. "Talk to your son," she ordered. "I'll check my schedule." She thrust the handset at Deon.

He accepted it happily. "Dad, are you coming here to the house?"

Arthur? Here? Charlie looked blindly down at the little black organizer that contained her entire life. She felt overwhelmed at the possibility of Arthur coming into her house again. She didn't think she could handle it. She tried to tune out Deon's hopeful voice as she snapped open her organizer, but she couldn't help hearing the plaintive undertone when he told his father, "You've never seen my room."

As she had expected, Charlie had nothing at all special planned for Tuesday evening. That was when she usually did laundry. If she lied and told Arthur that she was busy that night, she'd have to come up with something to do and somewhere to go. She couldn't sit at home with Deon doing housework. Her son would tell on her. He couldn't keep a secret if he tried.

She just couldn't face her ex in two days. She needed more time.

Charlie decided she'd go to a movie. Maybe Steve or Brenda would be free to go, too. If not, she'd go by herself. Her friends would cover for her. She motioned to Deon to bring her the phone. He finished up with his dad and handed her the phone.

"It's me, Charlie," she said. "I've got something Tuesday night. I'm sorry."

"That's okay," Arthur said magnanimously. "How about Thursday?"

There was no way she could lie twice in the space of less than two minutes, especially not with Deon looking right at her. "Okay," Charlie reluctantly agreed. "Thursday night."

"Where?" he asked.

She thought for a moment. "The Old Route Inn," Charlie told him.

"Great. Seven o'clock?"

"Let's make it eight," she suggested.

"Whatever you say," Arthur agreed. She wished he really meant that—she would have canceled the whole thing and put off seeing him for weeks, or months, maybe even years.

Unfortunately, that just wasn't an option. Charlie didn't think Arthur had any idea what a dilemma he'd created for her with his simple invitation, but that wasn't much comfort at the moment. It was his fault that she was in this situation, and she couldn't help resenting him for it.

At least she didn't have to tell him how thoroughly he'd upset her life. She could retain a modicum of dignity.

She hung up the phone and turned to face Deon and Gramps. They were both grinning like Cheshire Cats. Charlie knew just what they were thinking. She wanted to tell them, firmly and definitively, that there was no way in the world that what they were hoping for would ever happen. She despised Dr. Arthur Ross and wouldn't consider getting back together if they were the last two people on earth. She really wouldn't. But Charlie knew it wouldn't do any good. They wouldn't believe her, no matter what she said or did. They were going to go on hoping and dreaming forever.

Who was she to burst their bubble?

Four

Frementon, Virginia, was so small that there wasn't even a traffic signal at the busiest intersection of the biggest interchange in town, the junction of Routes 99 and 841. Two small blue signs, one reading ENTERING FREMENTON and the other LEAVING FREMENTON, were the only indications that this four-mile stretch of the country highway passed through one of the oldest incorporated townships in the county. Tom's General Store and Gas Station, located at the crossroads, was the only building in the rural landscape. Green pastures stretched back from the side of the road, interspersed with stands of native pine, yellow birch, oak, and maple, and beech trees that grew more abundant as they climbed up to the lightly forested ridges of the blue-green hills.

Charlie thought Frementon was beautiful, despite its size. Her Great-Aunt Emily, her Nana's sister, just couldn't take living in the tiny little town. Like so many Brown women, and men, before her, she found Frementon so confining that she left to move to the big city when her husband came home from World War I. Nana always said she regretted that she lost touch with her sister after Emily moved to Chicago, but, "I don't know why folks are always getting so excited about some big, dirty place where there's no grass under your feet and everyone's crammed in next to each other like sardines in a can. People weren't meant to live that way. We got everything we need right here in Albemarle County."

Within the boundaries of the town, there was one lawyer's office, a tack shop, two dentists, a few hunting and tool stores, and five or six private homes that boasted auto repair facilities in their garages or backyards. There was no mall, or supermarket, and the town's residents shared the schools, Darby Elementary and Roosevelt Junior and Senior High School, and the county fire station with the neighboring towns.

All of which made Tom's General Store, dinky as it was, a rather important fixture in the small country town.

"You're late, Mz. Brown," said her boss as Charlie entered the store on Monday morning.

She checked the watch on her wrist against the clock on the wall—set ten minutes fast today—but didn't bother to argue with him despite the fact that she was actually two minutes early for her shift. "I'm sorry, Roger," Charlie replied. She knew from painful experience that it was a no-win situation. Roger Wheeler seemed to need this little welcoming ritual, and whether the infraction was real or imagined, it was clearly important to him. If the clock on the wall had indicated that she was early, he'd have told her she wouldn't be paid for the time, and she should have spent it on her appearance.

"How are you today?" she asked cheerfully.

"Fine," he grunted, as usual. Then, a few seconds later, "Coffee's made."

Despite his constant complaints about her unprofessional demeanor, her habitual lateness, and her work habits in general, Charlie had managed to keep her job at Tom's for over three years. She worked from eight to four on weekdays, nine to one on Saturday, and eleven to three on Sunday. Roger was often there with her, and he always covered for her when she had to stay home with Deon because he was sick, or leave early to go to a soccer game. He had run the store for three days when she couldn't come in because her grandmother was dying. The store was open morning, noon, and night, whether she was able to work or not. Roger was always available to fill in. Tom's General Store and Gas Station was definitely his top priority. Her position at the general store was the first she had held where the owner of the company expected as much from himself as he asked from his employees.

She'd had jobs in, and been fired from, plenty of similar places over the past ten years and the same mind-numbingly boring, mundane responsibilities had proven to be too much for her to handle while caring for a bedridden elderly woman and a small boy. Roger Wheeler might speak to her with disdain, but he didn't treat her with the disrespect she'd received in so many other places where she'd worked. He didn't say as much, but she believed he had actually come to depend on her. More importantly, he didn't dock her pay as long as she had what he called an acceptable excuse for her absence. And he seemed to accept any excuse that involved caring for her family. Since that was *her* first priority, the job was perfect for Charlie. It was also less than fifteen minutes from her house.

After leaving her coat in the small back room that served as both the store's storage space and her personal escape hatch, Charlie went directly to the front of the store and rearranged the small display of cut flowers and potted plants. She had pleaded and pushed her pigheaded employer into allowing her to establish this small area of the store for a mininursery, but once he agreed to let her buy and sell a small selection of the vibrant, colorful merchandise, he couldn't seem to resist fooling with the stock. Every time she came into the store after he did, Charlie had to reorganize the garden section. Their little tug-of-war over the display kept her on her toes.

His beady little eyes kept darting from where she stood working, to the door. Charlie knew that if a customer entered the store while she was "fiddling with the goods," he'd be muttering about it under his breath for the rest of the day. But she was finished with the chore within minutes, and no one had so much as pulled up outside for gas when she stood back to admire her handiwork. She dusted off her hands and went about her business.

Charlie straightened the shelves and replaced items that had been purchased, swept the floor and wiped down the counters. There was a familiar, comforting flow to the busy-work. As she bustled from task to task, her thoughts were occupied with the SAT registration form she had filled out the previous night. It was a knee-jerk reaction to the return of her ex-husband. Whenever Charlie was upset about Deon or her job, or her paycheck or her life, she dreamed about chucking it all and going away to college. She had filled out that same form many times before, only to discard it after the late-registration date passed. She also ordered the college catalogues, and played with filling out the application—but that was only during major crises.

She smiled, thinking about what Roger would say if he read the things she wrote about him in those applications. In it, she had described him as the world's most compassionate employer, a master of diplomacy with the customers, and an expert in corporate finance. Charlie didn't think that he would even recognize himself from her description, but she was pretty sure that a recommendation from a man who seemed a combination of Gandhi, Churchill, and Gates would carry more weight with a college admissions board than one from a petty bureaucrat whose only saving grace was the soft spot she'd discovered in his hard heart for old women and small children. Charlie almost laughed out loud as she thought about it. Luckily, a customer came in, setting off the tinkling bells above the door with her entrance. It was Jeanine Donner, a high school classmate and one of the worst gossips in town. Her daughter was in Deon's class at school.

"Hi, Charlie," she said as she walked up to the counter.

"Hey, Jeanine. How is Bill liking the new job?" Everyone in Frementon, and in the county, knew everyone's business as soon as it happened, and they, and Charlie, knew Bill Donner had been ecstatic at getting a job managing a horse ranch right outside Charlottesville.

"Bill's good. How are you?"

"We're fine. Just fine. Thanks for asking," Charlie said, trying, and failing, to smile. Just as she knew all about Bill and his new job, she was sure Jeanine knew all about Arthur being back. Between Gandy and Deon, the news of her ex's return would definitely have started circulating by now. Everyone in town would be discussing her family.

There was nothing Charlie could do except ride it out. She certainly couldn't stop people from talking. She hated to be the subject of the rumors, but she had survived the raised eyebrows when she got married, when she got pregnant, and when she got divorced, and she would ride this out, too. In fact, this was nothing compared to that. She was older, wiser, and more mature. They couldn't hurt her.

After all, what could they say, really? As long as she was discreet, and maintained a dignified facade, there wouldn't be any juicy tidbits for the gossips to chew on. She just had to keep her cool. So, even as it became clear, from the growing number of comments made by the customers on Tuesday morning, that the news of Arthur Ross's return had already made the rounds, she managed to keep a lid on her emotions. She couldn't stand to be pitied.

By that afternoon, Charlie was feeling close to the edge. She escaped the watchful eyes of her neighbors by taking a walk through the woods to her house at lunchtime. She sat in the kitchen, eating a leftover chicken breast and trying to think about anything but her impending dinner with her ex-husband. Just as she was about to drown in self-pity, she looked up at the print above the mantel. It was a photo, called *Strange Fruit,* of a tree covered with sneakers hanging by their laces and was one of the very few pieces of modern art her grandmother had liked. Nana bought it in memory of her Great-Aunt Petunia, whose husband had been a local Indian boy who had been lynched. Charlie was ashamed of herself for making such a fuss about a little gossip. It wouldn't kill her.

On her way out of the house, Charlie grabbed the completed SAT application from the drawer where she'd hidden it beneath her maps. She walked swiftly back to work, thinking about how the rest of the afternoon was going to be even worse than the last day and a half had been. Deon would certainly have told at least one of his closest friends about her dinner date with his father. That would have made its way through the grapevine by now, and everyone who came into the store for the next few days would be watching her with avid curiosity. All she could do was to act cool and calm, and then go home and do the same with Deon. And then she would have to go and meet Arthur on Thursday.

When she reached the store, she went around the front to the mailbox before going inside. As she held the registration form over the mail slot, Charlie paused. She'd filled out the form, enclosed her check, and put two stamps on the official-looking envelope, but Charlie just couldn't bring herself to let it go. How could she consider taking the test after all this time? She was too busy for such foolishness. She didn't have time to study, she was a single, working mother. Most importantly, even if she scored 1600 on the college entrance exam, her dead-end job barely paid enough to cover the monthly bills and keep her son fed and clothed. Where the heck would she find the money for college tuition?

She tucked the envelope into her purse and went back into the store. It was impossible. She couldn't go to school. She was barely going to make it through the rest of the day at work. In forty-eight hours she was going to have to sit across the table from Arthur and carry on an actual conversation. She had enough to worry about without adding the pressure of thinking about taking the SATs.

Oh well, Charlie thought. *At least it will be over soon.* If not all of it, at least this day would be done. All she had to do was get through it. Charlie sighed. She'd gotten through worse than this before.

"I can't do this," Charlie said despairingly to Brenda as they walked into Starbucks. "I'm talking about me—not him," she added quickly as her friend gave her a warning look.

"*You* will be fine," Brenda said bracingly. The former Wall Street broker, who had retired at thirty-five to enjoy a quiet life in the country, now knew, as she said, more than she ever cared to know about Dr. Arthur Ross.

They were having coffee before the movie, after a dinner

during which Charlie had thoroughly exhausted the subject of her ex-husband. Charlie was not allowed to mention Arthur's name again. "I need your help here, Bren." She was desperate. "Please," she begged. "I need specific suggestions on what I'm supposed to do."

"You'll do *exactly* what you do with Deon, and Roger, and the PTA, and anyone else you need to handle. You'll take care of it, with style and grace, in a much nicer way than I ever could."

"Thanks," Charlie said, unconsoled.

While Charlie didn't dare to openly defy Brenda Tremaine's moratorium on any discussion of her ex, she did have more she had to say. "But this is different," she whined. "This isn't Roger, or Mrs. Comstock. This is—" She started to say Arthur, but she stopped herself. She needed advice, but she also needed to be very careful. "This is different," Charlie said again, tamely. She was walking a very thin line here, and she did not want to incur her friend's wrath. The woman was from Brooklyn, New York, had grown up on the mean streets, according to the stories she told, and was the toughest, smartest person Charlie had ever met. She was also an avid kickboxer.

Brenda said she needed the daily sessions with her punching bag in order to release the pent-up aggression evoked by life in a backwater town full of polite twits. "It's like living in one of those pastoral watercolors," she often said. "All blurry and washed out, with no sharp edges or really vivid colors." She actually sought Charlie out soon after she moved to town because she heard the gossip about her divorce from some moralistic old biddy. Disappointed as she was that the notorious Ms. Brown wasn't the rebel she'd been led to expect, she still became a friend.

"There is no reason on earth why you should be nervous," Brenda said now. "If anyone should be sweating, it's the jerk. You're not the one who left. You're the best person I know, sister." Brenda didn't call every woman of color her sister. She said she couldn't, especially not down here in the rural South.

"This isn't exactly Alabama," Charlie had pointed out to her, but the former New Yorker contended that the docile females being turned out down here on the farm were not members of her gender or species. She complained that they were breeding and raising a generation of macho male children and sweet, brainless, good girls, all spouting the conservative party line, including each and every hateful slogan coined by such pundits as Newt Gingrich and Pat Buchanan.

"These are black women! Sisters! What do they think they're doing?" she wailed. Brenda had always encouraged Charlie to ignore the hypocrites in town, and stand up against the self-righteous, churchgoing pillars of the community who thought she should be ashamed of her son and herself and hide away from decent people, and especially from the PTA in which she was so active.

"Girlfriend, you're approaching this all wrong. You should plan to bowl him over. He doesn't know you, hasn't seen you or talked to you in ten years. Knock his socks off!"

"Fine," Charlie agreed. "How?"

"Well, for starters, get a better attitude. If you walk into this like you're walking up the steps to the gallows, he's going to know you're scared."

"I am scared."

"Looking like a nervous wreck has never won anyone any battles."

"That's not true. I have been a nervous wreck during most of the key moments of my life and I never hid it well. For example, when my water broke I panicked so bad, I wouldn't get in Gandy's car. I was convinced that it would be safer to walk to the hospital than to drive, and I walked all the way to Route Ninety-nine with my neighbors lining up on the side of the road trying to talk me into getting into the car.''

"That's exactly what I'm talking about," Brenda said. "Grace under fire."

"Grace! Did you hear a word I said? There is nothing graceful about a hysterical pregnant woman waddling up the road while an old man follows her at two miles an hour in a pickup truck."

"You did it your way," Brenda said. "In case I haven't told you this before, you're my hero, Charlie Brown. So stop driving yourself nuts. You'll be great. He'll probably be tearing his hair out by the roots when he sees you again—wishing he hadn't blown it."

Imagining that scenario made Charlie feel slightly better, though she knew her friend would say anything to get her to shut up about her ex, even if it wasn't true. But Brenda did sound pretty sincere. "Thanks. You're my hero, too," she confessed.

"Ah, gimme a break," Brenda retorted.

"No, really!" Charlie insisted. "I love you, Bren."

"You know I love you, too, girl, but all this nonsense is going to make me ill. Come on, let's get to that movie."

"I'm there," Charlie said lightly.

They walked through the mall all the way from Starbucks to the Cineplex speaking of nothing but the film they planned to see. Charlie was still just as freaked out by the idea of meeting her ex-husband in less than forty-eight hours as she had been before, but at least she now knew she had two staunch allies on her side. Between Steve and Brenda, she figured she had a safety net now that she hadn't had when Arthur left her. He couldn't destroy her this time around.

* * *

Charlie waved good-bye to Brenda and turned, stumbling a bit, to walk up the footpath to Steve Parker's front door. She had definitely had too much to drink. Brenda was disgusted with her.

Charlie was embarrassed. She never could handle her liquor. She had only planned to have one little White Russian, to loosen up, as she told Brenda. She knew better, though. She couldn't take one drink without getting tipsy, and tonight that first creamy sip made her feel so relaxed and happy, and she'd been so unhappy when the glass was empty that she threw caution to the winds and ordered a second round. Two White Russians were one and a half drinks past her limit. The third one was the corker.

She let herself in to Steve's house, as quietly as she could, but as she was closing the door behind her, her purse hit the umbrella stand, knocking it over. Steve came out of the living room into the foyer, took one look at her as she tried, in vain, to reinsert the umbrellas in the wicker basket, and crossed his arms on his chest. She couldn't see very well, but he seemed to be smiling.

"Leave them," he instructed.

"Sorry," Charlie said, giving up immediately.

"What have you been doing?" he asked, as he quickly righted the umbrella stand. "As if I didn't know."

"Dinner and a movie," she said, trying to enunciate clearly, and not at all sure that she was succeeding. She leaned against the wall, to hide the shaky condition of her legs.

"Your little outing seems to have done you more harm than good," Steve commented.

"No, no!" she protested. "I feel better than I have in days." He took her arm and led her into the living room.

She held on to him tightly. She didn't want to fall and embarrass herself.

"How many did you have?" Steve wondered aloud.

"Am sh-sorry I'm late though. Sorry," she said again more carefully.

"Charlie, Charlie, Charlie. What am I supposed to do with you?" Steve said, helping her to sit down on his sofa.

"Just two." She held up two fingers as she answered his earlier question. Somehow her purse collided with the coffee table. "It's my metabolism. Booze goesh right to my head."

"Let's get you to bed," her best friend suggested.

"Is Deon asleep?" Charlie asked, surprised.

"It's one A.M. on a school night. What do you think?" Steve smiled dryly.

"Oh." She assimilated that information. "Let me just go give him a little kiss good night." She stood up, but she promptly found herself sitting down again.

"I tucked him in all nice and tight hours ago," Steve assured her. "Now it's your turn. Okay?"

He urged her to lie back on the sofa and took off her shoes.

"Okay," Charlie said. "Don't forget to kiss Deon for me."

"I already did," he told her. "Do you want to take off that coat?"

"Can I have a nice comfy blanket instead?" she asked.

"I think that can be arranged," he agreed.

Charlie held her arm straight up and Steve grabbed the cuff of her jacket and pulled until her hand was free of the sleeve.

"Turn," he ordered brusquely. She flopped onto her back, and he freed her other arm. "Lift, Charlie."

Charlie tried, but she couldn't seem to raise so much as

an eyebrow. "Can't," she told him. That struck her as funny, so she started to giggle. "Can't move."

He pulled the coat out from under her and stood. "I'll be right back."

She closed her eyes, and a moment later she felt him draping a soft, warm afghan over her. "Thanks, Steve," she mumbled, snuggling into the softness. "You're so nice."

"No problem, Charlie." His voice seemed to come from somewhere far, far away.

"Steve?" she called.

"Shhh, quiet," he commanded.

"Steve?" she whispered.

"Yes, Charlie. What?"

"Wait one minute and then I'll open my eyes and we can talk."

"We can talk in the morning," he told her. "Go to sleep now." He dropped a quick kiss on her forehead.

"Okay."

Charlie's last thought before she fell asleep was that Steve was a great guy. It had been a really long time since she'd been tucked in and kissed good night, and she liked it.

Five

As the zero hour approached, Charlie found herself going back to her closet over and over, changing her clothes, her jewelry, and her hairstyle, and—worst of all—agonizing in front of the mirror on the back of the door. She wasn't seventeen years old anymore. She raised her blouse and examined her midriff from the front and from the side as she dialed Brenda's phone number.

"Hey, it's me," she announced when Brenda answered.

"How are you doing?" her friend asked.

"Not good. I've tried on every single thing in my closet, and nothing I own will work for this dinner tonight," Charlie whined.

"What about your blue dress?" Brenda suggested.

"It makes me look old."

"You're twenty-eight," Brenda said in disbelief.

"Right! Last time I saw Arthur I was seventeen, my stomach was flat, my thighs were firm, and I won't even talk about my breasts. Brenda, I didn't have a single gray hair then.''

"You still don't have any.''

"I found one.''

Brenda continued speaking as if she hadn't interrupted. "And you've got a great body. You have *nothing* to worry about.''

"I'm not worried. I just . . . It would be nice if I looked even better than he remembered.''

"You do. Trust me. You were a skinny teenager. You have a woman's body now. Wear the blue dress,'' Brenda said confidently.

"Okay, thanks.''

Charlie knew she still looked pretty good. It wasn't like she was over the hill, yet. She was even mistaken for a college student the last time she drove into Charlottesville. But she didn't think she'd be mistaken for a teenager in her blue silk sheath. She looked at herself in the dress, and saw that it emphasized her bust and the curve of her hip. It ended just above the knee, and she liked that. She was proud of her legs.

She didn't usually examine herself so closely or so critically. She was a healthy, attractive woman—a bit frumpy perhaps, but then she didn't have anyone to dress up for. Deon didn't care what she looked like. She had it on the best authority that she wasn't bad looking, for a mom. The blind dates that she allowed friends to arrange for her on the average of twice a year had never inspired anything more than the purchase of a new dress, or maybe a day at the hairdresser, and, once, a manicure. They had never caused her to doubt herself in this way.

It was almost time to go, and she turned away from the mirror after one more quick look. Her hair was pulled back in a braid and coiled at the nape of her neck. She had decided against the sophisticated silk dress at the last minute, and chosen a satiny skirt with a gauze blouse. Charlie had seen the combination in a magazine and liked it—she thought the free-flowing style made her look younger. The outfit looked dressy, but not too formal. The electric-blue skirt swirled around her thighs, and the cream-colored blouse draped loosely over her bust and torso. Arthur shouldn't have any complaints. She'd even worn a little lipstick and mascara.

She had chosen the Old Route Inn near Charlottesville for their meeting because the restaurant was quiet, and because it was far enough away that she was relatively sure none of Frementon's residents would be there on a Thursday night. Not without her hearing about it, anyway. Just as everyone in town had heard about her date tonight, Charlie knew she would have been informed if anyone she was acquainted with were planning to dine at the inn. Luckily, there were no anniversaries, fiftieth birthday parties, or Lady's Garden Society dinners scheduled for this evening, so she figured she was safe.

Even so, Charlie found herself looking around warily when she got out of her little blue Honda Civic—as if she might have been tailed. It wasn't paranoia, it was perfectly justifiable. This was the first time in three days that she'd actually been out of sight and hearing of her nosy friends and neighbors, a large number of whom seemed to have taken it upon themselves to watch, listen, and advise her in this, her time of trial. Mr. Garrison at the Agfa had advised her yesterday morning that she should definitely consider remarriage. He knew a guy who married the same woman three times, and they were happy as clams. The kindly clerk was far from the first to dispense a helpful word or two. She'd been lectured on the dangers of raising her son without his father, and on the stupidity of trusting the same man twice, and everything in between.

There seemed to be two main camps among her advisors. The first believed she should rekindle her romance with Arthur with a view to remarriage. The second just as firmly advocated suing the man for back child support, and did not seem at all sure that Charlie should allow him unsupervised visits with his son. She tended to side with the latter group, but she was trying to keep an open mind. After all, she hadn't heard Arthur's side of the story yet. She didn't know for sure that he was the callous, unfeeling bastard that she'd labeled him ten years ago. Maybe he really did have a good reason for behaving as he had? She couldn't imagine what it might be, but she had every intention of giving him the benefit of the doubt. For her son's sake.

Finding nothing particularly suspicious in the parking lot, Charlotte went into the inn. Her first fear proved unfounded. He hadn't left town again. Arthur was actually there, in the bar area . . . waiting for her. She breathed a sigh of relief. She had made it, and he had made it. They were, to all intents and purposes, alone again. Finally, after ten years, he had actually shown up exactly when he said he would. It was a miracle. Or, if not a miracle, it was a beginning.

He was watching the door, and when she came inside he stood and smiled. Charlie gave him a weak smile in return. It was all she could manage. She looked him over as she walked toward the table at which he sat. He hadn't changed much. He was still long and lean, just under six feet tall, but his shoulders were wider, and his thin face was a more definite square. She saw the traits in him she'd recognized over the years in Deon: the hazelnut skin tone that was just a shade lighter and redder than hers, the oval eyes, the high bridge of his nose. He wore wire-rimmed glasses when he was sixteen, too, but back then he only wore them to read the blackboard or play baseball, like Deon did. Apparently he wore them all the time now. She wondered briefly if that meant Deon would grow more nearsighted, too, and have to wear his glasses constantly when he grew up.

"Hey, stranger!" She had been practicing the greeting in the mirror for the past three days, but somehow actually using it felt somewhat anticlimactic after all the buildup.

Arthur seemed happy to see her. "Hi, Char," he said, as if it were still 1990 and they were still themselves—the old Charlotte and Arthur—meeting up after school to go find some private place to talk, and neck, and dream of the future. Charlie didn't believe for a minute that he was so oblivious. He might act as if nothing had changed, but Arthur Ross certainly knew everything had changed—and he knew he was the one who was responsible for most of it. Especially the part where they hadn't seen each other, except in passing, in ten long years. He had to be playing it cool. Just like her.

Charlie felt a little uneasy at the thought that she might know how he felt, and that the reason she could guess at his emotions was that she felt the same way. She didn't want to empathize with Arthur Ross. The past ten years had provided her with ample proof that they had *nothing* in common. He had no right to share her feelings. They were hers. He would have to get his own.

She realized how ridiculous she would have sounded trying to explain this to Steve. Or to Brenda. She would sound childish . . . because she was being childish. But she had a right to be as immature as she wanted where her ex-husband was concerned. His immaturity had cost them a marriage, and cost Charlie a lot more than that as well. It was her turn now.

She tried to suppress her resentment. She would not let him get under her skin. She was here for one reason and one reason only . . . to set down the ground rules for any interaction he might want to have with Deon. The hostess showed them to their table in the dining room and Charlie used the short respite to compose herself. They looked over their menus, quickly decided what they wanted to eat, and ordered it. Charlie got a margarita as well. The sour taste would ensure she only sipped the drink. It might only give her Dutch courage, but she needed every little advantage.

"So how have you been?" Arthur asked, breaking the awkward silence that fell when the waitress left them alone.

"Fine," she responded, exasperated with herself and with him. "Just fine."

"I can't wait to see Deon! It's been, what, two years?" he mused.

"Almost three," she said, correcting him. "He's grown about a foot." It was the perfect opportunity. She had figured out a relatively simple set of instructions for him to follow in his dealings with his son. She hesitated as she reviewed them in her mind. She wanted to be very explicit.

"You've done a great job with him," he commented before Charlie could speak. She always felt patronized when he complimented her on the way she was raising Deon. No matter how he said it, it always felt to her that he was being condescending. If he had stopped at that, though, she might have kept a rein on her emotions. Unfortunately, he continued. "It will be great living so near you both." That was debatable, in her opinion. But she kept it to herself, and grew even more annoyed with him. "I'm looking forward to being a full-time father," he went on.

"Right," she said sarcastically. A full-time father? Him? She didn't think so. The opportunity for calm, rational discussion vanished as quickly as it had come. "You don't appear to me to have the slightest conception of what it means to be any kind of father," she said, incensed. The fear and anger that had taken root when she first heard

Arthur was coming home a week ago, and that had been compounded by her feelings of frustration and impotent rage as his presence here in Virginia had disrupted her life, finally boiled over. "You've seen him three times in ten years. That's your track record so far. Those are the facts."

She worked hard to maintain a safe, comfortable, stable home for her son. Arthur managed to upset that orderly existence without even trying. "You've got a helluva nerve talking about being any kind of a father."

"I—I'm sorry," he said, clearly taken aback by the violence of her reaction.

That made Charlie even more furious. He intruded on her space, and destroyed her peace of mind, and then he had the nerve to sit there looking shocked when she reacted, just as anybody would, with anger.

"This is my son we're talking about, and I don't want you making any promises to him that you can't keep. For years he's waited by the phone on every birthday, every Christmas, for that phone call you always promise him. Just a few lousy phone calls would have made so much difference, and you couldn't pick up the damn phone, let alone come and see him."

"I tried."

"How hard could it have been?" she asked incredulously.

"I was on call for days at a time. I've explained—"

She cut him off. "And he believed all of your excuses. Deon trusts you. He loves you. And I will not allow you to ruin that. You left us, and barely looked back." He started to interject, but she stopped him and went on. "I know, I know," she said impatiently. "Gandy told you how we were, what we were doing, and sent photos that he made us pose for. He painted this glowing picture of life on the farm and left out lots of little details. Like how demeaning it was to have to go to the welfare office every month and beg for a check. Or how badly Nana felt because she couldn't help with the baby. That, instead, she was the one who needed help. Gandy wanted you to come home, so he didn't tell you how hard it really was.''

"I didn't know," he blurted out.

"How could you know? You weren't here," she replied.

"Why didn't you say something?" he asked.

"And listen to even more of your excuses? I can't send money for karate lessons because my car needs to be repaired. I can't fly home for Christmas because the fare is too high. What was I supposed to do? Beg? He's your son, not a charity case. If you wanted to see him, you could have. Any time.''

"You're right. I'm sorry," he said. This time she believed his apology was sincere.

Charlie had not meant to lose her temper but it was a relief to have her feelings out in the open. "You should be." She took a deep breath, and let it out slowly.

"Feel better now?" he asked, just as if he read her mind.

"Yes," she admitted, somewhat sheepishly. "Much."

"Wow!" he exclaimed admiringly. "You've changed."

Charlie wasn't sure she appreciated the compliment. She certainly didn't trust the man who paid it. "It's been ten years. I'm a different person now."

"You were so sweet and gentle before."

"Thanks. I think," she answered.

"It wasn't just Gandy's photos and stories, you know. I was always sure you'd be a great mom."

"Please, don't." Charlie didn't like the direction this conversation was taking. "Don't try to win me over to your side. Whatever I was when you left, and the reasons you left, are questions that we aren't going to get into now. It's too late for all that. I just wanted you to know that I don't want Deon's life turned upside down. I don't want you telling Deon you're going to be different now. You changed your address, and that's all that's changed as far as I'm concerned. We'll see how it goes from there. Meanwhile, I want Deon to see you, but I don't want to have to worry that you're going to say stuff like that to him.''

"Like what?"

"Like you've changed, for example. Or things are going to be different now. Those kinds of statements are off-limits. Okay?''

"Okay, okay," he agreed. "I know I owe you guys. Big. I'm going to make it up to you, I promise." He met her searching gaze without flinching.

"Be careful what you say to him. I'm warning you, Arthur," she reiterated.

"I got it," he said. "I won't forget."

She didn't trust him, but it was going to have to do, for now. "So, here are the house rules. You can see your son whenever you want, for now, but you give me twenty-four hours' notice when you want to see him, and I know what you're doing at all times, as well as where you're going. You tell me first, not him, so I can decide if it's okay. No telling him about some treat first, so he can talk me into it."

"Fine," he agreed.

"We try to avoid weeknights, school nights, and when he's with you on weekends he does his homework first, then the fun stuff."

"Of course."

"It's harder than it sounds," she advised him.

"I believe you."

"And you show up when you say you will. Picking him up, dropping him off. I don't want to worry. Give me your cell phone number."

"Now?"

"Now."

He shook his head ruefully as he took out a business card from his wallet. He scribbled two numbers on the back, then handed it to her. "There you go. Home and cell."

"Thanks."

"I never pictured you as this . . . this mother wolf. You were such a pushover. Before."

She cringed inwardly, but answered him unemotionally. "Don't remind me."

"It's amazing. You're so—"

"Different," she finished for him. "You said that already."

"No, I mean yes, but that's not what I was going to say. You're incredible," he said, shaking his head in wonder.

"No, I'm not," Charlie replied.

"You still haven't learned to take a compliment though," he said, smiling, which took the sting out of it. "I bet that drives the boys wild. It would get me."

She wished she could believe him, but it had been a long time since Charlie had felt like the kind of woman who drove anyone's anything. He used to make her feel that way. For years, she missed that feeling. Then she got used to it. She had no illusions now. She was a single mother who worked in a small country store. There was nothing special about her. She was about as ordinary as a person could be.

As they finished their coffee, talk turned to mutual friends of theirs from high school. Charlie filled him in on those who still lived in town. Arthur told her he heard from Bobby Alvarado, who after college had gone on to teach at Boston University.

Charlie drove home in a pensive mood. She didn't have much to show for her life. She loved Deon, and the farm, but she felt stuck in the same old groove, doing the same old thing, day in and day out. She needed a better job, and she wanted to go back to school. She wouldn't be the first twenty-eight-year-old freshman.

Arthur admitted that he owed her. And he did. Now that he'd finished his residency and was a real doctor, maybe he'd actually start helping with the bills. Of course she wouldn't accept tuition money from him, but if he really was going to pay some sort of child support . . . her salary might stretch to cover a few books and things.

Maybe he would even pay for some of the time he'd missed. *Jeez!* Charlie thought. *What the heck am I doing?*

But on the way home, she stopped the car next to the mailbox in front of Tom's Gas Station. She'd been carrying the SAT registration around in her purse since she stood here two days ago and debated with herself over whether or not to mail it. She pulled out the envelope and looked at it again. Then she dropped it in the mail slot, and let out a long sigh of relief. It was done. She might regret it, but she couldn't take it back.

There was one thing she was very sure of. She didn't want to owe anything to Arthur. She preferred things the way they were—lopsided, but with the balance owing on her side of the sheet. For years she had felt superior to Arthur in this one area. She had been the sole supporter of their son. She was able to despise him with a clean conscience because she raised their son without financial help from his deadbeat dad.

The next morning, she read the classified ads while she ate her breakfast. She was going to have to work on her résumé over the weekend. It wasn't going to be easy. Her employment history consisted in getting, and leaving, one dead-end job after another. She couldn't imagine who would want to hire her after she told them what she'd been doing for the last ten years. But she had to try. She was Deon's mother, and that meant she just couldn't be a failure. It was past time for her to get on a career track that her son could be proud of. Charlie had to show him, and anyone else who might be interested, that she was just as capable of succeeding as Arthur Ross.

Six

The first time Deon spent the night with Arthur, Brenda and Steve showed up to keep Charlie company through the ordeal. It was such a sweet gesture that, and she couldn't bring herself to tell them that it didn't make her feel any better. Her self-esteem was at an all-time low. Arthur had done everything he set out to do when he left Frementon ten years ago. She, on the other hand, bore no resemblance to the seventeen-year-old girl who thought she was going to conquer the world. She was a clerk in a small country store, while her ex-husband was a doctor who saved people's lives. As she watched Deon grow closer and closer to his father, and listened to him sing the man's praises, she felt small in comparison. She hadn't done a single exciting thing in her entire life.

"There is no way I can compete with a man who loves fast food, drives a fast car, and plays laser tag like a champion," she told her companions as they sat around the kitchen table eating nachos and drinking daiquiris that Brenda whipped up in the blender.

"You don't have to compete," she said.

"Yes, I do." It had been only two weeks since Arthur's return to Virginia and already Charlie felt as if the special bond she shared with her son was growing weaker. It had always been just the two of them, but now suddenly it felt as if everything she'd worked so hard for were crumbling: her home, her family, and worst of all, her built-in excuse for everything that went wrong in her day. "I always thought that if Arthur had stayed here with me, I'd be able to do all the things I planned. I blamed everything on him. If I lost my car keys, I would swear that if he were there, they'd appear."

"You know the old Chinese proverb, be careful what you wish for," Steve joked.

"It's true," she said regretfully.

"I was joking."

"All those times I thought my life would be so much better if he were helping me raise our son, I was wrong. I always thought he got where he was today because I paid for his mistakes. But he didn't. He's a doctor because he worked hard. He's smarter than I am—"

As Brenda started to protest she amended that. "He's more educated than I am, okay? He's also more ambitious. I was the one who was too scared to apply to college. I chose to stay in that stupid job. He didn't force me to do it." Even before her grandmother's stroke, and her son's untimely arrival, made it so difficult for her to pursue her dreams, Charlie had to admit she hadn't exactly been raring to take on the world, or brimming with confidence that she could achieve anything she set her mind to. She was never feisty like her grandmother or intense like Arthur. All her life, Charlie felt she lacked that certain something that everyone else seemed to have—that personal trait that made them stand out from the crowd. If she had anything like that, she never figured out what it could be. She relied on Arthur to bolster her self-esteem, and when he left, Nana took over. Her grandmother had believed in her. Enough for both of them.

It seemed that Steve did too. "You signed up to take the SATs, right? And you started looking for a new job? So that proves you were right all along. As soon as he came back, you were able to change your life."

"Sure," she said sarcastically. "I'm on the fast track now." She dreamed of exotic places, but she had never been anywhere. She was perfectly happy sitting at home reading a good book. That wasn't Arthur's fault. It was on her.

This brilliant insight hadn't come to her all at once. As Arthur spent the time he had promised with his son, and tried his best to renew their friendship, Charlie realized she'd been vilifying him, to excuse her own failures.

"You're making yourself miserable," Brenda pointed out. "And you're bringing us down, too."

"I'm sorry," Charlie said, hanging her head.

"Joking, again." She grabbed her chin and forced it up. "Come on, cheer up. It's not the end of the world. Deon will be back tomorrow, and you'll be fine again."

"I don't think so," she said miserably. "I've had to face the truth after all these years. I've done nothing with my life, and he's talented and successful. All that I can do is face the facts. My life is boring and pointless."

"So he's perfect, and you're nothing? Is that what you're trying to say?" Brenda demanded. "Because that's crap!"

"You're depressed. You miss Deon, that's all," Steve said soothingly. "Tomorrow—"

"You keep saying that. Do you think when the sun comes

up tomorrow I'll suddenly be turned into . . . I don't know . . . a best-selling author or a college professor or something?''

"You'll have Deon back here where he belongs, and you'll feel better.''

"I'll never catch up," she put her head down on the table. "It'll be years before I even earn my college diploma, *if* I can get it at all.''

"That's not the real problem,'' Brenda announced. "You admire him and you don't want to admit it. . . .''

"Interesting.'' Steve looked at her speculatively. "You may have something there,'' he mused.

"Are you insane?'' Charlie said.

"You spent ten years inventing reasons to hate the guy—'' Brenda continued.

"Inventing reasons!'' Charlie spluttered angrily, but it didn't faze her friend.

Brenda persisted. "But it didn't work. As much as you wanted to hate him, you could never completely let go. Face it. He's the father of your child.''

"Which is the one good thing he ever did for me,'' Charlie argued.

"Deon's a great kid. And that's because of you. Just you. But I think you're still holding on to some adolescent fantasy that you and the doctor and Deon all belong together,'' Brenda concluded.

Charlie shook her head emphatically. "You're nuts.''

"Admit it. In a perfect world, *you* think you would all be a family. If you hadn't screwed it up, that is. You blame yourself, as much as him, or more.''

It was true that Charlie had been the one to ask Arthur for the divorce. But she wasn't going to remind Brenda of that. Her friend's cockeyed theory already clearly appealed to Steven. Charlie wasn't about to give either of them any more ammunition.

"Maybe a little teeny tiny part of me thinks I was wrong about him, but even if I was, I'm not interested in the guy now," she argued.

"That's my girl!" Brenda said approvingly. "Don't think it. Not for a second. Because you had it right. For ten years, you had the right idea. You have to get over him. He's a fool."

"I'm already over him. Completely," Charlie insisted.

"I always thought you might, I don't know, forgive him if he came back, hat in hand," Steve said. "But Brenda's right. Any man that would walk away from a woman like you and a kid like Deon doesn't have the sense God gave a gnat. Forget him."

"I can't forget him, that's the problem. He's here! That's what started this whole thing. And now he wants me to go to a party with him this weekend. They specifically suggested he bring a date, so he doesn't want to show up alone. Deon really wants me to go and I just know I will stand out like a sore thumb with all those doctors and professors from the university."

"Oh, we can take care of that," Brenda said confidently. "No problem."

"How?" Charlie asked.

"There's nothing like being the best-dressed woman in a room to give a girl confidence."

"Really?" Charlie felt a glimmer of hope. "Won't that take a lot of money?"

"Don't worry, doll, we're going to raid my closet. We're about the same size. And I have some really amazing stuff from my days of being a trendsetter in New York. I made a lot of money back then, and I loved to shop."

"This should be interesting," Steve said, sardonically.

"Very interesting," Brenda concurred.

Charlie looked from one bright, eager face to the other

and felt a pounding begin behind her temples. What was she getting herself into?

As it turned out, she got herself into Brenda's Ann Taylor dress and it looked great! She felt more confident the moment she slipped the linen sheath over her head.

"It's you!" Brenda said, nodding, turning her so that she faced the full-length mirror. By the time she smoothed the silky cream material over her hips, Charlie thought she might just make a favorable impression on Arthur's friends after all. In fact, she thought as she examined her reflection in the mirror, she looked so presentable, she might even impress the good doctor.

Not that she cared what he thought. Brenda's crazy notion that she still had any romantic illusions about Arthur absolutely missed the mark.

"All right," she admitted aloud to her friend from New York. "I do sometimes admire Arthur's accomplishments a little, but I think that what he did to achieve them was unforgivable."

"Methinks the lady doth protest too much," Brenda taunted.

"No, really. It took me a long time to get over what he did to me."

"You got over what he did. But what you needed to get over was Arthur."

"I am," Charlie maintained. "It's the truth," she added when her friend looked at her skeptically.

"I think you've been messed up about this for so long you can't see the truth anymore. And you need to face it, so you can put it behind you." Charlie glanced at her, exasperated. "By the way, Steven agrees with me. He thinks you're still in love with Arthur, too. The only thing is . . .

he's a romantic. He thinks it would be nice if you guys got back together.''

"Oh, great.''

"Although, if he sees you in this dress, he may rethink that,'' she said, raising her eyebrows suggestively.

"Steve? I doubt he'd even notice. And if he did, what do you want to bet he'd just laugh at me?''

"I doubt it,'' Brenda disagreed.

"Have you seen the women he goes out with?'' she asked, incredulous. ''They're beautiful and graceful and striking.''

"But who does he come home to?'' Brenda responded.

"I think you're the romantic,'' Charlie accused.

"Me, I'm a pragmatist. I see things as they are.''

"Right,'' she said sarcastically. ''First you say I'm still in love with Arthur; then you imply that Steve Parker could be swept off his feet by a dress. It's a nice dress. It's a great dress. But me and Steve? You're dreaming.''

Brenda shook her head.

"Why?'' Charlie asked.

"Because he's everything that Arthur isn't,'' she said cryptically.

"What is that supposed to mean?'' Charlie demanded.

"If you don't already know, I can't explain it. You'll figure it out. Or you won't.'' She shrugged. ''Either way, we have to decide what to do with your hair.''

The style she chose was very elegant. ''Black Jackie-O,'' Brenda called the smooth sweep of hair that coiled into a bun just above the nape of her neck. Brenda might not be the most astute psychoanalyst, but she more than made up for it with her other skills. Charlie loved the results of her makeover. She felt like a different woman. The designer dress made her feel slim and smooth and sophisticated. She could face anyone in it.

Arthur looked suitably impressed when he saw her. In

fact, the way his gaze traveled down her body made Charlie feel a little warm. She was thrilled to see his reaction and, for the first time since he'd come back, she felt that she wasn't completely powerless in this relationship. For a second he was the old Arthur—or rather the young Arthur— her Arthur, and she was the girl who knew just where to touch him to make him shiver. It was amazing what a little lipstick can do for a woman's ego, Charlie thought.

The party was a simple but elegant affair on the back lawn, overlooking the gardens, of a mansion in the wealthiest section of Charlottesville. Their hosts were Albert Wilson, the dean of medicine from U.V.A., and his wife, a surgeon. Albert was a tall, pale, spindly scarecrow of a man. Alice Wilson was equally slim, but it was a better look on her. She had a very pretty, ivory face, dominated by large blue eyes.

Their house was in an old enclave of stately old homes built of red Virginia brick and fronted by white-columned porticoes and manicured laws. Charlie had driven along the winding roads of this neighborhood before, admiring the antebellum homes and the huge old elms that shaded the ornate gates. Charlie was thankful the dean's property wasn't one of those that sported a lawn jockey. Even for Arthur, she didn't think she could walk past one of the racist lawn ornaments. This was an area where the tasteless, anachronistic statuettes of black boys in livery were considered traditional and, as such, sacrosanct.

Dean and Alice Wilson were not exactly typical examples of the old-money families that owned these homes. Both doctors, they were as driven to succeed as Arthur himself and probably had more in common with him—despite his background—than with others of their own class who were content to live off their inheritances and thought work was something to be avoided at all costs.

Charlie, on the other hand, had nothing in common with their hosts, or any of the other guests she met, all of whom were members—in one way or another—of the medical profession. Her clothes were perfect for the occasion, but she still didn't fit in with this crowd. Everyone there was not only white, but they all also had the look of people who knew that they belonged. She could only pretend she felt the same way, and she doubted that she was fooling anyone.

Not that anyone really noticed her. She might feel as if she stuck out like a sore thumb in this crowd, but these people were too self-absorbed to pay any attention. They were intellectuals, but their obsessions with their various fields and specialties made it difficult to converse with them. After each introduction, and the obligatory explanation that she was with the cardiac surgeon who had recently joined the team at UVa Health Systems, the discussion lagged or halted altogether. The attention of the person she was trying to speak with invariably turned to someone discussing the latest article in some medical journal about surgery, or diagnostic techniques, fascinating diseases or treatments.

Charlie gave up on trying to mingle and wandered off eventually to explore the garden. Almost hidden behind a trellis overgrown with grapevines and bougainvillea, an older gentleman sat on a wrought-iron bench. She'd have left him alone with a nod and a smile but he waved her over and offered her a seat beside him.

"Hi, my name is Gordon," he said after a moment.

"Charlotte Brown," she responded and offered him her hand.

He shook it, smiling. "Charlie Brown? Really? Your mother or father must have had a very active sense of humor," he said, but without malice. "Or did they just love *Peanuts?*" he asked.

She smiled and shrugged. "I don't really know the whole

story," she said. Charlie Brown didn't think her mother purposely named her after a cartoon character when she named her Charlotte Ann. She guessed that poor Sophie, like herself, didn't think of her own name, Brown, as her little baby's true name. Charlie was supposed to have her father's name, just as her son, Deon, was supposed to have his father's name.

For generations, the Brown women had given their sons and their daughters the surname Brown. According to the family legend, Sophia, the first Brown to own the farm, chose the name because she wanted to pass along to her children, and possibly their children, a pride in who she was, which included pride in the color of her skin. Whether or not the story was true, it was a lovely one, and more satisfying to believe in than not. Maybe the first Sophie just got stuck with Brown, through circumstances beyond her control, like her namesake, Charlie's mother, and like Charlie herself, but if she chose the name to affirm her belief in herself she created a heritage to be proud of.

Charlie still would have preferred the name Charlie Ross. So when she named her son Deon Ross Brown, it was an act of defiance. And it was one she had regretted for ten years. At seventeen she'd been angry, hurt, and humiliated, and she struck back at the boy she had married by refusing to give their child his surname. Nana said she cut off her nose to spite her face. When she thought about it, Charlie had to agree. Because she stopped calling herself Ross, and took back the name she had been so happy to finally get rid of. She became Charlie Brown again.

She couldn't tell this stranger all that, so she changed the subject. "Are you a friend of the dean's? Or his wife?"

"Not exactly. I'm an old friend of the family." He looked old enough to be his host's father, but unlike the dean, he had a sturdy trunk of a body and his skin had been tinged by the sun. He had the ruddy skin of a redhead though his hair was pure white. His thick white beard and round face made her think of Santa Clause, and his twinkling blue eyes added to the impression.

"So, you're not one of them." She waved her hand in the direction of the lawn where she had left the other guests. "Neither am I, to tell the truth. I came here with an old friend from high school."

"He can't be that old," Gordon said. "You've been out of school for what? A year or two?"

"Thanks." She acknowledged the compliment. "But I'm twenty-eight. He is, too. He's a heart surgeon." A note of pride crept into her voice without her volition.

"You like doctors," he stated, sounding somewhat disappointed.

"Sure, when I'm sick. Between you and me and this grapevine, though, they're not much fun at a party."

"Oh?" He smiled, his tone hopeful. "What makes you say that?"

She leaned closer, conspiratorially. "I don't know many people in the medical profession, but if these guys are typical, they aren't very interesting."

"I know," he said ruefully. "Here we are in this beautiful place, and all they talk about are medical procedures. They might as well be in their offices," he asserted, shaking his head. "It's a shame."

She liked this old man. He was a character.

"You might find this hard to believe, but some of the brightest young minds in the country are right here at this little shindig."

"I believe you," Charlie said. "So what would *you* like to talk about? Great books? History? Politics?"

"I can't talk about politics anymore. Doctor's orders.

That last farce of a presidential election gave me a permanent case of heartburn,'' Gordon explained.

"Books and history then," she suggested. "They go together."

"Yes." He looked happy, and Charlie suddenly felt content.

When Arthur found the two of them half an hour later, they were debating whether Shakespeare's comedies or his fantasies were better, having agreed that his histories were interesting and exciting but not nearly as much fun.

"Charlie, here you are," Arthur said, stopping short when Gordon turned to face him. "Mr. Watts. I—I hope I'm not interrupting. I was looking for my date."

For the second time that day, Charlie felt a flush of pleasure as her ex-husband gazed at her appreciatively. "Have you two met?" she asked the older man.

"Not officially," Gordon said. "I was part of the group that made him the job offer."

"So you're not just a friend of the dean's family," she chided him.

"I've known Albert's father since we were kids," he said, excusing his lie. By the casual manner with which he mentioned the dean of medicine, Charlie assumed Gordon was more important to the university hospital than he had let on.

"You're connected to the hospital," she guessed. "I thought you might be. You seemed to have such a strong opinion of the doctors."

"Mr. Watts is the hospital medical director," Arthur clarified in an awed tone.

"How important are you exactly?" she asked Gordon, teasingly.

He laughed. "Some people think I'm pretty close to God," he answered.

"And they're all here at this party, right?" she asked. Arthur looked stunned by her little joke. That, more than anything else, told her that she was right in thinking Gordon Watts was an extremely influential man.

"A number of them," he confessed.

"Tut, tut, tut," she scolded, playfully. Her ex looked as if he might have a seizure, but she knew the old man didn't mind her flippant tone. He liked it. "You've been naughty, hiding out here, talking to me."

"It was a pleasure, ma'am." He held out his hand to Arthur. "You're the lucky man who came with this fascinating woman, Doctor Ross? You should hold on to her. She could be a big help to your career."

Arthur shook Gordon's hand. "I'm afraid you'll have to ask Charlie about that."

Gordon turned to look at her. "So, what do you say, Charlie Brown? Are you going to help this poor man?"

"Maybe. If he's good," she retorted.

"I'd better go in," Gordon said reluctantly. He shook her hand, too, holding it for a moment between both of his large paws. "It really was a pleasure."

They watched him walk away; then Arthur turned to her. "Charlie, do you know who that was?"

"Gordon Watts. The medical director. And the most interesting guest at the party. He's fun."

"Fun? He practically runs the whole hospital."

"Well then, you had better be nice to me, because he likes me."

"What did you talk about?" he asked nervously.

"Nothing much. Shall we go back to the party?"

The rest of the party was much like the first part had been, but in the car on the way home, Charlie found she was in a much better mood.

"You probably shouldn't have taken me there, you

know." When Arthur looked at her curiously, she added, "I don't have anything in common with those people."

"How do you know that? You just met them. You don't know anything about them," he argued.

"Maybe not," she admitted. "But they've got one-track minds. All they talked about was work, work, work."

"The party was with, and for, their colleagues. Of course work was the main topic of conversation."

"The only topic, you mean. There are important events taking place in the world, things other people may know something about. There are even a few subjects other people might be interested in talking about." She considered mentioning that that was why Gordon Watts had taken such a liking to her.

He said it for her. "I can't believe you talked to Gordon Watts like that. No one talks to him like that."

"Maybe you should try it," she suggested.

"Yeah, right," he muttered sarcastically.

"You should take my advice."

"He only let you do it because you're a girl," he said, baiting her. It was as if they were in high school again. His tone, the silly insult, even the wording he used, was so adolescent that Charlie knew that he, too, was feeling the pull of memory. There was a familiarity to their situation. Ten years had passed since he'd dropped her off at home after a date, but at that moment she felt as if it had been just yesterday.

"You better be careful, buster. You've given me power over you now. I can make you or I can break you," she joked.

Seven

Steven Parker was exactly where he wanted to be. He felt completely at ease sitting in the comfortable, well-worn sofa that took up most of the floor space in the living room of Charlie's hundred-year-old farmhouse. It was long and deep and shrouded in a knobby, blue homemade cotton cover stacked high with pillows. Fronted by an equally worn area rug, with two scarred old oak coffee tables at both ends, the sofa faced a monstrous old television set, probably manufactured some twenty years ago, which sat on a wide shelf. Underneath that was an equally ancient stereo with both a turntable and a working eight-track tape player. Sitting next to it, incongruous, was a shiny black VCR and an ultra-modern Super Nintendo. Steve looked down at the two children sitting on the floor in front of him playing with their Game Boys. Content that they were happy, he tuned out their voices to listen for the sound of Charlie banging around in the kitchen.

She was upset. She'd been off-kilter since the day she heard Arthur Ross was coming back to their small corner of the state. Steven tried to empathize with her, but his situation was too different from hers for him to truly know what she was feeling. His wife didn't choose to walk away, she died. Charlie's ex left her of his own volition. Arthur Ross was a kid of seventeen at the time and chose to take advantage of a full scholarship at Boston University rather than struggling to support a family. A tough choice, and he chose wrong, but Steve could understand it. The man made a mistake. One mistake.

"Nobody's perfect," he told Charlie right before he had left her alone in the kitchen to come join their kids in the family room.

She was venting.

The two curly black caps of hair at his knee moved close together as the boys shared some juicy secret. Her son and his son. They were best friends. Just like Charlie and himself. She was a rare woman. Loyal. Loving. A lot stronger than she thought. She was resilient. She was going to bounce back from this. Even though she was under a lot of pressure, what with Arthur's return and all the old feelings that that brought back, she could handle it. He had faith.

He tried to be as supportive as he could. But this latest weirdness of hers was beginning to bug him. Why was she pretending to be something she wasn't? He wished that Brenda had never suggested that Charlie should fix herself up and strut her stuff. Now she was so caught up in "getting" Arthur, she'd lost track of why she was doing it. Why couldn't she just admit that, now that Arthur was back, finally fulfilling his responsibilities as a father, she was starting to soften toward him? Maybe she was on the way to forgiving him.

She loved the guy. Whether she knew it or not, she'd

been in love with him since she was Deon's age. It was true that he betrayed her, but he was trying to make up for it. If she was honest with herself, she'd admit it was working. The anger was starting to fade. She had scars, sure, but scars healed. Or they could if she'd let them. But she kept picking at the wounds, reexamining them, reminding herself how badly she'd been hurt. To punish Arthur, she decked herself out in Brenda's fancy clothes and flirted with his influential friends from the University of Virginia, trying to get under his skin.

Steve missed the old Charlie: the sweet, quiet, unassuming woman who cried every time she watched *Seventh Heaven.* Her son and his bet their allowances every week on how many Kleenexes she'd go through during an episode. Her record to date was four. She was the most softhearted person he knew. She just didn't have it in her to stay mad at Arthur. He was her first and only love.

They were still so young. At thirty-four, Steve felt years older than either of them, probably because of what he'd gone through when Gloria died. He wanted to tell Charlie straight out not to waste this precious time holding on to her bitterness. She needed Arthur, and he needed her, just as Steve needed someone to share his life and help him make a proper home in which to raise his son. Charlie was all for that. She'd been helping him ever since he decided to look for a new mate. But she couldn't, or wouldn't, see that she could use a partner herself. And Arthur was the perfect candidate, since she still loved him.

She wasn't ready to see that, though. He had to wait for her to recognize what was in her heart.

Steve was glad Arthur Ross had come home. By all accounts, they were one of those couples who were destined to be together. Arthur might have a lot to make up for, but he seemed like a decent guy. Steve thought she should give him a chance.

Steve hadn't actually talked with the doctor much. They'd been introduced twice. Once at school, and then again the first time Arthur came to pick Deon up to spend the night at his place. Steve was at the farm in order to help Charlie get through it. They chatted for a little—while Charlie said good-bye to Deon about twenty times. Then Steve pushed them out of the house and Charlie into the kitchen, where Brenda was waiting.

Brenda didn't like Arthur much. She'd been prejudiced against him before she ever met him and she was one tough woman—a big-city girl. Guys who left their pregnant wives did not get second chances in her book. Luckily, she believed that Deon would be better off with his father in his life, no matter how big a jerk he was, so she encouraged Charlie to see Arthur so they could eventually work out a legal custody arrangement. Otherwise, she and Steve would be working against each other and that would have made things even more difficult. If only she hadn't come up with this whole makeover deal, which was just screwing things up.

Arthur needed to get to know Charlie again, and she needed to get to know him, without all this game playing. Then nature could take its course and Steve could watch his best friend live happily ever after. Charlie finally came into the living room and threw herself down on the couch beside him.

"Have you got it all out of your system now?" he asked warily.

She ignored him and tapped Deon on the back of his shoulder to ask, "What are you playing?"

"Star Wars," her son informed her.

"Again? Did you rent it?"

"No. Shoshona loaned it to me. She's got tons of cartridges. She bought them.'' In typical ten-year-old fashion, Dean could not allow the opportunity to go by to nag his mother. ''She says her parents got a new cable contract and it's really cheap.''

''You watch enough television without all those premium channels,'' Charlie answered automatically. ''Shoshona, huh?'' she pressed. In typical motherly fashion, she couldn't let pass an opportunity to pry. ''So, how she's doing?'' Michael giggled. Steve nudged his son in the lower back with his instep.

''Fine,'' Deon said, turning his head to glare at his mother. Charlie, suitably chastised, settled back on the couch, leaning into Steve's side.

He was forgiven. ''Comfortable?''

''Very,'' she said facetiously. ''You?''

''I'm happy,'' he replied. And he meant it.

After a wild Connect Four tournament and much arguing and tickling, they tucked the kids into the bunk beds in Deon's room. Michael was spending that night and the next day with Deon and his mom, while Steve took the basketball team to the next county to play their arch rivals. Michael often came with him on these day trips, but Deon had asked if Michael could stay because he hadn't seen him much on weekends lately, and of course Michael jumped at the chance. Steve suspected his son missed both his best friend, Deon, and Charlie, whom he adored and whom he hadn't seen so much of since Doc had reentered their lives.

Steve wondered how Michael would react to Charlie's remarriage as he helped her to straighten up the living room.

''You're coming to Thanksgiving dinner, right?'' she asked.

''Sure,'' Steve said, without thinking.

''Great.'' She sounded relieved.

''Any special reason why I wouldn't?'' he inquired.

"No, no. Just . . . Arthur is going to be here and Gandy and, uh . . ." Her voice trailed off.

". . . He's not welcome." Steve finished her thought.

"It would be nice to have one man in the house who's not glued to the television set."

"Yeah, like you won't be running into the living room every five minutes to see the score," he said, mocking her. Every year dinner was hours later than planned because Charlie got distracted by the game. She loved football. She'd learned about the sport in order to share it with her son, and she'd gotten hooked.

"I thought I'd bring the little TV into the kitchen with us this year," she said, looking sideways at him from beneath her eyelashes.

Oh, yeah. He would definitely be there on Thanksgiving. Steve wasn't about to let her hide out in the kitchen all day avoiding her ex. "Charlie—" he started.

"Don't say it," she warned.

"I just wanted to point out that—"

She cut him off. "Don't, Steve."

He brought his hands up to her neck and pretended to throttle her. "Woman, will you shut up for a second and listen to me?" He looked into her eyes, his hands resting on her shoulders, and saw in her expressive eyes that she wasn't going to give an inch.

She stood still, looking back up at him, and calmly said, "I already know what you're going to say. It's the same thing you've been saying. Give the man a chance. He's not such a bad guy."

"He can't be that bad," Steve said with feeling. "Not when he's capable of making both you *and* Deon fall in love with him."

"Yeah, yeah, yeah," she intoned. "Look, I'll work out

visitation and custody and all that, but Arthur Ross is not going to charm me into anything else.''

''You just keep your guard up, girl. I'm sure he'll give up eventually,'' Steve lied.

''I hope so,'' Charlie said.

He hoped the man wasn't fool enough to actually fall for her act. ''If he does, I hope you don't end up regretting it,'' he warned.

She moved out of his grasp, toward the door. ''I won't. Don't worry,'' she assured him. She handed him his coat and turned on the porch light to light his way to the car. He walked out the door feeling vaguely unsatisfied. He hadn't made a dent in the wall she'd built up around herself.

Charlie had been hurt. It was understandable that she'd try to protect herself. It was going to take time, and patience, to get through to her.

If *he* was this frustrated, he could only imagine how Arthur must be feeling.

Dr. Arthur Ross didn't make it all the way from the family's dilapidated farm in Albemarle County to his beautiful split-level apartment in Charlottesville by taking no for an answer. He had the money, the career, and the home that he'd dreamed of as a boy. He had the brains and the determination to make it through the most difficult residency at Boston General, and he'd gotten himself the job he'd always coveted at U.V.A. He'd watched and waited for an opportunity, and luck had gone his way, as it so often did when you were ready and waiting.

Now it was time that his wife and son became a part of the picture-perfect life he had created for himself. Deon was perfect. He adored the kid. He was charming, beautiful, and intelligent. Luckily, the boy was equally enamored of him, and had dropped right into the palm of his hand. Charlie was coming around, too, though more slowly of course. He was so close to getting every single thing he'd ever wanted that he could taste it. It was true that it was going to be a challenge to win back his ex-wife's trust, but he'd never been afraid of hard work. He had proven that. He had made it.

He hadn't had anything handed to him. He earned scholarships, took student loans, and more student loans, worked wherever he could, and applied for every possible grant and fellowship he could find. Lack of money wasn't the only obstacle he came up against either. Another major stumbling block was the competition he faced. The little schoolhouse in Frementon had provided a good basis, but he'd had to beat out some of the best-educated people in the country in college, then medical school, and finally on the job itself. He managed to do it, too. To excel at it, in fact.

Because he kept his eye on the prize. Because he never, ever accepted a compromise. He went all the way. Arthur never took any shortcuts. He honestly believed there weren't any. Everything that was worth anything in life took either time or money, or both. He'd been short of those commodities, but he worked his butt off and he made it. He was a successful doctor. A heart surgeon. He planned to be one of the best. It was a difficult calling, with the highest alcoholism and suicide rates after dentist and cop, but it was worth it. He could handle the stress, the insane hours, the competition. He knew he could. He already had. He couldn't tell Charlie—not yet, at least, and perhaps not ever—but it had even been worth giving her up for a time, in order to get to where he was today.

He kept planning, all along, to come back and get her and Deon, but somehow ten years had gone by and he hadn't been able to pursue that goal until now. It was an uphill battle, but he knew he would win in the end. She'd waited for him. That meant the biggest obstacle she could have put between them—another man—wasn't something he had to waste time on. Not that a husband or boyfriend would have stopped him, but it would have slowed him down considerably.

She was open to taking him back. He just had to show her that she had not waited all this time, suffered all that hardship, in vain. He had to convince her that they were still perfect for each other. He'd made a lot of headway in the short time he'd been home. She despised him at first, he could see it in her eyes, but it didn't take long before that changed. Deon paved the way for him. Arthur knew Charlie wouldn't deny her son a father. Even if she had hated him, she wouldn't let Deon go through what she had endured—being abandoned by her mother and her father, never sure who or where they were, or whether they ever wanted her. She couldn't bear to see her son hurt that way.

Sometimes, she watched them together with a glow of satisfaction in her eyes, as she did tonight while they sat around the dinner table celebrating Thanksgiving. He swore he saw her wipe away a tear when Deon thanked God for having both his mom and his dad with him this year. She'd always been very softhearted. Lucky for him, that hadn't changed.

"Is everyone ready for dessert?" Charlie asked as she stood up to clear the last course from the table. Groans and polite refusals were her response. The dinner had been a masterpiece. She served the old, traditional fare side by side with new, exciting dishes. The wine was excellent. She might not have a college education, but she had learned a lot since he left. She would be the perfect wife for an up-and-coming doctor. She'd demonstrated that already. The very first time he took her to a business function, she charmed the hell out of the most important man there.

If he pulled this one off, he'd have it all: a beautiful home, a great career, a bright, beautiful wife, and a charming, affectionate son. They could even keep the farm as their country getaway when they moved up to D.C., where someday he planned to hold an American president's life in his two hands.

Arthur could see it all so clearly. He had no doubt he could make it happen. All he needed, as he'd demonstrated time and again, was to be able to picture his objective, and focus on it with all his strength, and it would become reality.

The two boys and he moved into the living room after dinner, while Charlie and Steve cleared up. Arthur was sleepy and he had an early call in the morning, but he was absolutely determined to speak to Charlie alone tonight, so he settled in to wait everyone else out. Steve and Michael Parker had been there all day, so they would surely be leaving soon. Deon looked about ready to drop where he stood.

Which didn't stop his son from asking, "Do you want to play Nintendo football with us?"

"I don't know how," he demurred.

"We'll show you," the boys offered.

Awkwardly, he sat down on the floor with them and they tried to explain the game to him. It was late, they had eaten a lot of food, and they became grumpy when he couldn't seem to get the hang of the game. Soon they gave up on him. Arthur scooted back up on the couch and watched them play until Steve came out of the kitchen and told Michael it was time to go home.

"Bye, Doctor Ross," Michael said politely.

"Bye, Doc," his father echoed. Steve winked at him as he followed his son out of the door left. Arthur liked that guy. He couldn't help noticing that Steve tried to arrange things so that Charlie could spend some time with Deon and him. Charlie hadn't seemed very happy with Steve's machinations.

"He seems like a good man," he told Charlie when she came back inside after seeing them off.

"That's what he says about you," she murmured sardonically.

"A good judge of character, huh?" he teased.

She didn't rise to the bait. "Uh-huh," she answered noncommitally.

Left alone, with only Deon to serve as a buffer between them, Charlie gravitated toward the couch, where his son sat next to him watching a cartoon. *Peanuts* again, Arthur noted. Deon had a collection of all of Charles Schultz's holiday stories, and Arthur was surprised to learn he and his mother watched "It's the Great Pumpkin, Charlie Brown" every Halloween. He didn't try to join in on the banter between mother and son. Clearly, it was a private joke. She had always hated having the same name as the cartoon character Charlie Brown.

Arthur couldn't wait to give her his name again. Charlotte Ann Ross had such a nice ring to it. Deon snuggled up against his side and Arthur sensed, rather than saw, Charlie's gaze on them. He looked up to find her staring, her expression torn between pleasure at the sight of the two of them, and jealousy at the bond forming between them. He wanted to tell her she'd been a good father to the boy as well as a good mother, but he'd tried before to praise the job she'd done raising their son and learned that that kind of comment seemed to irritate her.

He wasn't allowed to say anything nice to her. Not about Deon, and certainly not about her.

He tried anyway. "That was a fantastic dinner."

Charlie grimaced. "Thanks," she said shortly.

"You're going to have to work on that," he said.

"What?" she demanded.

"Not getting all bent out of shape when someone pays you a compliment."

"I thanked you. What else do you want?" she asked contentiously.

"A little sincerity."

"I meant it," Charlie said grumpily.

"That's much better." His sarcastic tone made her smile.

"Okay, I admit you may have a point," she conceded.

"Thank you," he said graciously.

"Show off," she accused.

"It's an art. I'm serious, Char," he added as she laughed. "Stop laughing. I'm going to pay you a compliment now and I want you to respond naturally and gracefully and not as if I'm making it up."

She carefully arranged her features into a neutral expression. "Okay, I'm ready."

"Okay, here goes." Arthur cleared his throat. "Charlie, I wanted to tell you that . . ." He faltered.

"Just make something up," she whispered helpfully.

"I don't have to make something up," he answered. "There are a lot of nice things I could say about you. I'm just trying to choose one."

"Okay," she said, but she didn't sound convinced. "Go ahead."

"You see, that's exactly what I'm talking about. That right there. I could compliment your looks, your brains, or your heart. You're a good person, a wonderful mother, a charming hostess, a great cook. I could go on, but you won't believe any of it. When I say I like something about you, you assume I'm lying. Why is that?"

"Oh, I don't know," she replied, exasperated. "Maybe

because in the real world people don't go around saying things like that to each other.''

''Sure they do. It happens all the time.''

''Not to me,'' she insisted.

''You just don't hear it. You choose not to hear it. Right now you are changing the subject, avoiding the moment of truth.'' He had done this to her. Maybe not alone, but he had helped. She had not known her own worth when she was seventeen either, but back then Charlie was willing to believe him when he said she had everything going for her. She didn't have that anymore. She had no faith in herself or in him.

''Hey, I thought you were supposed to say something nice to me. What happened?'' she asked, still smiling.

''You distracted me.''

''Fine. I'll shut up now.'' It was at least three full seconds before she spoke again. ''I think Deon's asleep.''

Arthur abandoned his plan to trick her into listening to what he had to say. He was going to have to use a more direct approach. It was just that she'd set up so many barriers between them. She had even suggested they see a lawyer to get a custodial agreement regarding regular visitation and uniform child support. She kept calling herself his estranged ex-wife. In part, he believed, she did it to remind herself of their past and he supposed he should take it as a good sign that she needed the reminder, but he was fast losing patience. He wanted to move ahead with this. With her.

He had to keep pushing. But not too aggressively. He didn't want to scare her away. ''So, have you been seeing anyone?''

''What?'' Charlie asked, looking blankly at him, then down at Deon.

He followed her gaze, and found he was gently stroking Deon's soft curly hair. He hadn't been conscious he was doing it. She smiled. Perfect. "I asked if you were dating," he repeated. "Anyone special, I mean."

"Lately? No," she said. "I probably would have mentioned it if I were."

"Oh, yeah," he said, suddenly feeling embarrassed. "I guess you . . . um, would have to explain me, I mean, introduce me, or something."

"Something," she agreed.

"So, how about before?" he persisted, though he felt incredibly stupid asking her about this stuff. He hadn't expected this to be so awkward. He forced himself to go on. He had to know. "Have you, um, met anyone you thought you might . . . like?"

"In ten years?" She was staring at him as if he were insane. "Do you really think you have the right to ask me a question like that?"

"Just . . . curious," he mumbled. This wasn't going well.

"You have no right," she started to say, her voice rising. Then she appeared to think better of it. "But, hey, if you want to get into this . . . what about you? Have you been living like a monk for the past ten years?"

"Me? I—" He loosened his tie. "Not exactly a monk, no. . . ."

"But you figured I was sitting around here, pining after you," Charlie accused him.

"It isn't that. It's—you're so beautiful, more beautiful than I remembered, that's all I was trying to say," he sidestepped. Better, Arthur thought.

"You did not," she replied. "You were fishing."

"I thought, maybe, just, Gandy never mentioned you were seeing anyone, and I hoped that meant that I—" He faltered. "I might have a chance to—" Her icy expression froze the words on his lips.

"Chance to what? Go steady?" She laughed, but there

was no humor in the sound. "You want to recapture the past, Arthur?"

"No, but—"

"I have got a newsflash for you. I'm not interested in anything you have to offer, Doctor Ross. If you think—" Deon murmured and turned in his sleep. Charlie looked at him and halted midsentence. Then she looked back up at Arthur and shook her head. "I can't do this," she said softly. "I'm sorry."

"No, I'm sorry. I didn't intend to make you uncomfortable, or hurt you. I've missed you. I regretted what happened between us. Ever since I saw you again, I thought maybe there was a possibility that you could forgive me. That we could, at least, be friends again. Or something. We both love him." Arthur put his hand on Deon's shoulder, resting it gently on this tangible evidence of the love they once felt for each other. "That's something we have in common, something we share. It could be something to build on. I was hoping we could, maybe, put the past behind us? Try to make things better in the future?"

"Sure," Charlie agreed, passively. "I want that, too. For Deon."

"I'm more selfish than you are. I want it for me, too," Arthur confessed.

Part Two

Eight

Charlie's life was a mess. She didn't really mind studying for the SATs after all. It was even fun, in a way, thinking about taking the test and wondering if she'd do as well on it as she had the first time. But she was almost thirty, and she felt as if she were back in high school again, trying to find time to study, and reacquainting herself with mathematical formulas and rules of grammar. This was not what she had in mind when she decided to change her life. She didn't want to go backward.

Perhaps she was just too old for all this stuff, but she didn't like feeling anxious and uncertain most of the time. Maybe she never did enjoy it. Maybe in hindsight it seemed more exciting than it was at the time. She remembered being nervous and elated when she first started dating, her palms sweating and her heart pounding while she waited for Arthur to kiss her good night. But she remembered it as being more fun than it was now. Whether or not she liked this roller-coaster ride the first time, she didn't appreciate it these days. She wanted to be on secure ground again.

Even Steve admitted, during the postmortem she held with him and Brenda, that her Thanksgiving dinner was a pretty embarrassing affair. And he didn't know about what happened after he left. He had only witnessed her minor blunders, such as when she dropped the cranberry sauce so it splashed up onto her blouse and she had to go and change into a new outfit. She also broke her great-grandmother's serving platter. Then she inserted the blades in the electric knife upside down so that when she tried to carve the turkey, the knife didn't cut through the tender meat, but instead made the eighteen-pound bird wiggle and jiggle until she realized what she was doing wrong. That was not to mention the verbal gaffes that had plagued her throughout the evening. And, of course, she was mortified that everyone saw her tear up and sniffle through Deon's heartfelt Thanksgiving toast.

"Yes, there were some snafus," Steve confirmed. "But the food tasted great."

"I burned the pie," she told Brenda. "It actually set off the alarm before I noticed the smoke seeping out the sides of the oven door."

"Honey, you need to do more than *wear* those clothes you've been borrowing from me. You've got to live the part."

"I'm trying," Charlie said through clenched teeth. "Believe it or not." She glanced at Steve. "I try, but . . . I feel like an idiot. Arthur comes into the room, and I'm seventeen again, and brain-dead."

"It was pretty pitiful," Steve admitted. "I think the big guy is trying to tell you something." He pointed at the ceiling and mouthed G-O-D.

"You could have helped," Brenda exclaimed, exasperated.

"I did," he maintained.

"Right," Charlie said dryly. "Good old helpful Steve here was busy playing Dolly Levi all night. I didn't know what he would do next. That made me even more nervous. As if I needed any more pressure."

"Just trying to move things along," he said without an ounce of remorse.

"Well, hello, Dolly," Brenda said, regarding Steve with a quizzical expression.

"What are you thinking?" Charlie asked her warily.

"Yeah, what?" Steve looked equally nervous.

"If you want to give her the benefit of your experience, why don't you tell Char what she can do to make this guy sit up and take notice?"

"Leave me out of this. I'm not going to help you two mess with Doc's mind." Steve dismissed the idea instantly.

"I thought you were my friend," Charlie whined.

"I am, and I'm telling you that you're going about this all wrong. Just be yourself—the sweet, charming woman who puts everyone *else* at their ease. Once you stop playing all these games, you won't feel so self-conscious and you'll get comfortable with him."

Brenda looked at him speculatively. "I'm surprised to hear you say that, Steve. The women you go out with all seem like pretty serious game players to me. Now, if they were a little more like Charlie here—sweet, sensible, smart—I could understand it, but the ones I've met . . . like that girl you brought to my barbecue on the Fourth of July . . ."

"Melissa?"

She shook her head. "Gorgeous, but I wouldn't use the

word sweet to describe her at all. Obnoxious, maybe," she added.

"She wasn't that bad," he argued.

"She had a pretty unappealing personality. So what in the world makes you choose a woman like that instead of going after, say, old Charlie here?"

"Charlie?" he said, as if Brenda had suggested that he should date outside of his species. "There is no comparison. She's real, and genuine, and that is her appeal. This whole act is not her at all, and she shouldn't pretend it is."

"That's great," Brenda said sardonically. "Good advice, bro. If you want him to walk all over her. Again."

"He's not going to do that. He wants back in. Let him get to know you again," Steve said to Charlie. "The real you."

"Okay, say I do that," Charlie posited. "Say he even likes the real me. What comes next? What if some opportunity comes up in California, or Timbuktu? Do you think he's going to pass that up for us? I mean, for his son? Because I don't think so. He's made it pretty clear that he doesn't think that way."

"You'll deal with it together. That's what couples do," he explained patiently.

"Arthur and I are *not* a couple. We *were* a couple. Ten years ago. But we haven't been together in so long that I can hardly remember what it was like." She sighed.

"You remember," he said knowingly.

Charlie hated admitting he was right, but . . . "All right. Yes. I do remember," she said slowly. "That doesn't mean I want to go back. Arthur wasn't what I thought he was. That I remember very clearly. You're the one who seems to have forgotten."

"He's trying to change," he insisted.

"Why do you keep pushing this? I've got Brenda on one

side saying that I have to be on my guard every minute, and you on the other acting like Arthur is your new best friend, and Deon, who is the only one who really matters here, to look after. You're not helping. Brenda's not helping. I've got to trust my own judgment, and it's hard enough to do that without all these conflicting opinions from my friends.''

"Okay, Brenda and I might have different goals, but we both agree on one thing. You still care about him. No matter what you say, I know, *we know,* that you do. We can see that, even if you can't.''

"Steve, I don't want to fall in love again. Is that okay with you?'' Charlie said, growing irritated.

"You can't help loving someone. It's not something you can turn on or off with the flip of a switch.''

"I'm pretty sure I can control myself,'' she said dryly. "All I have to do is remember what he did to us.''

"You don't really want to do that.''

She was annoyed at his assumption, but she tried not to let it show as she answered him. "Yes, I do, Steve.'' She took a deep breath. "Honest. I may still love him somewhere deep down. But I hate it when he makes me feel like I was fourteen again.''

"You hate it so much that you're doing everything you can to make him fall in love with you again.''

She would have liked to wipe that self-assured expression off of his face, but she had to settle for saying, childishly, "I am not.''

"I bet he'd love to go jogging with you and Deon sometime. You could wear your sweats, and put your hair in a ponytail. He could see you as you really are, when you're not dressed like a department store mannequin . . . and breaking everything you touch.''

"Steve, I'm sure you're trying to be helpful, but Charlie doesn't need that kind of advice,'' Brenda argued. "Be yourself!'' She snorted. ''She's not fourteen and this isn't her first date. She's a mature woman, with a child, which means she's lucky to have a date at all.''

Charlie nodded. ''Not that I'm actually dating Arthur,'' she reminded them. ''But we do have to see each other and discuss our son regularly, and I'd rather not act like some tongue-tied teenager every time that happens.''

''I'm telling you, you're making this more difficult than it needs to be. You have the upper hand here. He's not in a position to win,'' Steve declared.

Brenda shook her head, sadly, looking at him as if he were some kind of retarded child. ''I told you before, it's a very different ball game for men and women. You've got what women want—decent job, decent house, decent personality, and a nice butt. Men are looking for more in a woman, they want their fantasy to come to life, whatever that may be.''

''We're guessing in this case . . .'' She paused, thinking, her eyes on the ceiling. She continued, ticking points off on her fingers as she made them. ''. . . Arthur wants the wife who can entertain his hoity-toity friends from the university and the hospital, who cooks like a dream for himself and his son, and knows how to dress for every occasion. What man wouldn't want that?''

''Not this one,'' Steve said.

''*You're* the one who likes to go jogging. Arthur isn't really the type. If you're not going to give us more useful information, like the kind we asked for, I don't think you should speak at all,'' she said, dismissing him.

''Just trying to give you the male perspective,'' he said, offended. ''Isn't that what you asked me for?''

''I asked you what makes you date the women you do. Tell her''—she inclined her head toward Charlie—''what makes you drool?''

"I, it, I . . . I have no idea," Steve said, abashed.

"Well, think about it and get back to us," Brenda ordered. "Meanwhile, I just got a great idea."

As usual when Brenda had one of her brainstorms, Charlie was scared to hear it. But she was willing to try almost anything after that disastrous dinner. She wanted her life back under her control. She wouldn't mind throwing Arthur off balance for a while, either. She needed him that way, not just to revenge herself, but because she needed to be on equal footing with him when she discussed their son and his future.

Not that she would mind if she could also get back a little of her own. He had his chance, and he'd thrown her away. Now he was back, and, for two months now he'd been tormenting her, culminating in the Thanksgiving fiasco. It was her turn.

Brenda's suggestion, however, was a little strange. "Start dating someone else," she said. "There is nothing like the possibility of another man in the picture to make a guy feel possessive."

"Don't do that. I'll help you," Steve suddenly blurted out.

"You will?" Brenda and Charlie exclaimed at the same time.

"You'll be the other man?" Brenda asked.

"No, but I'll help you with Arthur. Dating him," he clarified, looking quite pleased with himself. "Making him drool was how she put it, I think." He nodded toward Brenda.

She nodded back. "Good."

"Steve—" Charlie started to argue.

"Never look a gift horse in the mouth," Brenda advised, with a self-satisfied grin. "This should be interesting."

"I'm not sure what you want me to tell you," he said.

"What gets your juices flowing?" Brenda replied without batting an eye.

"Brenda!" Charlie exclaimed, shocked, but Steve didn't seem at all fazed.

"Hmm, I'd have to think about that." He closed his eyes, thinking back, she assumed, to his sexual experiences. It didn't take long. "I've got one," he announced. "Do you remember Clarissa, the woman who worked at the DMV?"

"I thought you didn't like her," Charlie commented.

"I didn't, but she was still hot. She did this thing women do sometimes. She touched up her lipstick after dinner, when she thought I wasn't looking. I was supposed to be looking at the dessert menu, I think, but I love watching women apply lipstick."

"Nana told me it was rude to do that at the table. She taught me to excuse myself and go to the ladies' room to fix my lipstick."

"Nana knew," he said, nodding.

"Nana knew what?" Charlie asked.

"I'm guessing she knew how provocative it is. When you pretend you're not aware that I'm watching you, but I know that you know I am watching, it's irresistible." Charlie watched, fascinated, as he licked his lips. "Then all you can think about for the rest of the evening is kissing the lipstick off."

"Hmmm," Brenda murmured. "Calvin likes to watch me put on my makeup, too. I like to watch him shave. There's something intimate about it. Good one. So what else?"

Steve stood up and walked a few steps away from the table, then pivoted to look at them. "Well, um, high heels are sexy."

"Everyone knows that," Brenda told him. "Why do you think we wear them?"

"I hate them," Charlie complained.

"Tough," Brenda said. "You've got great legs and you know what they say . . . if you've got it, flaunt it."

Steve's eyes went to her legs and Charlie shifted in her seat, tempted to hide them under the table. "Okay, okay," she gave in.

But Steve continued to examine her as if she were something under a microscope. "You've got a great neck." He came back toward them slowly. "You should bring attention to it. Touch it." He reached out and raised her chin a little. "Stroke it." His fingertips grazed her throat. "Here."

She watched as his eyes traveled downward and felt herself grow warm under his speculative gaze.

"Your skin is a beautiful color," he said pensively. He walked around her chair and stood behind her and put his hands on her shoulders. "You should show off these shoulders . . . and your back. Exposed skin is very sexy." He was really getting into the spirit of the thing now. Charlie sat very still, mesmerized by his voice as he went on. "Stockings, not panty hose," he said definitely. "And a flash of lace or satin peeking out from behind a woman's blouse makes a man want to see more."

Brenda watched them, an amused smile playing around the corners of her mouth. "Anything else?" she asked, when he stopped speaking.

"Maybe one more thing." Steve squatted down beside Charlie's chair and put his hand on her knee. "I don't know if everyone likes this, but I love it when I'm talking to a woman and she curls her long legs up under her on the couch, so all I can see are her knees." He stood up. "That's all I can think of, at the moment."

"That's enough," Charlie said hurriedly. "For now, anyway."

"That should do it," Steve said, looking down at her. "If Arthur is anything like me, she'll drive him crazy."

"Arthur? We're not doing all of this for his benefit," Brenda said scornfully.

"Why not?" He appealed to Charlie. "It'll work."

"You've met him what? Twice? Three times? And you're so sure you know him. Why is that?" Brenda asked.

"I can tell. Take it from me, he still cares about Charlie. He's back to make it all up to her. Give him a chance."

"He can have all the chances he wants," Charlie said impassively. "I'm not going anywhere."

"Except on a date," Brenda hurried to add. "There's no crime in that, is there? I'll bet you the heart surgeon hasn't been celibate all these years."

"What difference does that make?" Steve asked, disgusted.

"Ask her," Brenda suggested, pointing at Charlie.

"It makes a difference," she told him. It was true.

For years she sat around, waiting for Arthur to come to his senses and come home. Then, one day, she realized that he had moved on. On to a new life and on, she was sure, to other women. That was when she decided to date again. She was not going to stay home alone, trapped on the farm, while he did whatever he wanted, with whomever he wanted. Unfortunately, her dates hadn't been all that successful. She just didn't seem to click with any of the men she met. Frementon didn't offer many choices.

"You're sure you wouldn't want to take her out?" Brenda inclined her head toward Charlie.

"No," Steve said firmly. "What's important is whether Arthur has feelings for her. That's who she needs to go out with. That's what Charlie needs to find out for herself."

"I can get my own dates, thank you," Charlie said, stung.

"You can?" Brenda questioned. Charlie flashed a look

of reproach at her. "Sorry, sweetie. I didn't know," she said, excusing herself.

"So now you do. Don't you forget it, either. I'm not completely without resources."

When Charlie had seen Gordon Watts last, at a reception at the university, he offered to introduce her to one of the professors he knew, if things didn't work out with Arthur. It was obviously a joke, but she had told him to point the man out, and he actually found the man and introduced her to him. Bruce Anderson was an adjunct professor in the English literature department and he was not bad looking. Charlie told Brenda she would seriously have considered dating the professor, except at the time she hadn't wanted to antagonize Arthur. In light of Brenda's proposed plan of action, Bruce was the perfect candidate. There was no one whom Arthur was more in awe of than Gordon Watts. The fact that he introduced Bruce to her would probably be enough to rattle Arthur's cage, all on its own.

"Besides," Charlie told Brenda and Steve, "I was tempted to ask Bruce out anyway. This just gives me that little extra added incentive."

It was Steve's turn to snort in disgust. "I can't believe you'd consider using the guy like this."

"I just *said* I considered going out with him before this even came up."

"Yeah, but you didn't, because you still have feelings for Arthur."

"No, I don't," she said firmly.

He was definitely wrong. Arthur Ross might affect her more than she liked, but Charlie wasn't interested in having any kind of relationship with him at all. "Even if I do have feelings for him, it's not like anything healthy can come of it. There's too much history between us." She was absolutely sure of that.

"You're wrong," he said, just as certain. "You loved him for a long time. You may still. Don't you think you should find out?"

"Why? What do you picture happening here? A happy ending? That's not very likely."

"So why are you dressing up for him? Flirting with his boss? Trying to make him jealous? And don't tell me it's because you want revenge. All you had to do to hurt him was be nasty, or stomp on his ass, or even ignore him."

She wished she could be as sure as he was that she had that kind of power over her ex. "So maybe I wanted to see if I could still push his buttons."

Steve didn't buy it. "You've already proven that," he argued. "The man is obviously interested."

"I never said—" she started to protest.

"He isn't the only one," he said definitely. "You're tempted, aren't you? You'd like to see what it would be like to be with him again, wouldn't you?" Charlie hadn't realized that she had given herself away so completely.

She might not be sure of how she felt about her ex-husband, but she wasn't going to discuss that with Steve Parker or with anyone. Not at this point. "Look, you can think what you want, but this is my call," she told him.

"Just be straight with him. Tell him what you want," Steve persisted. "Dress up if you have to to make yourself feel better, but don't bring some innocent bystander into this."

"I'm not going to shoot the guy, Steve. I'm just going to ask him out on a date."

"If you do this, you're going to regret it," he warned.

"It will be fine," Brenda said soothingly.

"I'm not going to stick around to see this one fall apart," he warned.

When he left, Charlie called the adjunct professor. He was thrilled to accept her invitation to dinner.

"Mission accomplished," she reported, after hanging up the phone.

"Let's go choose your costume," Brenda suggested, actually rubbing her hands together in anticipation.

"You make it sound like a play," Charlie replied.

"It is, in a way. Mostly improvisational in nature."

"So what happens if I really like this guy?" Charlie asked her. "I mean, what will I do about Arthur then?"

"That's a whole other can of worms. Which we can worry about later." Brenda dismissed her concern.

"Okay, Scarlett. Let the future take care of itself." She waved her hand airily. "Let's deal with the current situation."

"What we need right now is a battle plan," Brenda said.

What Charlie really needed was for Arthur to go back to Boston or wherever and leave her alone. She was afraid that if there were too many more scenes like the one on Thanksgiving night, she might soften toward him, even forgive or forget what he had done. She couldn't get the image of him and Deon cuddling together on her couch out of her mind. "What I need right now is a drink."

"You need a clear head," Brenda remonstrated. "This is Deon's future we're trying to protect. You *have* to get the upper hand with Arthur, or he'll be able to beat you out of child support and cheat his son like he's done for the past ten years. You need an airtight agreement that will provide your son with what is rightfully his, whether his father feels like giving it to him or not. If Arthur could desert you once without a dime, he could do it again. You've got to protect yourself. Take care of it now, while Arthur is in this family values phase."

She knew Brenda was right. She believed Arthur meant

to take care of them from now on, but she knew she had to take advantage of his current mood and this inclination he seemed to feel to become a part of their lives. If things didn't work out, she didn't want to be left high and dry. She couldn't let pass an opportunity to insure Deon's future. "I know, I know. I just feel like taking a break," she said.

"Steve did this to you," Brenda said soothingly. "Him and his fair play. Don't let it get to you."

It wasn't Steve, she wanted to tell her. It was Arthur. Arthur and his regrets. She almost felt sorry for him, for the guilt and pain he suffered. Almost. She was shocked by the intensity of the feelings his confession evoked in her. She shouldn't have been so affected by simple words coming from the man who had hurt her more than anyone else ever had.

Maybe there was something to what Brenda and Steve said after all. Maybe the fire between herself and her ex-husband had not died out altogether. She felt way too much when he said he missed her. She felt sorry for him.

If anyone ever told her that there would come a time when she'd feel sympathy toward Arthur Ross, she'd have told them they were insane. But she did pity him, a little. She didn't know how she could have the capacity to feel for him. If it came from loving him, from still loving him despite all he'd done to her, she was in trouble. Because she couldn't live through another romance with that man. It had nearly destroyed her the first time.

She didn't want to love him again. There was too much at stake. She couldn't afford it. If Brenda's dire predictions had a grain of truth in them, her son definitely couldn't afford it. She couldn't let herself be sentimental about this. She had to be strong, completely in control, hard, and calculating. She had to be totally ruthless.

Nine

Steve called her the next day to apologize. "I still think you should deal with Arthur like you would with any other human being, but I had no right to come down on you like that," he said.

"Apology accepted," Charlie said. "Flawed though it was."

"So you wanna get together for a study session?" Charlie knew perfectly well that he didn't really think it was necessary for her to cram any more for the SATs, that it was just his way of offering her an olive branch.

"Sure, thanks," she acquiesced. "I can use all the help I can get." She was scared to death about taking the four-hour test. She had discovered, in taking the practice tests, that she had forgotten a lot of basic mathematical formulas on top of the algebra and calculus that she had always had trouble with. When Steve came over that night, she discovered that he did not suffer the same memory loss.

"You're really good at this. Why didn't you teach match?" she asked as they sat having a cup of coffee after a couple of hours of reviewing test material.

"I like teaching physical education," he replied.

"I got that," she said dryly. "I meant why don't you teach both? You teach other classes. You taught Deon social studies last year."

"The Darby school created the culture and community courses that we teach. I don't need credentials to teach them, since I was hired by the PTA, not the school board. I'm only qualified to teach academics at the kindergarten level," he explained. "I left school before I received my certificate to teach the higher grades."

"You never told me that," Charlie said.

He shrugged. "It never came up before."

"So is that why you've been so supportive? You regret not getting your certification?"

"No. I don't regret it," he said. "Gloria and I made a deal when we started dating. We both had our bachelor's degrees, and had been out in the workforce for a couple of years when we met, and one of the first things that we noticed we had in common was that neither of us was happy with our careers. Civil service seemed like a good idea right out of college, and my job in the public school system in Richmond and her job at the post office both offered security and, of course, great benefits, but we weren't satisfied. Before we got married, we both agreed that we wanted to follow our dreams, even if everyone else thought we were crazy for trying. We'd be a team. So we made a plan. First I got my certification in early childhood education; then she got her master's in fine arts. When I went back to school for my master's degree, she got pregnant. I changed my focus to physical education so I could graduate earlier. At the time we thought I could get work in the school system, figuring I'd go back and get another master's, and maybe even a doctorate in a couple of years, when she was able to go back to work.'' Steve didn't need to say that Gloria died before he could go back to school, leaving him with a child not yet two years old. Charlie already knew that part of the story.

"I'm sorry. I didn't mean to bring up bad memories.''

"No, that's all right,'' he reassured her. "I don't mind talking about it. Those were good times. And I like teaching phys ed. I'm good at it.''

"Yes, you are,'' she asserted. "Deon thinks you're the best teacher at the school. And he's not an easy grader.''

"I know.'' Steve smiled. "He's a tough little guy, your son.'' He looked at her speculatively, then continued. "That's part of the reason why I've been so . . . hard on you about how you deal with his dad.''

Charlie was feeling too good to argue with him about Arthur. "Forget it. I know you meant well.''

"I did. I want you to feel comfortable talking to Doc. Deon picks up on your feelings, whether you tell him what's going on or not.''

"I know that,'' she replied. The subject was a touchy one. She had spent ten years trying not to let Deon know that his father had abandoned them, or that she hated him for it. In a little over two months, it had become clear that she'd be unable to hide from Deon how unsure of herself she felt around Arthur Ross. She didn't want her son to sense her resentment of the man he admired so much, or make him feel that he had to take sides. She couldn't lie to her boy, though.

"Can't you just . . . I don't know . . . try to treat Arthur like you would anyone else? Other people have taken advantage of you, hurt you even, and you've always been very straightforward about it.''

"With you, I have. Not with them. Usually when someone screws me over, I walk away. I don't have the time or the energy to deal with anyone who doesn't respect me."

"You worked things out with that Candy woman," he reminded her.

"She was my boss. She couldn't really hurt me. I didn't care what she thought. I just wanted her to treat me with respect. Since I couldn't get her to do that, I left that job as soon as I could. It's different with Arthur. He can hurt me."

"I understand. I really do. But going out with some other guy isn't a good idea," he said.

"What would you suggest then, Steve? You saw for yourself how I am whenever he's around. I can't spend the next ten or twenty years breaking things whenever he's in the room. That wouldn't be any good for Deon either."

"What about your original idea? You can continue to *act* like you feel confident and self-assured around him. Eventually it will become true. I promise."

"I'm not that good an actor," Charlie said. "I just can't do it."

"I can help," he persisted.

"You did help," she replied immediately. "But it's not enough. Putting on lipstick and wearing backless dresses might help to divert his attention from my klutzy behavior, but I guarantee you, it won't change how I feel. I'll still know how clumsy I feel whenever Arthur looks at me. Dating someone else is easier than pretending I can handle him."

"You *can* handle him—that's what I've been trying to tell you. You can't see it, but you've already gotten the upper hand. All that's left is for you to realize it. He's done everything but wave a white flag."

"Well, I want the white flag," she said stubbornly.

"So try being nice," he urged.

"Nice? To Arthur? Where will that get me?"

"If I'm right about your true feelings for him, it will get you exactly where you want to be, which is back together again."

"Even if that were true, which it isn't, I don't see exactly how that would work?"

"The same way it always did. You smile, show him you're interested."

"You're saying I should seduce him?"

"What else?"

"Do you honestly believe that all I have to do is put on a pair of high heels and a backless dress?" she asked doubtfully.

"You'll have him eating out of the palm of your hand," he confirmed. "Oh, and it would help if you didn't spill anything on him. I could . . . give you a few more pointers. Maybe if you figure out why you're so nervous around him, then you'll get over it?"

"I already know why I'm so nervous around him. He broke my heart."

"That was a lifetime ago. He can't hurt you anymore."

"He's the father of my son, which gives him the power to hurt me more than anyone else in the world."

"You think he'd try to take Deon away from you?" he asked.

"Not really. No."

"Face it, Charlie. You're upset because you have to share Deon with him, not because you're afraid he's going to take your son away from you."

"But he could."

"I barely know the guy, but I don't think that thought has ever entered his mind. Do you honestly think he's suddenly going to fight for full custody?"

"I don't know. But he could. He could definitely try to get visitation."

He clearly wanted to continue arguing the point, but he decided instead to reason with her. "I still don't see how trying to hurt him, or control him, could help. You don't want to antagonize him, do you?"

"Not exactly. I just don't want to feel so unsure of myself around him."

He thought about that for a moment. "Okay, pretend I'm Arthur."

"What?" she exclaimed.

"Just try," he pressed. "I'm not me, I'm Doc. Okay? What do you really want to say to him?"

"What is this, the amateur psychology hour? I can't do this."

"Charlie, I want to see Deon every other weekend," he said, ignoring her refusal to participate in his ridiculous role-playing exercise. "Is that okay with you?"

"I can't—"

"Come on, it's not a difficult question," he continued.

Charlie knew he wasn't going to give up, so she tried to play along. "Deon and I sometimes make plans on the weekend, so I'll need you to be a little bit flexible, Arthur." Surprisingly, even though it was just Steve, she felt almost as tense as if she were actually having this discussion with Arthur Ross.

"I think we can work around that."

"What makes you think he'd say that?" she inquired.

"It's a reasonable request. He'd sound like an idiot if he said no, and from everything you've told me about him, he isn't an idiot," Steve answered.

"Okay," she conceded. "That makes sense."

He resumed playing the role of her ex-husband. "What about the holidays?"

"You can have Groundhog Day, Arbor Day, and Memorial Day. How's that?" she responded, only half joking.

He was completely serious. "What about Christmas?"

"No way."

"But you celebrate Kwanzaa."

"And Christmas, and Hanukkah, and every other holiday of the season. You have never even come to visit over the holidays. They can't be that important to you," she said.

"They're important to Deon," he countered.

It was the stuff her nightmares were made of. "Stop, Steve. I don't want to do this anymore."

"I know it's not easy, but you know there are some issues that won't be so easy to resolve," he pointed out. "If we come up with some answers—"

"We still won't have a clue whether he'll agree. I told you I can't do this, and this is why. It's too painful."

"You're just scared," he argued.

"Yes, you're right. I admit it. I'm scared," she said resentfully.

"What are you really afraid of, Charlie?" he pressed.

"I thought we just figured that out," she said angrily.

"I don't. I don't think you're afraid that he'll want to see his son in the future, I think you're afraid that he won't want to see you."

"That would make things difficult, don't you think? Certainly, as far as Deon is concerned. You said it yourself, he picks up on what I'm feeling. What do you think he'll think of me, if his father can't stand me?"

"I don't think that has to happen. But doing all this stuff you've been doing isn't going to help the situation at all. You're going to bring about the very thing you're trying to avoid."

"Why would I do that?"

"Because you're just as afraid that Arthur will come back

into your life as you are that he'll leave it again. You don't need to pull some poor sucker into the middle of this. You can handle it.''

"I don't see how," Charlie said hopelessly.

"Pretend I'm Arthur."

"Not again."

"No arguing this time. We're going to practice being nice to the man."

"How nice do I have to be?" she asked suspiciously.

"You were his first love, too. It shouldn't take too much to remind him. A look, a smile, a touch." He hesitated. "A kiss," he muttered.

Charlie couldn't believe he was actually suggesting she seduce Arthur. "You're not serious about this?"

"Absolutely."

"Kiss him. Just like that. I couldn't."

"Of course you could. You and Arthur have plenty of chemistry between you. Deon is proof of that."

"That was a long time ago."

"It will come back to you."

She couldn't believe she was discussing the possibility of becoming intimate with Arthur again. Even more unbelievably, she was discussing it with Steve. *But why not?* Charlie thought. *We've spent enough time talking about his love life.* He'd given her running accounts of his dates— not in detail, of course, but enough for her to get the gist. Why shouldn't they talk about her and Arthur kissing?

"I'd probably end up missing his mouth and getting a split lip," she said.

"I doubt that. It's simple. You just wait until the moment is right and . . . go for it."

"Simple? For you maybe. I'm not as expert at these affairs as you are. I haven't had a lot of experience in these matters, and recently there's been nothing. Even if I could have done this at one time or another, I'm out of practice.''

"If it's practice you need . . .''

"Are you suggesting that I . . . ? That you . . . ?'' she spluttered inarticulately.

"It's no big deal,'' he said.

"I think this is taking the role-playing a little too far.''

"Try it. Come on,'' he urged.

"You want me to kiss you?'' she asked incredulously.

"Just as if I were him.'' When Charlie just stared at him in utter disbelief, he took her hand. "Follow me.'' He led her out onto the front porch, then turned back to the front door. "I'm Arthur, dropping you off after your date.'' As Charlie continued to stand there, bemused, he snapped his fingers in front of her face. "Thanks, Char. I had a good time,'' Steve prompted her.

"Me, too.'' She moved closer to him. She couldn't believe she was actually thinking about kissing him. But he seemed to think it was a perfectly rational plan.

He turned to face her. "Good night,'' he said.

Charlie reached up and gave him a quick kiss on the cheek. Then she stepped back.

"No.'' He reached out to grasp her upper arm and pull her back into him. "If you have to kiss him on the cheek, stay close, so he can feel you against him.''

"Okay,'' Charlie said. "Then what?''

"If he doesn't take the hint and kiss you back, you'll have to kiss him again. And not on the cheek.''

"This is ridiculous,'' she said. "I'd have about the same effect on him that I have on you.''

"I *am* him,'' he insisted. "Try to remember that.'' He pulled her close and kissed her full on the mouth.

When Charlie would have pulled away, he put his hand

behind her head and held her in place. She couldn't move. After a moment, she didn't want to.

He lifted his lips from hers. "That's what he'll do. I'm telling you. If you give him half a chance."

Charlie could still feel the warmth of Steve's mouth on her own. "You—you can't know that," she said, faltering.

"Trust me," he said. "I know."

But she couldn't trust him. He clearly thought nothing whatsoever of the kiss that they had just shared, while her heart was pounding like a drum.

If anything, Steve's little experiment made her more sure than ever that she didn't want to get into any kind of compromising position with her ex-husband. Arthur had always had the power to make her go weak at the knees. If she were to be really honest with herself, she'd admit that he still did. She couldn't take a chance on his being able to turn the tables on her with a kiss that would mean no more to him than it had meant to Steve.

He might think he knew Arthur Ross, but Charlie really did know the man, and she wasn't going to try and seduce the good doctor into giving her what she wanted. Maybe she could have done it ten years ago, when he was as naive and inexperienced as she was herself. At this point, though, there wasn't a chance that she was more skillful at the art of seduction than he was. Between the two of them, Charlie wasn't making any bets on her sexual prowess. Steve had been able to make her senses reel, and he was just a friend. She didn't want to even think about what might happen if Arthur kissed her like that.

She was better off with Brenda's plan. She might not be absolutely sure that it would rattle Arthur's cage, but she knew one thing—dating the professor wasn't likely to get her all hot and bothered. That was more than she could say for any plan that involved seducing her ex-husband. Bruce

Anderson was a nice, safe guy. She would be comfortable dating him, even if she did feel a little guilty about why she was doing it. Charlie figured that, crazy as it was to go out with a guy just to needle her ex-husband, at least she wasn't really hurting anybody. And, this way, she couldn't get hurt either.

Ten

The adjunct professor was a charming, intelligent dinner companion. They had dinner at a cute little restaurant near U.V.A.—a cozy Italian place that seemed popular. On that Friday night, Bruno's was lively, full of young people and families. Charlie felt right at home.

"This is a great place," she told him.

"You've never been here before?" he asked.

"No, I never heard of it."

"I'm glad I brought you here then," he said.

"Me, too," Charlie replied. She and Bruce Anderson seemed to agree on just about everything. He loved the same books that she loved. He even understood her desire to go back to school.

She surprised herself by telling him about that. She hadn't even told Arthur yet. She was afraid Arthur would think that she was overreaching herself, or worse, that she was being silly, but Bruce thought it was a great idea.

"In a way, you're lucky," he told her. "I sort of wish I'd been older when I went to college. I'd have appreciated it more than I did."

"Why?" Charlie asked, curious.

"Because I went straight out of high school, so for me it didn't feel like much of a privilege to go. Don't get me wrong, I enjoyed it, but I went mainly because my parents expected it, and I only worked as hard as I had to. I'm a different student now, in grad school. I want to do good work—the best I can—because I know I'm there for me, not for my parents or anyone else."

"Going back to school at my age doesn't sound so crazy when you put it like that," Charlie said appreciatively.

He had a solution for each of the obstacles she faced. No money? Apply for grants and scholarships. He could turn her on to a couple of sources. No time? What about nights and weekends? Her son couldn't take up every minute. People with kids went to college all the time. Which was exactly what Charlie wanted to hear. If she had met Bruce before Arthur came home, this relationship might have had a future, she told Steve at their weekly breakfast the following Sunday morning.

Apparently Bruce enjoyed himself as well as he called on Monday to ask her out again. "We can go to a show or something."

"I'd love to go," she told him. "But I'm not sure when."

"My schedule is wide open," he answered promptly. "You choose the date and the time and I'll be there."

It was a nice change of pace to have a man who was so eager to please. Charlie couldn't help but feel flattered. "Well, umm, this weekend is my weekend with Deon." She and Arthur hadn't consciously worked out a schedule for Deon's visits to his place, but one had evolved naturally. Her son spent every other weekend with his father, and one night a week after school—usually Tuesday or Wednesday. "I might be able to get away next Tuesday evening. Deon is supposed to go to his father's place for dinner."

"That sounds fine," Bruce said. He sounded happy. "I could pick you up at your place."

"Or we could meet at the County Café on Sixty-six, at around seven," she suggested.

"Sure," he agreed. "Whatever works for you."

"Okay," Charlie said, somewhat flustered. "I guess I'll see you next Tuesday."

She hung up the phone feeling elated, and nervous. This very nice man, who had brains, personality, and everything else a girl could ask for, seemed pretty intent on dating her. She'd explained—as best she could—about Arthur, he knew about her son, and she told him about her dull-as-dishwater job, and still Bruce wanted to date her.

She wondered if her grandmother would approve. Nana had always suggested that she try to meet "a nice young man." Ruby Brown didn't seem to expect Arthur Ross would return, but she never believed that Charlie would end up alone. Charlie herself, however, had begun to think she might follow in the family tradition. One Brown woman or another had chosen to raise her children on this little farm without any man to help her, including the original Ms. Brown, the freed slave Sophia, and most recently Ruby herself, as well as plenty of others in between. Charlie's mother might have done the same, but in her case, apparently, she couldn't cope without a man.

Charlie didn't know why the farm couldn't seem to support the men of the Brown family. Perhaps it was a curse. Great-Great-Aunt Imelda had a husband, but during the Depression he couldn't get work of any kind, forcing her to sell off half of the acreage to keep the wolf from the door. After keeping the family together through the worst of the economic blight, her husband left as soon as the Browns were back on their feet. Somehow they managed to do without him.

There had been another aunt, the sister of the widowed Petunia (whose Native American husband was lynched in 1899), whose husband had decided they should also move away—but to more exotic locales, such as Paris, where supposedly she sang or danced, or did something on the stage.

The family stories that had been passed down for over one hundred years all included variations on this theme. Women alone seemed to be capable of nurturing life on this small farm. She and Deon might be better off, Charlie sometimes thought, without a third party around the house to confuse things. Men had never done her much good. But Bruce did seem nice. She was more than tempted to spend another evening with him. It was just a shame about the timing.

"When it rains, it pours," Brenda said when Charlie called to tell her the news that night after Deon was asleep. Brenda was thrilled for her. A little too thrilled. Charlie began to suspect she hadn't been completely honest about her motives when she suggested dating someone besides Arthur. Once she started thinking about it, it didn't take Charlie too long to figure out that Brenda had never intended for her to get the upper hand with her ex-husband by dating other men. She had some nefarious reason of her own for suggesting that Charlie should ask someone out.

"Brenda, what do you think is going to happen here?" she asked.

"What do you mean?" her friend replied innocently.

"Bruce is a nice guy and all, but—but I'm not in a position—"

"You're free, single, and over twenty-one. You're in the perfect position," Brenda said, correcting her.

"I'm too . . . confused to consider starting anything like that at this point in my life," Charlie protested.

"So who told you to start anything?" Brenda said. "Just try to stay open to the possibilities."

"No," Charlie said, but even so, her second date was going nicely until Steve and Arthur showed up at the County Café and sat down at the next table.

Charlie couldn't believe her eyes when she looked over and saw them. "Oh my God," she cried involuntarily.

"What?" Bruce jumped.

"Sorry, it's just . . ." She waved a limp hand toward the table where Arthur and Steve were sitting. Bruce looked over in time to see Steve nod and Arthur wave back at her. "That's my ex," she explained.

"The big guy with all the muscles?" he asked warily.

"No, that's Steve. He's a friend of mine. Or he was," she said, glowering at him as she spoke to Bruce out of the corner of her mouth.

"So, what do you think they're doing here?" he asked. Luckily, he didn't seem to mind the intrusion. In fact, he smiled at them, amused.

"I don't have a clue," Charlie said. "Arthur is supposed to be with Deon." She raised her voice enough for them to hear her at the next table. "Where are the boys?"

"They're at my place," Arthur replied.

"Alone?" she asked.

"We just stopped in here for some dessert and coffee," he said casually.

"Make it to go," she commanded.

"Okay, okay, we weren't planning to stay," Arthur said.

"It's for all of us. The kids, too," Steve added.

"Good," Charlie told them. "You never know what the

kids could get up to while you're here *spying on me*." The
last came out in a low growl. It had a galvanizing effect on
Arthur, who jumped out of his seat and gestured to the
waitress. Steve stood up more slowly.

"It was nice to meet you," he said cheerfully to Bruce.

"Yeah, sure," the younger man said, laughter in his eyes.

Steve followed Arthur up toward the front of the café,
where they intercepted a waitress and, presumably, placed
their order.

Charlie dropped her head into her hands. "I'm so sorry,"
she said.

"Don't worry about it," Bruce responded. "They're
probably just trying to watch out for you. I have a little
sister. I know how they feel."

"I don't care how *they* feel. They're being jerks." Arthur
and Steve stood near the door, waiting for their order and
watching her and Bruce.

"I'm sure they didn't mean to embarrass you."

"Well, they did. And I don't have the same respect for
their motives that you do," Charlie retorted, annoyed.
Steve's and Arthur's actions were irritating, but Bruce's
defense of them really irked her.

"Why are you getting so upset?" he asked. "It's over
now." He waved toward the door, and she turned her head
to see that the spies were leaving.

"I'm not getting upset," Charlie spluttered. I'm just . . .
I don't think it was funny, what they did."

His smile disappeared. "Okay," he said seriously. She
could tell he was just humoring her. That annoyed her all
over again.

"Look, Bruce," she began.

"Uh-oh," he said. "Here it comes."

"What?" she asked.

"The speech," he said, shaking his head.

"I'm not going to make a speech," she denied.

"You're not?"

"No."

"Good," he said, smiling.

"I just wanted to say one thing."

"Not a speech, though." He was still smiling.

"No, just . . . this is a complicated situation and I don't know how fair it is to get you involved in it."

"Okay," he said, nodding.

"So . . ."

"So why don't you let me decide?" he said.

"Decide what?" she asked.

"Whether I want to be involved."

"But you don't understand the situation."

"I can live with that," he said. "Let's just see what happens. Okay?"

Charlie let it go. This was only their second date. There was no need to beat it to death. Bruce seemed like a nice guy. He handled her friend's and her husband's spying with aplomb. She liked him. Maybe she would see him again. Then again, maybe she wouldn't. Nothing had to be decided right away.

It wasn't him she was angry at, really. It was her ex, whom she never planned to speak to again, and her best friend, whom she planned to call as soon as she got home.

"Steven Parker," she barked into the phone. "What in the world were you thinking?"

"Sorry, Charlie," he said immediately. But he didn't sound very apologetic.

"How could you?" she demanded.

"It was a spur-of-the-moment thing. We didn't plan it or anything."

"Believe it or not, that was pretty obvious," she said. "I had to explain to my date that my ex-husband just started his career as a stalker. He's not too good at it yet."

"He's not a stalker. He's . . . an interested party."

"I can, sort of, understand Arthur's behavior, but what the heck were you doing there?"

"We were there to get coffee. That's all. Anyway, I thought the whole idea was to make Doc jealous." He excused himself. "You should be happy. It worked."

"So that's why you were there?" she asked skeptically. "To help me?"

"We-ell." He drew out the word.

Charlie took a deep breath. "Why were you really there, Steve?" she asked, calmer now. "Why did you tell Arthur about my date? I wasn't going to mention it yet."

"I didn't." He licked his lips.

"Right!" she said in disbelief.

"It's true," he protested. "He called me."

"Then how did he—" Halfway through the question, she knew the answer. Deon. Of course.

"Damn," she muttered. "Why didn't you tell me about Deon?"

"I just found out tonight. When Arthur called. You see why you can't fool around like this? All kinds of problems can come up," he enjoined.

Charlie didn't appreciate his tone of voice. He was the one who was in the wrong, not she. "Look, I know you don't think I should do this, but I can't do it your way. I *can't* seduce *Arthur*. Even if you're right, I just can't do it. But I need to level the playing field somehow. You've got to understand that. I've explained it. I need him to be off balance, whether because he's jealous, or indignant, or whatever. I just . . . I want to have the upper hand. Instead you made me feel like an idiot, having to explain to Bruce who you were and what you were doing there.''

That obviously hadn't occurred to him. "What did you say?" Steve asked, genuinely curious.

Frustrated, she asked, "What do you care, Steve?"

"I care about you. And Deon. I don't want to see either of you hurt."

"So you and my ex follow me around? That's very helpful," she said sarcastically.

"It's not like it was a big secret, you had planned to tell Arthur sometime. I mean, the whole idea was to let him know, right?"

"I think you've been living in this town too long. Everyone thinks they have the right to butt in to everyone else's business."

"Not everyone's business, just family," he said as if that justified everything.

"This was private. Not for general consumption," Charlie said angrily. "When I want you to know my business, I'll tell you. You don't have any right to *spy* on me. No one has that right. Especially not Arthur, that . . . creep."

"You make it sound like he's some kind of psycho. He just wanted to get a look at the man you were dating. We weren't peeking around doorways or anything," Steve protested.

"That's all right then, I guess," she said wryly.

"I have to admit I was . . . curious, too," he said without contrition.

"Why?" she asked wonderingly.

"Because of the way you talked about the guy."

"His name is Bruce."

"Bruce," he repeated. "I haven't heard you say you wanted to date anyone in a while, and I just wondered what he was like."

"You wondered?" She was momentarily at a loss for words.

"I didn't know whether it was him or the situation. I thought maybe you were just teed off because Brenda suggested me as your date and that's why you were suddenly so interested in this guy."

"You're trying to protect me from myself?" she asked incredulously. "Who do you think you are?"

"The same thing I've always been. Your friend. So do you forgive me?"

"No," she responded. "Not yet, anyway." But she wasn't as angry as she had been. She had allowed this to happen. She had asked for his help. "I'm not a child. I don't need your protection. I can take care of myself."

"I know."

"Obviously not," Charlie said, contradicting him.

"I realize it now," he declared. "I just . . . forgot. I've gotten so used to thinking of you as . . . family. You came to me for advice and then refused to listen. I guess I lost my head."

"Well, you can be sure that I won't be asking for your advice anymore."

"Don't be like that, Charlie. I'm really sorry. I would never do anything—"

"No, you won't. You won't have the chance." As he started to protest, she interrupted him. "Look, this was partly my fault. I did come to you. You were the first person I thought of when I heard my ex-husband was coming back. I think of you as someone I can talk to about anything, especially about Arthur. The first person I told. Even before Deon. It's hard to find a friend you can really confide in in this town without worrying about everyone hearing about it. You and Brenda were the only ones in town who didn't know him, who didn't see me when he left me in a bloody mass of pulp. I think of you two as my . . . family, too."

"I'm glad you think of me that way."

"Thanks, but—" She had to tell him the whole truth. "I was using you, too. You more than Brenda even. Because you're a man. I thought you could give me some insight into what I was up against."

"We're not choosing teams here, Charlie. If we were, I'd be on your team. All the way," he assured her.

"I believe you. But I think I'd better handle this on my own from now on."

"But—"

"No buts. I appreciate your desire to help. Really. I just don't need it."

"Charlie!" He started to argue, but thought better of it and started again. "I don't want this to hurt our friendship. Or anything. You are very important to me."

"I don't want this to screw up our friendship either," she echoed.

"Good, I guess," he said hesitantly.

He sounded so uncertain. She hated that. "You're forgiven, buddy. Okay?"

"I promise never to embarrass you again," he vowed.

"Uh-huh," she said warily.

"Swear to God. Never." She pictured him holding up his hand as he swore.

Charlie smiled to herself. "Good." She couldn't stop thinking that nothing would ever be the same again. She had always been able to talk to Steve about anything, and now there was this big gap between them. They shared the same fundamental beliefs in almost everything: parenting, politics, movies. He was her best friend. She knew he only wanted what was best for her. It was just that they so completely disagreed on what that might be. He wanted her to get back together with Arthur. She was going to break his heart.

Eleven

Charlie couldn't decide whether she should invite Bruce to the Christmas festival at Deon's school that Friday. It would have been perfectly natural to ask him, even though they had only spoken once since that disastrous second date. Pretty much everybody in Frementon attended the annual party, thrown on the last Friday before Christmas. It was a town tradition, and she loved the whole day. She was certain Bruce would enjoy it, too. There were games and hot spiced cider at the school, a living nativity scene at the little Baptist church, and strolling carolers, as well as musical performances by the church choir and anyone else who wanted to perform in the school, the churches, and the firehouse. Best of all was the tree-lighting ceremony.

"But Arthur will definitely be there," she told Nana, when she visited her. "He's going to be at Deon's school for the kids' concert, and probably at the church singing hymns, like he did when he was a kid." She didn't really want another embarrassing incident, like the one at the County Café. ''Bruce really will think he follows me around,'' she said.

Charlie had no doubt that her grandmother would tell her she was playing with fire. Which was why, in the end, she decided not to stir up the coals by inviting the new man in her life to a function that she'd attended from the age of seven to the age of seventeen with her first love. Maybe she was just saving face, but she couldn't stand the idea of showing up at the town's premier social event with both her ex-husband and a guy the inhabitants of Frementon hadn't met before. It was going to be difficult enough to bear the scrutiny and field the questions of her neighbors. Charlie had absolutely no intention of providing more grist for the rumor mill.

When festival day came, she was glad she'd made that decision. Deon seemed very happy to have both of his parents there, for the first time ever. Little as she wanted to feed any fantasy he might have about the chances of a reunion between herself and his father, Charlie didn't put up any resistance as Deon dragged Arthur about by the hand to meet his friends and proudly reintroduce him to their neighbors.

The doctor got a lot of curious looks and even a double take or two, while Charlie was on the receiving end of some very pregnant glances. Hearty shouts of ''Where have you been?'' and ''What have you been doing with yourself?'' usually accompanied the greetings of those who had known him during his childhood. A wink at Charlie or Deon accompanied questions like ''So, are you back to stay?'' or ''How long are you in town for?''

Jeanine Donner couldn't resist mentioning that he missed their high school class's tenth reunion just that past summer. Charlie remembered that the woman had asked her for his current address. ''I know we sent you an invitation,'' Jeanine scolded. "It was fun. People came down from Washington, D.C., and everywhere. Evelyn Tremont even came all the way from San Francisco."

"Did she really?" Arthur answered, opening his eyes wide.

"Evelyn's got six brothers and sisters that live within an hour of here," Charlie said to him, sotto voce. "She comes home to visit every summer."

"Jeanine, how is Evelyn?" he asked, smiling.

"She has six children, including a set of twins," Jeanine informed him. "She married someone nobody knows, and his job took them to Frisco. She misses home, that's for sure."

"Don't we all," Arthur said, nodding sympathetically.

The person he seemed to enjoy meeting the most was Brenda's husband, Calvin. It was the oddest thing. Arthur and Calvin took to each other right away. Brenda was disgusted. She kept giving her husband dirty looks throughout the evening. He seemed oblivious of her disapproval and he and Arthur were the best of friends by the time the festivities ended. As one of the organizers of the events, Charlie had to stay and make sure that everything got cleaned up.

"I'll take Deon home," he offered.

"I'm sleeping over at Michael's house tonight," his son told him. "Right, Mom?"

"Yeah. That's the way we planned it," she agreed. "He does it every year. The boys do their Christmas shopping together."

"Okay," Arthur said, deflated.

"Bye, Dad," Deon said, throwing his arms around his middle. Arthur hugged Deon, and their son ran off, completely happy.

"Well, I guess this is good-bye, then." It was more than

obvious that he didn't want to leave. Charlie empathized with him. It had been a great day. Deon's enthusiasm was contagious. She still felt invigorated, too. On the other hand, she still had work to do. He was just going to go home to an empty apartment. It had to feel emptier than ever after a day like today. She should have been elated, euphoric even, at the thought of it, but Charlie felt sorry for him.

So, apparently, did Calvin. "Why don't you come on over to our place and have a drink?" he asked, ignoring his wife, who was silently mouthing *No!* and gesturing emphatically with her hands.

"Great," Arthur said, unaware of the undercurrents between husband and wife. Charlie laughed out loud at Brenda's annoyed expression. Calvin didn't know it yet, but he was going to be in big trouble when she got him alone.

"Charlie, should we wait for you?" Calvin asked, oblivious.

"No, no, you go on," she told him. "I'll meet you later."

She didn't rush to get to the Tremaines' house, but instead took her time, checking with the janitor about their clean-up operation, directing the parents who had volunteered for clean-up duty, and, finally, helping the security guard make sure the building was secure. Charlie used the short drive to the Tremaines' house to gear herself up for seeing Arthur in yet another setting in which she had never expected to spend time with him—Brenda's homey country kitchen. She had a pretty strong suspicion that Brenda would be fuming by the time she arrived.

As it turned out, Calvin was keeping Arthur company and Brenda was nowhere in sight. Neither man appeared to be missing his hostess. They were deep in conversation. "The thing I missed most while I was away was that feeling of a united community who all looked out for each other," her ex was saying as she came into the kitchen. "Hi, Charlie," he greeted her perfunctorily, then went back to their discussion which Charlie listened to for a moment before leaving them to find Brenda. They were chatting about the charms of rural Virginia, which they were both rediscovering after long absences. Arthur had barely been home since he left for college, and Calvin had spent the last decade trying to make it as a corporate lawyer in New York City after growing up in North Carolina.

"The city isn't conducive to socializing either, at least not for me," she heard Arthur say as she walked down the hallway toward the back of the house.

Brenda was closeted in the spare room, flipping through a pile of paperwork that she'd chosen to deal with rather than trying to make casual conversation with the heart surgeon she so despised.

"You don't have to hate him on my account," Charlie told her.

"I don't hate him," Brenda replied. "I barely know the man. But from what I do know about him, I don't feel any desire to get to know him any better."

"Calvin likes him. They're in there right now comparing notes on coming back to the farm," Charlie reported.

"Male bonding," she answered, snorting contemptuously. "I don't know what is wrong with that man. It's like he's forgotten what that bastard did to you."

"Steve thinks Arthur's here to make up for all that. Maybe Calvin agrees with him."

"Don't you worry, Charlie," said her loyal friend. "Calvin wouldn't dare agree with that crapola."

"I'm sure he won't . . . after you're through with him," Charlie said, grinning.

"Damn straight," Brenda assured her.

"So, shall we go out and confront the enemy?"

They joined the two men in the kitchen, who were still

talking about country life, and its attendant joys and sorrows. "I can't believe the traffic. There is none," Arthur was saying. "In Boston, cars don't even move out of the way for fire trucks and other emergency vehicles. Here, friends will stop and say howdy in the middle of an intersection."

"True," Charlie responded. "But that isn't always a good thing. It may seem nice and neighborly now, but wait until you've been home awhile and it will start to drive you crazy."

"I don't think so," Arthur said. "I'll never get tired of having people treat each other with respect and courtesy."

Brenda must have taken exception to his tone, because she shot him a dirty look and stood up to go to the refrigerator. Charlie thought she heard her friend mutter something like "You should try it some time." Then Brenda stuck her head in the icebox.

"Is anybody hungry?" she asked. "I've got a cheesecake in here somewhere." She slammed the refrigerator door shut and swung the freezer door open with so much force that it slammed back against the counter next to it with a loud thump.

Calvin finally noticed his wife. "Do you need any help, honey?" he asked, solicitously.

"No, I've got it," she answered, tossing the cheesecake into the microwave to defrost.

Her husband ignored her body language and took her at her word. He turned back to his new friend. "It's true that there usually isn't any traffic, but I do miss public transportation," he commented.

Brenda placed four small dishes, dessert forks, and a long, slim knife on the countertop. "You can cut the cake," she half asked, half ordered, as the timer on the microwave binged at them, signaling that the timer had reached zero. Calvin didn't respond and Charlie could see that her friend was nearing the end of her tether. Brenda brought the dessert over to the island that separated the kitchen from the living room and reached for the knife. "Fine," she said. "I'll do it."

"No," Calvin argued, snatching the stainless steel blade up off the counter. "I can do it."

Apparently, however, he couldn't. The knife slipped and he cut himself instead—right across the wrist. Blood spurted from the wound. Arthur was by Calvin's side instantly.

"Oh my God," Brenda cried.

"You must have nicked a vein, Calvin. Come over here by the sink so I can wash this out and see what damage you've done. Brenda, help me get his shirt off."

"Ow," Calvin exclaimed. "That hurts."

"Sorry, but I've got to keep pressure on it. It's a very nasty cut." He turned to Charlie, his hand going to his pocket from which he pulled a key ring. "Please get my medical bag out of the car," Arthur said calmly, throwing her his keys.

She caught them and turned on her heel. "Be right back."

Behind her as she rushed out of the kitchen, she heard him speaking calmly to the panicky couple. "Brenda, do you have a first aid kit?"

"Yeah, somewhere. I'll find it."

Charlie found his bag of medical supplies in seconds and ran back inside. The two men were alone. She assumed Brenda was still looking for the first aid kit. Rather than stand idly by, she soaked a rag with cold water and cleaned up the blood that had fallen on the counter and on the floor.

Arthur spoke soothingly but firmly to Calvin. "There's no artery entry, but you do have a serious venous injury. We've got to take you to the hospital and get this stitched up. Can you bend it, like this?"

"I can." Calvin groaned. "But it hurts like the devil."

Watching her ex-husband in action made Charlie feel a

twinge of pride that he was hers once. She watched, fascinated, as Arthur tied a strip from his bag around Cal's forearm.

"I think I'll be fine now," Cal said, through clenched teeth.

"You definitely need stitches." Arthur insisted.

"He's phobic about hospitals. The only doctor's office he'll visit is his pediatrician. He's been going to the man since he was born," Brenda said briskly as she entered the room carrying a small blue plastic box with a red cross on it and a handful of boxes and bottles she must have scrounged from her medicine cabinet. "Can you take care of it here? Then I can take him to have it looked at in the morning by Doctor Carey."

"It's not exactly . . ." he started to say, but stopped to steady Calvin as he swayed slightly on his feet. Arthur looked from him to Brenda and finally at Charlie. "I guess we could do that. You have to promise not to sue me for malpractice if his arm falls off," he joked.

"I promise. Just so long as I don't have to go to the hospital," Cal agreed.

"Can you use any of this?" Brenda asked, setting the supplies she'd gathered on the counter.

"Yeah," Arthur said. "That alcohol to sterilize my hands."

"Can I help?" Charlie asked. She had wiped up all the spots of blood scattered about the room and put the sleeve of Calvin's shirt in some cold water in the sink to soak and couldn't think of anything else to do that would be useful.

"You can hold this," he said, motioning her toward him. He put her hand on the thick gauze pad he'd clamped onto Calvin's cut. "Keep pressure here."

He went to the sink. "Brenda? The alcohol." She brought the bottle to the sink and poured the isopropyl alcohol over his hands. As he walked back toward Calvin and herself, he suddenly blurted out a question. "Do you ever wish we could turn back the clock and do our whole lives over differently?" Brenda and Calvin ignored him. They must have sensed that the question was meant for her, not them.

"Huh?" Charlie's mouth dropped open. "What?"

He didn't look at her as he came over and looked down at the wrist she held. She followed his gaze. The red stain on the gauze was slowly spreading under her fingers. Blood was still oozing from the cut.

"I do," he said, busily removing various items from his medical bag. "In the past ten years not a day has gone by that I haven't thought about you. Missed you," he said as if it were the most natural thing in the world to suddenly bring this up here. Now.

He spread out the materials he'd been preparing on a clean white cloth napkin, and put it on the counter next to Calvin.

She started to get up, out of his way. "No, stay there," he ordered. "I could use your help. Dip each of these sutures in the iodine, and then hand them to me when I ask for them. Okay?"

Charlie felt as if she were going crazy. Or he was.

"What about me?" Brenda asked bravely.

"You can hold Cal's other hand," he said, not unkindly. He positioned himself in the small space between Calvin and Charlie. "Cal, don't move, okay? Charlie, you can take the gauze off now."

He had taken a small clamp out of his bag, and when she took the bandage off the cut, he quickly attached it to Cal's arm. Charlie blanched, but didn't move. She held her hand over the needles she was supposed to hand to him.

Arthur examined the cut carefully, poking at it a little. "This lidocaine with epinephrine will numb the area," he said, then used a hypodermic to inject the anaesthetic into the skin around the wound. Each time he pricked Calvin with the needle, the other man hissed in pain. "Sorry, Cal. But it's over now," he said. Then, without missing a beat, he stated with slightly less emotion, "I still love you, Charlie." He didn't even look at her but kept his gaze on Calvin's mangled wrist. "Hand me the suture scissors from my bag, will you?"

The little scissors were next to the sutures on the napkin. She gave them to him. "Did you hear me?" he asked.

"What?" Charlie asked, dazed, watching as he pulled the edges of Cal's wound open a little, cutting minute slivers of his skin away here and there.

"I said I still love you," he repeated.

"Uh-huh," she murmured, fascinated as she watched him work, and befuddled at the idea that he could appear to be completely focused on the wound he was preparing to sew closed while initiating a conversation about their relationship.

"I love Deon, too. You know that." She couldn't think of anything to say to him, but he didn't wait for a response anyway. "I was stupid. I didn't know what else to do." He handed her the scalpel. She put it back on the napkin. "Vicryl, please. That's the three-O silk. One of the small ones." She handed him one of the small silver needles through which he'd threaded short lengths of silk. "I'm not trying to make excuses." His hands moved deftly over Calvin's forearm as he put the stitch in and tied it. "I agreed to the divorce even though I knew you didn't really want it, because it seemed like the only way out." He handed her the needle. "Another suture. I was a coward. I know that."

Charlie didn't doubt his feelings. His tone of voice was just as intense as his concentration on Calvin's injury.

"Okay." He removed the clamp and waited for a moment. "That's done."

Fascinated as she was by his revelations about the past, the dramatic events unfolding in front of her were just as intriguing. "How do you get those out of there?" she asked.

"They'll dissolve inside him in a while, and by then the vein will have repaired itself."

"Cool," Charlie said, impressed.

He looked up at her, a smile playing around his lips. "Yeah," he agreed. "Hand me the larger suture needle please." She gave him what he asked for and he bent back over the site of the wound. "This four-O silk will have to be removed by a doctor, though," he explained to Cal. "Why did you ask for a divorce?" he asked, without looking up at her.

Charlie was getting used to this strange conversational style of his. She thought back to when she'd been seventeen, alone and scared, and waiting for him to come and rescue her. It all came flooding back to her. "I was spending a lot of time in the library, and Mrs. Chambers and I talked about the situation. She suggested a do-it-yourself divorce as one of my alternatives. It was a shock to me to hear the word. I thought it might shock you, too . . . into choosing me and our baby. I didn't think you'd ever actually consider signing it."

"I've regretted it ever since. At the time I thought it was either you or medical school."

"You were probably right," she said. It was the first time she'd thought about that moment without feeling diminished by the fact that he had chosen to continue his education over staying with her. "I don't think we could have managed to pay for college and everything else with Nana and Deon to take care of, too." It didn't seem so terrible, suddenly, that he took the way out she had offered. He was only seventeen.

"Maybe I should have tried. I love my work. But I'd rather be digging ditches than spend another ten years without you in my life. There,'' he said, satisfied, handing her the needle he'd been stitching with. After she put that with the others, she looked down at his handiwork. It looked perfect to her.

''At the moment, I'm very glad you're a doctor,'' she said sincerely.

''Me, too,'' Calvin chimed in. Charlie had almost forgotten he was attached to the wrist that Arthur had been repairing.

''I think if he doesn't lie down, he's going to fall down,'' Brenda said, looking from her husband to Arthur.

''Let me just . . .'' He reached over and retrieved another gauze pad from the countertop and quickly taped it in place over his handiwork. ''You can take him to bed,'' he said. Brenda helped Calvin up out of his chair, and steered him toward their bedroom.

Arthur started to clean up the area where he'd been working. Charlie watched him, bemused. She didn't know how to respond to all of this. After a moment, he spoke, still without looking at her. ''I know I blew it, but if you could try to forgive me, a little bit, and get to know me again, maybe we could have a future together.''

''I don't know,'' she finally said. He waited, expectantly. Charlie hesitated, at a loss for an honest answer for him. She was confused and unsure of herself and of him. The whole incident had been so surprising. It didn't feel real. ''I can't just erase everything that's happened between us.''

''Don't erase it. Just . . . put it away for a little while,'' he begged.

Charlie was given a reprieve as Brenda came back into the room. ''He's asleep already,'' she said.

''He'll probably need these, in the morning.'' Arthur fished a bottle of aspirin out of the pile of medical supplies on the counter and handed it to Brenda. ''Keep the bandage dry,'' he admonished.

"Thank you," Brenda said. She held out her hand to him, and when he took it, she covered it with her other hand. "I really appreciate what you did for us."

"It's okay. All in the line of duty," he joked. "Well, I guess I should be going," he said to his hostess, but he looked directly at Charlie. She knew he was still waiting for her answer.

Brenda didn't seem to notice the undercurrents between them, though she couldn't have missed his declaration of love. He'd said it out loud, for anyone to hear. Charlie watched her walk away, but Brenda didn't even glance in her direction. "I'll get your coat," she offered.

"Mine, too," Charlie called after her retreating back. She looked around the kitchen, to make sure they hadn't left a mess behind. To her amazement, it looked just as it always did. There wasn't a single outward sign of the evening's momentous events. Inside, she was a mass of conflicting emotions: pride, nostalgia, frustration, and hope.

"Thank you for inviting me over," Arthur said politely when Brenda came back with their coats.

"Thank you for coming," she replied just as courteously as she handed them their overcoats. Arthur put his tweed on, and picked up his bag; then Brenda led the way to the door. Charlie followed behind them both and watched Arthur exit, then hugged Brenda good-bye.

"He may not be as bad as I thought," Brenda whispered in her ear.

Arthur had done it again, Charlie thought as she followed him down the path to her car. He'd managed to disarm his severest critic. There was no chance that she could manage to hold out against him all by herself. She might as well give in right now. Even if Steve and Brenda and everyone in Frementon was wrong, and Arthur was just going to take her on another roller-coaster ride like the last one. She had one very good reason to risk it. She owed it to Deon. Her son would be overjoyed if things actually worked out between them.

He was waiting by her car door. "Well?" he asked. "Is there any chance that you and I can become friends again, Charlie?"

"Of course," she responded. "You're the father of my son. I always wanted us to be friends."

"I don't want another truce just for Deon's sake. I love you, Charlie, I've always loved you. Just, please, give me a chance to prove it to you."

"All right, all right," she gave in.

Arthur smiled. Then he bent his head to give her a quick peck on the cheek. "You won't be sorry," he promised.

Charlie wasn't sure she agreed with him, but she nodded. They stood facing each other in the dark, and she felt overwhelmed again with the feeling that they'd regressed somehow ... traveled back through time to their high school years. She was glad he couldn't see her clearly. She didn't think she could have hidden her nervousness in the full light of day. She rubbed her hands against her legs, to dry her sweaty palms. She clamped her jaw shut, to stop her teeth from chattering aloud and giving her away.

Apparently, her feelings were communicated to him anyway. "God, I feel like I'm thirteen again, dying to ask you out on a real, official date and scared to death to do it." They always had been on the same wavelength. That had been one of the good things about their relationship. She felt like he understood what she thought and without her having to tell him. He just knew.

"Fear can be a good thing," she said. "It keeps you safe."

"I don't want to be safe," he retorted. "I want to be with you, to reach out and touch you." He reached out and brushed his hand against her cheek. "I want to hold you again."

"Well, that certainly wouldn't be safe."

"I'm shaking like a leaf," he confessed.

"That's good. I mean, it's only fair," she said, hastily correcting herself. "I'm terrified."

"Of going out on a date? With me?"

"That, aaand . . ." she responded, dragging the word out as she tried to decide how much she should tell him about her feelings. ". . . I'm not sure about that other stuff you said, either."

"What?" he asked. "Getting back together? Would that be so bad?"

"Not bad, exactly." She could still feel the spot where his fingers grazed her cheek. "More like . . ." There was only one word that really described it. ". . . dangerous."

"Maybe that's what the two of us need," he suggested. "Maybe a little danger is just what we need to get us out of this stalemate we've been in."

"Not me," Charlie said. "I've already taken enough risks in my life to last a lifetime."

"Does that mean you wouldn't go out with me if I asked?" He took a step closer. "If I promise there'd be no risk involved?"

"I'd have to think about it," she said gravely.

"Take a chance, Charlie," he urged. He leaned over and kissed her, full on the mouth. Even with his lips closed, and his hands at his sides, that kiss still felt like trouble to her.

When he stepped back, all she could do was stare at him, her jaw dropping to her chin. She knew what she must have looked like—wide-eyed and gaping at him—but she could not help it. She'd never been very good at hiding her emotions, and at that moment, she was too busy trying to sort through all the feelings that kiss had evoked to worry about what he might think of her. Charlie couldn't figure out whether it was passion that heated her blood, or anger at his presumption.

There was only one way to find out. "Do that again," she ordered.

This time Arthur didn't hold back. His arms went around her waist as his mouth slanted over hers and his tongue found the slight dip where her lips met and gently coaxed her to open up for him. Her bulky parka was no barrier to the heat emanating from his body and she was engulfed in his warmth. Memories of earlier times flooded through her. It had been so long. She threw caution to the wind and kissed him back.

When he finally lifted his head, she kept her arms locked around his neck, and looked up into his eyes, wondering if he felt the same way that she did—that something had changed between them. The kiss was different than she remembered. Something was missing. But he looked thoroughly satisfied. He beamed down at her, disgustingly pleased with himself.

"Mmmm," he murmured, as if she were a hot fudge sundae that he'd just taken a bite of. Charlie gently disengaged herself and stepped back.

"You were really impressive tonight. With Calvin." She looked back up at the house they had just left.

"Impressive enough to take you out to dinner tomorrow night?" he asked. "I'm supposed to go out with some friends anyway, so there shouldn't be any risk involved."

She looked up at him curiously. "You're not thirteen anymore?" Charlie asked.

"I'm all grown up now," he said happily.

She let him wait for a few seconds while she thought about whether she was really going to do this. "Okay," she agreed.

Twelve

The evening had not started out at all well. First Deon acted rather strangely when she told him she had a date with his father. She thought he'd be ecstatic. Instead, he seemed almost bored. As she was preparing for the evening, he came into her room and sat on her bed, watching her with a morose expression.

"How come you're going out and leaving me here alone at night?" he asked accusingly. Charlie was surprised at the question. He usually begged her not to get a sitter. That was why, when she couldn't find one, she'd decided he could stay home alone for the very first time. Arthur had agreed that he was old enough—and promised her he'd get her home by nine.

"I'll be back in a couple of hours. Then we'll do the tree."

"Why do you have to go to this party?" he asked. "I thought you didn't even like Dad much."

''Your dad and I are trying to work on that. I thought you'd be happy about it.''

''I am, but why do you have to act so weird around him?''

''I don't act weird,'' she argued.

''Yes, you do. At Thanksgiving I thought you were going to bust a gut.''

''Where did you learn that expression?'' she asked, in order to cover the mortification she felt on realizing that her young son had noticed what a dolt she had been around Arthur. ''Anyway,'' she went on, when he didn't answer, ''I was nervous. It was a big meal and I hadn't ever cooked for your father before.''

''So?'' he said, nastily.

''Soooo, I wanted to make a good impression.''

''Well, you didn't,'' he said. ''Even Michael noticed, and he thinks you're perfect.'' This was news to Charlie. She knew Steve's son was attached to her, but she figured that was because he was starved for a woman's attention.

''He does?'' Since she saw quite a lot of him, she tended to fuss over him a bit because he didn't have a mother to do it. He seemed to like it, unlike her own ungrateful child.

''You better not tell him I said anything,'' Deon warned her, realizing that he'd betrayed his friend's confidence.

''Don't worry, I won't.'' But it felt good to know the boy liked her. At least she wasn't a complete dud with the opposite sex.

Deon wasn't finished with his critique. ''You didn't ever used to borrow Brenda's clothes. You used to say they weren't very practical.'' When she got over her surprise at the fact that her ten-year-old son had any idea what she thought of her friend's clothing choices, she dealt with his comment. ''I didn't mean for you to hear me say that, and I would appreciate it if you wouldn't repeat it. Ever,'' she said in her most dire voice. ''It wasn't kind of me to say something like that, and it would definitely hurt Brenda's feelings if she heard you say it."

"So why are you wearing them?" Deon asked.

"Because your dad's friends are very . . . sophisticated and I want to fit in," she tried to explain. Deon didn't seem satisfied with her explanation, but she didn't have time right then to discuss it further with him. Arthur was due at any moment. "We'll talk later, okay?" She made a mental note to have a talk with him as soon as she had the chance and finished preparing for her date. This time she'd borrowed a very pretty, formal dress from Brenda. Not the standard little black dress, but a red silk, form-fitting sheath with a slight flare at the thighs so it swirled around her legs when she moved.

Deon dragged himself out of her room, obviously unsatisfied, and for a change, he didn't come out of his room to see his father before they left. Charlie realized that she had made a mistake. She shouldn't have allowed Arthur to influence her decision. She was Deon's mother, and she knew her son; he wasn't ready to spend an evening by himself. But there was nothing she could do about it right then. She couldn't cancel her first official date at the last minute. Charlie was sure Deon would be all right alone for a couple of hours, even if he wasn't too thrilled at the prospect. If she hadn't believed that, she wouldn't have planned the evening the way she had, no matter what Arthur had said. In the future, though, she would get a sitter, whatever anyone else might say.

After that rather unsettling incident, she wasn't particularly happy at being lectured by Arthur about giving his friends a chance this time.

"I promise I won't sneak off by myself," she finally promised him, as they drew up to the restaurant where they were going to meet a group of the doctors and their wives for someone's birthday dinner. Some of his friends had been at the dean of medicine's lawn party and they recognized her right away and tried to include her in their conversation. Unfortunately, she put her foot in her mouth almost as soon as she joined in with the conversation.

The gentleman seated to her left told her, "Dennis has been saying that he prefers riding Arabian horses to the native breeds because they're more responsive to commands from their rider. What do you think, Ms. Brown?"

Charlie answered him. "Horses aren't native to Virginia, or this continent, so there are no native breeds. But, if he means breeds like the Morgans or Tennessee jumpers, which were first bred here in the states, I'd have to say that I think that breeds that were created for riding are just as sensitive to their riders as Arabians, in general."

Arthur gave her a look that warned her that her opinion wasn't exactly welcome, although the silence that greeted her response left her in little doubt that her comment hadn't been considered appropriate.

"It depends on the horse, and the rider, of course," she added, hoping to make up for her blunder.

Dr. Jonas Appleby—which, she discovered during the introductions a moment later, was the name of the man who'd asked her the question—was no longer listening. He became engrossed in his conversation with Dr. Dennis Johanson, who was sitting across the table, and he didn't solicit her opinion again that evening.

There were others at the table, however, who were more charitable. They ignored her faux pas and included her in their wide-ranging discussion of everything from finding baby-sitters to good antique furniture. A lot of the conversation revolved around shopping. The doctors, male and female, liked to talk about buying big-ticket items such as cars and houses. The spouses, and a male and female nurse who were married to each other, discussed food shopping and interior decorating.

Charlie quickly learned that they didn't want to know where to buy what they wanted, but where to shop for it.

"They *really* like shopping," she told Arthur on their way home. "The process. Not buying stuff, but finding neat shops and browsing and all that. It's amazing that they all found each other."

"That was just polite conversation," he informed her. "It's safer than, say, politics or religion, and they all have to work together. When we're socializing, we don't want to discuss anything controversial."

"Such as what?" she asked. "Abortion?"

"Yeah, that would be a subject we'd avoid," he said, with a wry grimace.

"Who makes these rules? The A.M.A.?" she asked.

He laughed, but didn't try to explain it. Instead he changed the subject. "I hope you had a good time."

"It was okay. It's going to take a while to learn how to have a real conversation with your friends."

"They're not close friends," he said. "We work to-gether."

"You said that already," she pointed out. "What is so important about working together?"

He had to think about that for a moment. "It's very de-manding, and it's difficult to make a life that isn't centered on your hospital schedule, so you sort of end up with a group of friends that aren't . . . high school pals, or college buddies, or whatever. They are the people who are free when you are and who understand when you can't shuffle your schedule to suit their convenience. Friends from work. You don't share your political views, or family problems, or your spiritual life with them, just your free time."

"It doesn't sound like the basis for a very satisfying friendship," she commented.

"It can be. If you're lucky. I had a good friend when I was an intern at Boston General, Jim Tolin. It turned out that he was from a very similar background, and we had a lot in common."

"Where is he now?" she asked.

"He's still in Boston. He's hoping to open his own practice. Plastics are his specialty."

"Do you miss him?" Charlie inquired.

"Yes, sometimes. But, you know, I've been really busy lately, trying to get a life, as Deon would say," he joked. "We e-mail each other occasionally."

"Maybe he can come down and visit sometime," she suggested.

"Maybe," Arthur said doubtfully. "I think he likes to spend his vacations in the islands."

"So? What, you're never going to see each other again?" she asked.

"Who knows? We could end up working in the same hospital. I could go back to Boston, or he could come down here."

A moment ago, Charlie had been concerned by Arthur's lack of real friendships, but her attention was diverted by his casual tone when he mentioned going back to Boston.

"Go back to Boston? Why would you do that?"

"I have connections there. If a good position on the cardiac team became available, they might offer it to me."

Charlie couldn't believe he talked so dispassionately about a move like that. She might have understood it if he'd sounded homesick for the place, since he had lived there for the last decade, but there wasn't even a hint of emotion in his voice when he said Boston. It was only when he mentioned the cardiac team that he sounded excited.

"So let me get this straight. You'd go back to Boston if they offered you something like that? I thought you wanted to stay here at U.V.A."

"I do," he said. "But I couldn't pass up a great opportunity like that. I may have to wait years for a permanent position on the staff here."

"What about us? What about being a part of our lives?" Charlie asked, trying to keep her voice from betraying her feeling of fear.

Apparently, he didn't hear it. He answered her in the same detached tone. "It's not very likely that anything like that will happen." He looked down at her, and she saw a gleam of speculation in his eye. "If it did, and we were together, you guys would come with me, I guess," he added, hopefully. "Wouldn't you?"

"Uh-huh," she murmured, distracted. They were almost at home by then, and she didn't have to say anything more, which was good since she was at a loss for words.

She couldn't believe he was so unconcerned about where he might live in the future. Clearly, he planned to go wherever his work took him. He felt no strong connection to his roots. It should not have been a surprise to her. All he ever wanted, when they were kids, was to get out of Frementon. But as a teenager, his dream had been to be a doctor at U.V.A., and when he came back, she assumed that it was to fulfill that dream. Now she didn't know.

Charlie didn't notice when he reached her house and parked the car. He'd turned off his Jeep and turned to her before she realized that they were sitting in the darkness, frigid air slowly seeping into the SUV and mixing with the overheated air inside. His eyes glinted in the black night as he reached for her. Through the window she saw thousands of stars sparkling in the slate-gray sky behind his head, before she closed her eyes to savor the taste and feel of his mouth as it opened over hers. His palm caressed her cheek as he gently sucked on her lips. Charlie felt his teeth against the tip of her tongue as she slipped it into the warm, velvety depths she hadn't explored in so long. Her worries forgotten already, she surrendered to the strength of the feelings he was arousing with his mouth and hands.

The nostalgia she had felt when they first kissed was gone, replaced by the strange feeling that it wasn't Arthur Ross who evoked this passionate response, but a complete stranger—one whom she had never touched or kissed before. Her memory imbued him with the power to make her knees weak and her blood sing, but this man didn't do to her what she expected. His body felt good against hers. His strong hands and full lips awakened feelings within her that she hadn't felt in a long, long time, but it was as if she'd never been intimate with him. The body, the hands, the lips, could have belonged to any of the men she'd dated for the past ten years and found lacking because they couldn't compare with him.

His hand roamed across her back and slid around the back of her neck, and a shiver ran down her spine at the touch of his long, masculine fingers against the sensitive skin at the nape of her neck. He felt her quiver and he smiled against her lips; then his mouth moved down over her cheek and chin. She sighed, and smiled herself. Familiar or not, this man's touch was magic.

It had been a long, long time. She forgot all about her son, waiting for her inside the house, as her breathing grew heavy and harsh, and Arthur's hands, and hers, sought for and found flesh beneath coats and scarves, shirt and dress, until she was brought back to earth by the sight of her porch, including the swing, empty flowerpots, and all. The porch light was on. It hadn't been when they pulled into the driveway some twenty minutes before. She didn't know when it had been turned on, but she knew who had done it.

"Stop, now. We've got to stop," she panted, pulling herself out from under his torso, and trying to untangle her arms and legs from his.

"What?" He didn't seem to comprehend what she was saying as he craned his neck, trying to follow her retreat away from the driver's side of the car.

"We've got to cool it, Arthur. I've got to get inside. Our son is waiting and he knows we're here." He straightened up and peered out of the window at the house.

"Huh? How do you know?" He tried to straighten his collar and his tie.

"The porch light is on. It wasn't when we drove up." She buttoned her shirt, which had somehow come open to the waist.

"My God!" he exclaimed. "Do you think he's watching?" He gave up on his tie and pulled it off.

"No, I don't think he would. Or anyway, I don't think he can see anything. The light is behind him, and it's completely dark out here. And we seem to have steamed up the windows a little."

"Well, ummm," he murmured, clearly at a loss for words. "Do you think he's going to be upset?"

"Yes, I believe so," she answered. He had been unhappy when she left. Perhaps if they'd gone straight into the house when they arrived home, he would have felt better about them going out without him. As it was, she imagined, he wouldn't be too happy about their extracurricular activities.

"Well, we'll just explain to him that we're adults. We—you and I—have a right to, um . . ."

"Fool around?" Charlie supplied. "I don't think that's a good idea. He's already angry with us."

"Us? What for?"

"I don't know. Maybe he's a little bit jealous of our date tonight. Whatever the reason, I think I'm in for it tonight."

"Do you want me to come in with you?"

"Nah. I can handle him. I hope."

Arthur looked sympathetic. "Is there anything I can do to help?" he asked.

"I'm going to promise him that we got a little carried away but we're going to control ourselves from now on. You can apologize when you see him," Charlie said.

"You can't be serious," he replied.

"I am completely serious. We're not teenagers anymore."

"Of course we're not. That's why I don't think there's anything wrong with ... what did you call it? ... fooling around. At our age, it's not like we'll make the same mistake again."

"That's not funny," she chided him.

"I know," he said apologetically.

"That's why I don't want to rush into a physical relationship with you," she said.

"You don't trust me yet," he said sadly.

"I guess not," she said. "At least, not enough."

He covered her hand with his. "It's okay. I understand."

She turned her hand over in his so she could curl her fingers around his palm. "I am glad." She gave him a kiss on the cheek. "Call me tomorrow. I'll tell you how it goes." She opened her door. "No, don't get out," she added as he started to open his door as well. "Good-bye, Arthur."

She caught his muffled response, " 'Bye," as she closed the door behind her. Charlie hadn't felt the cold until now, but as she ran up to the house, she realized the temperature had dropped steeply.

Deon was waiting for her in the kitchen when she came in. "You were supposed to be home half an hour ago," he scolded.

She went directly to the stove and turned the gas on under the kettle. "I was only a few minutes late," she said, excusing herself.

"I was worried, so I watched for you out the window. I saw you drive up. What were you doing in Dad's car all that time?" he demanded.

"I'm sorry, but that's none of your business, young man," she said repressively.

"Anyway, I know," he said, clearly disgusted. "You guys were making out."

"That's enough of that," Charlie said firmly. "This is not something that I'm going to discuss with you."

"Why not?" he asked petulantly.

"You're the child. I'm the mother. I don't have to explain myself to you. But, as a matter of fact, I wanted to tell you that your father and I are not going to be ... making out like that again."

"You're not?" He sounded genuinely surprised.

"No, we're not. We are just starting to date again and work all this stuff out. Tonight we got a little carried away, but we're not going to do that again, okay?"

"Yeah, sure," her son said, trying to sound nonchalant, but looking quite pleased with himself.

However, over the next few days, it became clear that Deon obviously didn't care for the new arrangement. He made obnoxious little remarks, whenever he thought he could get away with them, and he was downright rude about any touching, hand holding, or kissing. Charlie wasn't thrilled by Deon's attitude, but she figured he was going through some kind of adjustment. She could understand that. She was finding it a little difficult to get used to Arthur's proprietary air herself. At least Steve was happy. Apparently, her son had let him in on what was going on, and he called to congratulate her.

"Thanks, bud," she said. "I was worried you wouldn't approve."

"Of course, I approve," he said. "I've been telling you all along that this was going to work out."

"Don't be so smug," she said. "You might have warned me that Deon wasn't going to like it."

"He'll come around," Steve insisted. "Wait and see."

Thirteen

On Christmas Day, Arthur showed up with his car trunk full of gifts. "He must have bought every single thing Deon ever showed a passing interest in," she said to Brenda as the men carried a mountain of boxes and bags into her house and stacked them around the tree. Everyone helped to open them. He had bought Nintendo games Charlie hadn't even heard of, and football gear, and soccer and baseball, and, of course, basketball paraphernalia, including socks, sweats, jerseys, protective padding, posters, trading cards, autographed balls, and more. He also gave his son a Walkman, a set of weights, and sweat bands for working out. The list went on and on, including ridiculous gifts like cans of Goop and Silly String, toy cars and videocassettes, board games and puzzles. Last, but not least, there was a model rocket set, which Arthur promised to help Deon build and launch.

"He's nuts," Brenda proclaimed.

"He's making the most of this opportunity to show his

son how much he loves him," Steve said softly to Charlie after he helped carry some of the unwrapped booty out to Arthur's car to be brought back to Deon's room in Arthur's apartment. It definitely wouldn't all fit in Deon's room in the farmhouse.

"Aren't you worried that Michael—" Charlie started to ask.

He cut her off. "He won't be jealous. I've taught him better than that. Besides, he knows he'll get to play with all this stuff, too. I can practically guarantee that all he's feeling right now is happy for his best friend."

Deon himself was obviously overwhelmed, but he didn't seem as enthusiastic about his father's generosity as Steve had been. He was, of course, thrilled as he opened package after package containing gifts he couldn't help but appreciate, and he hugged his father, and kissed him, and thanked him again and again, but Charlie knew her son well enough to know that he wasn't as impressed by this largesse as he had been when his dad gave him a teddy bear on their first night together. He'd slept with it ever since even though he'd outgrown stuffed animals a couple of years before. Poor Teddy, she noticed, had been migrating steadily from his pillow to the foot of his bed over the past few days, but he hadn't kicked it off the bed. Yet. This morning, though, he let his father choose which of his shiny new toys would stay at the farm and which would grace his bedroom in town. He didn't seem to have any preference, one way or the other. She found it curious, and a little bit unsettling, but he was being so stoic about it that Charlie left him alone rather than asking what was bothering him.

She found out after lunch. He excused himself after only one helping of eggs, grits, sausage, and ham, and Steve followed him out to the family room. Everyone else was still eating, and she was too busy serving her guests to focus her full attention on the two of them, she saw through the window that they'd gotten their coats and gone outside. They were tossing a football back and forth when she went out to the backyard to tell them that she had made Deon's favorite dessert, a chocolate pecan pie. They didn't notice her right away, so she overheard what they were saying.

"I liked everything, but how come he got me so much stuff?" Deon asked as she came out the kitchen door.

"I think that shows that Doc really paid attention to you when you talked to him about what you liked," Steve answered. "Don't you?"

"I guess," her son agreed. They tossed the football back and forth a couple more times, and just when she thought that that was the end of the conversation, Deon asked another question. "Why didn't he just choose one big thing, like Mom always does?"

"Maybe he's trying to make up for all those Christmases and birthdays that he missed," Steve replied. Charlie winced. She had bought something and pretended it was from Deon's dad for every special occasion in her son's short life. "I would do that, I think."

"You wouldn't. You would never miss Michael's birthday. Or mine." The plaintive note in the ten-year-old's voice made Charlie's heart ache. She thought Deon had grown accustomed to his father's absence when he was five or six years old. It appeared she was wrong. "I wish he was more like you, or my other friends' dads. Even the divorced ones. I don't know why he gave me all that sports stuff. He doesn't even come to see me play anymore."

"He has been spending a lot of time with you, though. Right? I know Michael and I don't get to see as much of you since he's been home because of the weekends you guys spend together."

"Yeah," Deon drawled. "But . . . he only likes to do

things in town, like go out for ice cream or go to the movies, and stuff like that.''

''Stuff, huh?'' Steve repeated. ''Stuff like laser tag, and Disney movies. Stuff you always liked to do before.''

''Yeah,'' Deon said, smiling meekly. He knew he wasn't being very reasonable. Charlie was glad that Steve had managed to get him to admit that.

''So, what's the problem, buddy? He's not like the other dads, because he's *your* dad. He's special. You're getting to know him. I think that's pretty cool.''

''I guess so.'' Deon nodded, throwing the ball back with renewed energy. ''He likes that rocket set. He said we could build it together. That would be good.''

''Good, what do you mean, good?'' Steve scoffed. ''It will be great!''

''Uh-huh,'' the boy said. He wasn't completely convinced, but he seemed a bit happier. ''When it's done, will you and Mike come to the launch?''

''You bet, Deon. We'd love it!''

A week later, on New Year's Eve, Steve came up with yet another brilliant idea to bring Deon and Arthur closer together. He attempted to arrange for Arthur to give Deon a belated Christmas gift, one that Charlie was sure it had taken him a lot of time and trouble to obtain. Steve had gotten Deon's hero, Julius Irving, to autograph and write a personal inscription on a photo of himself, and not just any photo, but one of him in his New York Nets uniform from his days in the A.B.A.

Steve was not very good at covert operations, Charlie discovered. He got Arthur's phone number from her and, though he refused to tell her why he wanted it, it wasn't hard to figure out once Arthur gave Deon the unusual gift.

''Didn't you go to school with Doctor J's son?'' she asked Steve when she saw him next.

"Yeah," he answered slowly.

She nodded, satisfied. "I thought so."

"Why did you want to know that?" he inquired.

"Just . . . curious," Charlie replied, and didn't say anything more.

Deon wasn't fooled by Steve's little ruse either. She didn't know if that had anything to do with his rudeness toward his father, but he made it clear that he still didn't approve of his parents' revised relationship. Over the next few weeks, they fell into a routine where, on the weekends when Deon stayed with Arthur, Charlie often joined them for part of the time, either Saturday night, or Sunday during the day. On the weekends when Deon was supposed to be with her, he usually slept over on Friday night at Michael's and Steve's house, while she and Arthur went out.

Steve more than made up for her son's lack of enthusiasm. He vetted her outfits on Friday nights when she dropped Deon off on her way to meet Arthur, and he offered to keep Deon as long as she liked on Saturday morning, so she could have the time to "catch up with old friends." On Sunday, at their breakfasts, he pumped her for details, and nearly rubbed his hands together in glee with every positive comment she made. He didn't seem at all concerned that the situation between Deon and Arthur was getting worse and worse.

It came to a head when Arthur came over to take them out to dinner, and Deon objected, vociferously.

"Why can't we stay home and order pizza and watch TV?" he demanded. "Why do we always have to go out?"

"I wanted us to have a special evening," Arthur tried to explain.

"This is our life," Charlie had interjected, trying to smooth things over. "Every night doesn't have to be an event. Who can live that way?" Neither of them responded.

"I know you're trying, Arthur, but it's hard to dress up and go out all the time. At home we can spill food on ourselves and not worry about it."

"All right," he agreed, suddenly. "Let's stay here."

Deon seemed surprised, and pleased, that he had won the argument, but Charlie could tell he wasn't completely mollified. That night was the beginning of a new phase in Arthur's and Deon's relationship. He treated his father with respect, appreciated his gifts and treats, but he didn't seem to trust the man, despite Steve's machinations. Arthur did not seem to be picking up on his son's feelings at all. He thought that it was his apartment that Deon didn't like, that that was why Deon tried to get out of visiting with him. Charlie had tried to talk to him about it, but he just said that he and Deon would work things out.

Unfortunately, they didn't seem any closer to an understanding two weeks later when Arthur asked them both to his house for dinner instead of inviting her on their usual Friday night date.

"I'm supposed to go to dinner with Michael," Deon told his father, his chin set.

"You go to Michael's house every week," Arthur countered. "I bought burgers and franks for you and salmon for your mother and me."

"You know I always go to Michael's house on Friday. You planned this just so that you can split us up because you don't like my friends," Deon accused.

"Yes, I do," his dad argued.

"You never come to school anymore to see me play basketball."

That night, Charlie settled the matter, announcing that they were going to Arthur's place so the two of them could talk it out. She told Deon he could see Michael on Saturday. Deon sulked, while Arthur tried to get his son to talk to

him. When he couldn't get him to respond, he gave up. They
barely spoke to each other all evening.

She didn't know if Deon told Steve about the argument,
but after that he started treating Arthur a little more coolly.
By the end of January, he seemed to have changed his mind
about Arthur and herself . "Why don't you wear your own
clothes?" he asked one Sunday morning at their weekly
breakfast. She was dressed to go out and meet Arthur and
his friends at a horse show.

"You sound like Deon," she retorted.

"I do?"

"Yes, you do."

"Well, he's right. I thought you two were supposed to
be getting to know each other again. Arthur can't get to
know you unless you show him who you really are."

"I am. He likes these clothes. He asked me to wear them."

"This specific outfit? He chose this for you?"

"Sure. He knows where we're going and I've never been
there before, so he gave me some advice. Anything wrong
with that?"

"Nothing really. I don't understand why he would do
that, that's all. He doesn't seem ... I'm just surprised that
he isn't spending more time here with you and Deon together,
that's all."

"He will," Charlie said. "When he gets used to being
home. I'm *sure* he will." She kept telling herself that Arthur
would get comfortable in her house again. If he didn't feel
at home there, Charlie was afraid he'd be looking to leave
at the first opportunity. She told herself that he'd relax and
settle in as the two of them grew more comfortable with
each other, but it did worry her.

Apparently, it made Steve nervous, too. "What's wrong
with that guy?" he said the first Sunday in February. "He
hasn't been to a b'ball game in weeks."

"What's changed?" she asked him. "You used to like Arthur."

"I don't understand him. You've got a great place here, a great kid. His kid. If I were him, I'd hang with you guys here every chance I got. If he can't see what a wonderful life you have, he doesn't deserve to be a part of it and I feel sorry for him."

"You don't act like you feel sorry for him. You act like you're angry at him. And at me," she pressed.

"I thought you wanted to make something of yourself."

"And I thought you wanted me to get back together with Arthur."

"I did. I do. But not at the expense of everything you had planned. Come on, Charlie, you just got started on all this. College. A good job. A future. You don't want to lose momentum now, do you?"

"No, of course not, but I've been pretty busy studying."

"I went through the classified ads for you." He picked the newspaper up from the table. "Some of these jobs sound pretty good. I circled the best of them," he said.

Charlie groaned. "I can't deal with this right now," she told him. "I have to concentrate on the SATs."

"Okay, but as soon as they're over, you're going to get serious about the job search, right?"

"Right," she promised.

"Good," he said, but he didn't seem completely satisfied. "Keep the paper."

Charlie couldn't worry about Steve's strange change of heart, though. As her SAT test date approached, she grew more and more distracted. By the eve of the big day, she felt as nervous as a cat. Deon was no help. He seemed to have picked up on her nervousness. He flung himself around the house, banging into walls and throwing things that made great bumping noises that she kept having to ask about.

Finally, she asked him to take a bath so that she could get a little peace and quiet. She ran the bath for him, then called him in to take it, while she made herself a cup of tea. She drank it, staring at the test preparation book she'd bought.

Fifteen minutes later, she went and knocked on the bathroom door. "Hey, Deon?"

"Yeah, what?" he called out to her.

"You want to go to a movie?"

"Now?" His voice squeaked, he was so excited. "Yeah, mon."

"That's Mom, not mon."

"Whatever," he said, but without the usual scornful undertone. "What are we going to see?"

"Whatever you want," she yelled. She heard the water splashing onto the floor as he got out of the tub, and a moment later he opened the door wearing his terry-cloth robe. She drank in the clean little-boy smell of him and felt, for the first time in days, like she was actually doing something right. She'd put him through a lot in the last few days, or weeks, or months. It was about time she started to make it up to him.

Later that night, when he was in bed, and she'd gone back to staring at the SAT book again, she realized she had forgotten to ask Steve an important question. Without thinking, Charlie reached for the phone.

"Huh, hello?" Steve's sleepy voice echoed through the phone line.

She'd wakened him. "When I get to the test I have to fill out a form telling them which colleges I want the results sent to and I can't decide whether to have the test results sent to the colleges I'm applying at, or to wait and send them myself after I see if I do better or worse than I did the first time."

"Wait," he answered immediately. "I'm sure your scores will be higher, but you don't lose anything if you wait."

"Okay, thanks." She hung up without saying good-bye, she realized a moment later. "Rats!" she said to herself. "I'm losing my mind." She debated whether she should call again, but decided it would be odd to call him back just to say good-bye. She'd call Steve later. When the test was over.

The day of her SAT test dawned bright and clear. It seemed wrong, somehow, that the earth continued to spin, the sun to rise, and the birds to sing, when she felt the icy fingers of impending doom approaching. She drove in a haze to the high school where the test was going to be administered. Charlie couldn't believe she was about to do this to herself. She looked around at the nervous, young, excited faces around her, and felt completely out of place. What was she doing here?

Once the test started, she lost track of everything else. It was only she, two number-two pencils, and the test paper with its columns of A,B,C,D,E in their little red circles, interrupted briefly by an uncompromising test monitor with a steely voice who called, "Time's up," over and over again, until finally she said, "Lay your pencils down and pass your test papers up to the front of the class, please."

As she walked out into the parking lot, Charlie felt as though a huge weight had been lifted off of her. It was done. Now she could go home and relax.

She'd asked Steve to take the boys for a play date and sleep-over anticipating the need to go home and collapse after her ordeal. She walked into her house and threw her SAT preparation book into the garbage, then sat at her kichen table, thinking about the blissfully peaceful afternoon and evening she was going to have. The last thing Charlie expected was a phone call from Professor Bruce Anderson, but he called a couple of hours after she arrived home from the test.

She had completely forgotten that she'd agreed to go out with him to celebrate after she took the SATs. It wasn't until she heard his voice on the phone that it came back to her.

"Hi, Bruce," she said in response to his greeting, her heart falling.

"Hey, girlfriend, how did the test go?" he asked.

"It's over. That's all I care about," she answered. "I meant to call you before this, but what with studying and all I forgot." She had intended to explain to him the next time he called that she was dating Arthur, but she hadn't gotten around to it, what with all the upheaval in her life.

"That's all right," he said airily. "We still have plenty of time to plan the evening."

"Uh, well, there may be a minor problem. Remember I told you that my ex-husband was back in town?"

"The heart surgeon, right? How could I forget? He showed up at dinner. That was one date I won't forget for a while."

"Well, it may sound strange, but we've decided, that is, I've decided to . . . see him again."

"This sounds serious," he said, sardonically.

She winced at his choice of words, but had to admit, "I guess it is, sort of."

"Oh?" he prompted her

"Serious," she clarified.

"Oh," he said, getting it. There was a pregnant pause, dead silence on the line; then he spoke again. "So, let me be perfectly clear here. Are you trying to tell me that you're not available for dinner?"

"N-no, but, well, I . . . I mean, I'm available, I guess," Charlie stuttered, surprised that Bruce still seemed to want to go out with her.

"Have you taken a vow of some sort?"

"No, but I am seeing him again," she repeated.

"So you don't want to see me?" he asked, sounding a little disappointed.

"I just didn't want to give you the wrong impression—" she tried to explain.

"I'm not afraid of a little competition," he said, interrupting her. "And you did promise we'd celebrate when you took the SATs, remember?"

"I'd like to, but everything else aside, I don't think I'd be very good company, Bruce. I didn't get much sleep last night."

"You dissin' me?" he asked. "You dissin' *me?*" His impression of Robert De Niro was horrible, and it wasn't improved by his use of ghetto talk, but it did make her smile.

"I would never do that," she assured him.

"Hey, wench, I thought we were gonna get jiggy with it tonight."

"I don't think I know how to get jiggy," she answered, laughing.

"Don' worry about it," he said. "We'll do sometin'."

"Now you're a Rastafarian?" Charlie teased.

"Hey, there's only so much you can learn from one Spike Lee movie. I'll roll on by your crib at seven, aw'ite?"

"Aw'ite," she agreed, chuckling as she hung up the phone.

Fourteen

Charlie's daily routine had changed so drastically that she sometimes felt as if she were living someone else's life. Who would ever have thought that at brunch that Sunday they would not be talking about Steve's date of the previous night, but hers.

"I thought I might fall asleep on him, after staying up all night worrying about the test, but he took me to this beer joint that all the students go to and there wasn't any chance I was going to conk out in the middle of all that noise."

"Sounds like you had a good time with the boy professor," he said in a snide tone. She had never condemned *his* dating habits, no matter how ridiculous, but Steve made it clear that he still disapproved of her relationship with Bruce Anderson, despite the change in his feelings toward her ex-husband.

"What do you have against Bruce?" she asked him straight out.

"Nothing. I don't even know him, but his timing is really bad," he said dismissively.

"That's not his fault," she pointed out.

"No, it's not," he agreed, directing a meaningful look at her over the top of his coffee cup.

"It's not *anyone's* fault." She defended herself against his unspoken accusation. "That's just the way things happen sometimes. Ex-husbands reappear."

"And ask you to give them a second chance," he taunted.

She stared at him in disbelief. "And your obnoxious friends tell you you should give it to them," she retorted, then stuck her tongue out at him. He was the one who told her she should take a chance on Arthur.

"Only if they really seem right for you," he said, self-righteously.

Charlie wanted nothing more than to wipe that self-satisfied expression off of his face. "And you knew, the minute you saw him, that Arthur was right for me," she said sarcastically. "How is it that you can do that, coach? Figure out who's right and who's wrong for a person without knowing anything about them?"

"I know you," he said, as if that vindicated him. "I know you were still in love with Arthur even after all those years, and that the two of you deserved a second chance. I can't help it if Doc is blowing it with you by trying to impress his buddies at the hospital."

"Hey, I know. You can write a book! How about Match-making 101? It would be the perfect job for you. Those who can't do, teach." She regretted it as soon as she said it, but Charlie was tired of being told what she should do. It had been his advice that had led her into the mess in which she now found herself.

"Okay, okay. I'll back off," he said, holding his hands up, palms out. Surrendering to her.

"Where have I heard that before?" she jeered.

"I mean it this time. I'm not going to say another word about your men. You can handle them on your own."

Charlie liked the sound of that. Her men. Plural. She suddenly realized that she was actually dating more than one man at the same time. It was a first for her. She should try and enjoy it. It would probably never happen again. "Whatever happens," she told him. "I'm going to make the most of the situation. In my own little way."

"So, now that that subject's been declared out of bounds, let's move on to a more important topic," he proposed. "Work!"

Charlie had been expecting something like this. She'd gained a temporary reprieve a week earlier when she begged him not to bother her about the job search until after the SATs were out of the way. But she'd taken the SATs yesterday. She had no more excuses for delaying the inevitable.

"Okay, but I'm not looking forward to this," she commented.

"Why not?" he asked, raising his brows inquisitively.

"I hate quitting," she said as he cleared off the table in front of them.

"Tom's Gas and General?" Steve was honestly surprised. "You hate working there."

"I know, but . . . it's home," she whined. "Anyway, I've quit worse jobs, and I always end up feeling horrible."

"That's because you never had anything better lined up. This time we're going to find you the perfect position. Something with a future," he promised.

Charlie resigned herself to becoming the subject of Steve's newest pet project as he pulled the classified section out of the Sunday paper on the seat next to him and spread it on the tabletop between them. "You know what's worse than quitting a job?'' she asked. He looked up inquiringly. ''Interviewing for a job,'' she said with a sigh.

Charlie's life suddenly became a roller coaster: Job interviews were scary and often demeaning, her life was too boring to write about in the essays required by college applications, and, most frightening of all, the more time she spent with Arthur, the more she realized that he was nothing like the boy she remembered. He was suave, self-assured, and he could be fun to be around, but his life revolved around his profession. All of his friends were doctors like him, accomplished, established, and socially adept. The more time she spent in his circle, the more she realized that she didn't want to get to know these people. It seemed they lived on a different planet—light-years from her small country farmhouse.

Her most pressing concern was Deon. She tried not to let the pressure she was under affect the way she treated him, but it was impossible. Her son had to bear the brunt of her frustration simply because he lived with her and because he was ten, which meant that he was loud and he was demanding, particularly since he was hurting. She just didn't have the energy to cope with his frustration and her own at the same time.

Worst of all was his ambivalence toward his father. Nothing she said to her son seemed to make him feel any better about his father, or her relationship with him.

''He's probably jealous,'' Brenda theorized. ''It was bound to happen sometime. He's had you all to himself his whole life, and here comes this big, strange man who takes up lots of your time and energy.''

''But he was fine when Arthur first came home,'' Charlie argued.

''You didn't like your ex back then. Deon only started

acting this way after you and Arthur started dating again, right?''

"Sort of," Charlie answered. She thought back over the past few months. ''He was starting to act a little strange after Thanksgiving, but I guess it came to a head after he saw Arthur kiss me good night.''

"Classic oedipal conflict," Brenda said, smiling.

"It's not funny," Charlie remonstrated.

"No, it can be very serious. What is Arthur doing about it?'' she asked, putting on a mask of concern.

"I don't know," Charlie answered gloomily.

Arthur was compounding the problem with his obvious delight at the way things were going between him and herself. She just couldn't understand it. Didn't Arthur see that Deon flinched every time he gave her a kiss hello or good-bye? Did he think that it was normal for a boy Deon's age to be so glum? she wondered. He had to remember how his son acted when he first arrived. Didn't he miss that excitement—the wonder in the ten-year-old's voice when he heard that Arthur's boyhood bedroom had been painted blue, too? Was he truly unaware of the change in Deon's attitude toward him? Or was it possible that he was embarrassed to admit that he didn't know what to do, or too proud to ask for help? She couldn't believe that he hadn't noticed. On the other hand, if it hadn't been for Deon, she might have become preoccupied with him, too, she thought. They were doing a lot of necking these days. It was just like being back in high school, except that he didn't wear Brut anymore, and instead of Nana waiting up to scold her for staying out late, she had Deon scowling at her over breakfast.

For the last ten years, Valentine's Day had been a sort of sad little holiday as far as Charlie was concerned. When she was a child, and throughout her teenage years, Valentine's Day had never passed without her receiving a token of Arthur's love. The year that he had chicken pox, a friend of his, Harvey Allen, had shown up on her doorstep with a box of candy. She threw it in the bushes by the front porch before he could tell her it was from Artie. Then she had to pick up the candies out of the dirt and kiss them to God before she ate them. Charlie was seven months' pregnant the first year she celebrated Valentine's Day without Arthur. She bought herself a red rose and a box of candy and cried over the first while she ate the second.

When Deon was a baby, she took him out to a romantic restaurant every year on the evening of February 14, usually with another single mother and her children. The year that he was three, she even dressed him in a suit, which complemented perfectly the little red dress that his twenty-two-month-old date wore. Afterward, she destroyed the pictures and never told him about it.

The year she met Steve, it all changed. With his coaching, Deon learned to bring her flowers and she, of course, gave him toys and sweets. They made a bit of a mini-Halloween out of the holiday, each trying to collect more candy than the other, and Steve and Michael joined in. Steve had been unable to avoid going on dates on the single most romantic night of the year, especially in the last couple of years, since he had been on his quest to find the perfect mom for Michael. He had always managed to join Deon, Michael, and her for some portion of the festivities, though . . . even the previous year when he had been on date number two with a gorgeous woman with a lot of mommy potential, but had managed to get home by ten and watch the end of *Sleepless in Seattle* with Charlie and the boys.

This year, it was her turn. Not that she begrudged Steve Parker any of his amorous adventures, but Charlie was looking forward to the most romantic Valentine of her life. Arthur was home, and he was in love with her again. He was being mysterious about the whole thing—and that had raised her expectations even higher. She was anticipating the day with so much pleasure that Charlie was almost sorry when it actually arrived. She made Deon heart-shaped pancakes with strawberries for breakfast. He gave her the card that he had made himself.

She was so excited about the evening that even a job interview couldn't dampen her spirits. In fact, that she had her first-ever *good* interview—for a job she really wanted, as assistant manager of a bookstore called the Book Nook in Washburn, a little town halfway between Frementon and Charlottesville. She liked the woman who owned the store, Rose, and then when Rose called in the manager, Mary Ann, half an hour after the interview started, Charlie liked her, too. They talked books and shopkeeping and childrearing and politics. She planned to go back and visit them, even if she didn't get the position. She felt like she made some new friends.

It's probably just because it's Valentine's Day and I actually have a date for the first time in a decade, she thought. She was pretty sure Arthur would bring her flowers and champagne, maybe even a piece of jewelry. Charlie didn't consider herself a mercenary woman, but she would really have liked to get some sentimental token to remember the day by; a gold locket with tiny photos of Deon and Arthur in it would be perfect.

She had told Arthur about how Deon and she had exchanged gifts and made a contest out of getting free candy from friends and relatives, so he would be sure not to pass the day by without getting Deon something. So she wasn't at all surprised when she heard through the grapevine that Arthur had appeared at Deon's school, armed with pink and red cupcakes for the entire class, as well as goody bags that had to have been professionally assembled—they were so perfect, and extravagant. She was shocked, however, when he showed up at Tom's that afternoon at four and told her they were going out right then and there.

Charlie had already taken time off that morning for the job interview and it had gone so well that she was an hour later getting back to the store than she told Roger she would be. So she didn't think he would be happy about her leaving early for her date.

"I arranged this with him days ago," Arthur told her.

"You did?" She looked at Roger in amazement, and the man actually smiled. It wasn't a big smile, and he wasn't exactly sparkling with pleasure, but it was genuine enough: She'd have sworn he looked glad for her, pleased with himself, and embarrassed at the rare display of emotion. She might have been reading quite a bit into a simple smile, but she could hope. It was Valentine's Day after all. Harder hearts than Roger's had been softened by the romantic holiday.

"Get out of here," he shouted, but with affection. She was sure of it.

"He really likes me," she said in wonder as she and Arthur left the store.

"You're easy to like," he said simply, opening her car door for her with a flourish.

There was a big pink Valentine's Day card on the passenger seat, which she picked up before she sat down. She opened the envelope slowly as Arthur pulled the car out onto Route 99. She read it and smiled at the hokey sentiment inside. Her heart swelled with joy. Arthur had actually surpassed her expectations for this day. It was turning out to be just perfect.

They had headed out of town and were on Route 29 North before she thought to ask where they were going.

"D.C.," he said happily.

"Washington?" Charlie asked, surprised and a little alarmed. "That's a two-hour ride."

"We're going to a concert, and dinner, and we'll be staying at the Woodward Hotel. Separate rooms, of course," he announced. He looked like the cat that swallowed the canary.

"But, but," she spluttered. "What about Deon?"

"Brenda's going to take him for dinner. She's got it all planned."

"Arthur, I told you this has always been a special day, and night, for Deon and me."

"I know. But you've got a real date now. You don't need a stand-in anymore."

"What is he going to think when I don't come home tonight?"

"Brenda said she'd explain everything and make sure he understood." Charlie knew Brenda didn't approve of the way she and Deon pretended to be each other's dates sometimes. Her friend thought Charlie and Deon were too dependent on each other, too close. She was probably a most cooperative ally when Arthur came up with this scheme. Brenda was always warning her about how hard it was going to be when Deon reached adolescence and had to separate his life from hers. They had argued about it before, but had agreed to differ on the subject and Brenda let it drop, except for the occasional rumble.

"Pull over. I've got to call Brenda. I'll tell her we'll be there before he goes to sleep."

"There's no way, the concert won't be over until eleven or twelve, and it's at least a two-hour drive."

She couldn't refuse to go to the concert. As ill advised

as his plan was, she couldn't say no at this late date, especially since he had put so much time and effort into arranging the evening. Charlie didn't feel any such compunction about canceling the hotel stay, however. "Yeah, right, well . . . first thing in the morning, then," she said, dialing the Tremaines' number.

"You don't need to call Brenda," Arthur insisted. "She's going to make sure it's a really great night for Deon. You don't have to worry, honey."

"I didn't even say anything to him about not being there. My God, Arthur, you have to know this is not the best plan to win him over. Haven't you noticed that Deon's not exactly thrilled about our relationship? I think he's already afraid that you're going to take me away from him. This won't help the situation."

"I think you're too close to the situation to see what's really happening. It's time you loosened the apron strings. I talked to Brenda about this—"

"Brenda? Brenda doesn't—!" Charlie exclaimed. "She means well, but Brenda was raised by wolves! Her idea of a good mother is a woman who doesn't eat her young."

Arthur ignored her. "She agreed with me. Deon will be fine."

"Fine," Charlie agreed, knowing she couldn't win this one. "But we are not staying overnight. Deon and I always exchange gifts on Valentine's Day. If we're going to delay that, then I'm not delaying it any more than I have to. I want to be there when he wakes up in the morning."

It wasn't the perfect solution, but it was the best Charlie could do. She would call Deon, and explain. She would go to dinner and a concert with Arthur. And she would sleep in her own bed tonight. At some point. Hopefully, she could still salvage the situation.

Everyone might be happy in the end, but she knew no

one was going to be completely satisfied. Not Arthur, not
Deon, and not she. It was a shame. How could Arthur have
come up with this harebrained scheme? Didn't he see what
was going on with his son, with her? Didn't he understand
anything? Valentine's Day could have been the perfect
opportunity for them to spend time as a family—for Deon
to see romance as it could and should be, as it was when it
was shared by his father and his mother.

After she called Brenda and got her to swear to enact
certain rituals that Charlie considered essential to Deon's
enjoyment of this holiday, she managed to relax a little.
Arthur was sweet and very conciliatory, even though she
knew he still felt she had overreacted to the whole affair.
She forgave him for his thoughtlessness by the time they
reached the capital. Dinner was romantic, the concert even
more so, and she felt very mellow, almost tranquil, as they
started home.

"We could have spent the night and left early in the
morning," Arthur said stolidly.

It was midnight and she knew he had a point, but Charlie
wouldn't concede defeat, even in her current, more relaxed
mood. "This way, we'll get home by two and I can get four
good hours' sleep and be at Brenda's by seven A.M. when
they all start to wake up—with donuts and bagels in hand."

"You know we could be sipping champagne at the Woodward Bar right now, don't you?" he asked.

"Champagne, huh?" she said. "That would have been
nice." She wanted to make him feel better, but she was too
happy to be headed home to regret her choice now. "Give
me a rain check, okay?" She leaned her head back against
the headrest and closed her eyes.

"Right," he said, but there was a hint of sarcasm in his
tone. "I'll keep a bottle of Piper on ice."

"I'm really sorry," Charlie murmured, sleepily. "I'll make it up to you somehow."

"I can think of one or two ways you could do that," he said, gruffly.

"Good."

"I'm going to hold you to it, too," he warned.

"Fine," she muttered, right before she dozed off. "Great."

Brenda had followed her instructions and picked up Charlie's gift for Deon on her way to pick her son up at school, and had given it to him, and Deon accepted her apology gracefully enough the next morning over breakfast. Charlie didn't know if Arthur's plans for Valentine's Day had caused any further widening in the rift between himself and his son, but Deon didn't want to visit his father that weekend and she didn't force the issue. Arthur agreed to switch weekends, and left it at that.

She brought Deon over to Steve's house on Friday night. Michael must have been listening for the car, because he was waiting for them when they reached the front door of the house. "You look beautiful, Charlie," the boy said admiringly. She was dressed for dinner with Arthur.

"Thank you, Michael."

"Gimme a break," Deon muttered and he grabbed his best friend's arm and pulled him away. Charlie listened to their feet thumping up the stairs to Michael's room.

She turned to Steve and raised her eyebrows at him. "And they say chivalry is dead?"

"That's my boy! He's going to be a real lady-killer. And he's right, you do look beautiful tonight. Is that one of Brenda's designer outfits?"

"No, actually, I bought this one. I'm glad you like it. I didn't think you would approve."

He looked her up and down. If she didn't know better, she thought, she'd think he was mentally undressing her.

"It's not that I don't like your new look. You look good in anything you wear. But as good as you look in Brenda's fancy outfits . . ."

"Yes?" she prompted.

"You'd look better out of them."

"Steve!" she exclaimed, shocked to find that, apparently, he *had* been mentally undressing her.

He wasn't done. "Frankly, I think you look best in your . . ." Despite herself, Charlie found herself leaning toward him, waiting, as he drew out the moment. ". . . jeans."

"Thanks," she said wryly.

"No, I mean it. You look good in them."

"Good-bye, Steve," she said, ending the conversation. His flattery was intended to make her feel good, she was sure, but Charlie grew nervous when her old friend Steve started paying her compliments out of the blue. She enjoyed the occasional harmless flirtation as much as the next girl, but not when it was her best friend that was making suggestive comments. Steve was her friend, her buddy, her pal. He wasn't allowed to think about her as a sexual being, let alone talk to her that way. As far as their friendship was concerned, they were both without gender. That was how it had always been, and that was how Charlie wanted it to stay. It was too weird to think about changing that. It was too difficult to make the transition in her mind, from thinking of him as good old Steve Parker, buddy, to thinking of him as a man— with all the usual wants, and needs, and urges that led to flirting and . . . other things.

She was dealing with enough changes in her life already— too many changes, in fact. Charlie was just dying for a break from all the upheaval in her formerly orderly life—what with the job search, her burgeoning relationship with her ex-husband and the long-forgotten feelings that aroused, and the turbulence between Deon and Arthur, she was feeling a lot of friction—and there was no end in sight. She didn't need her friend Steve adding another disturbing dimension to the situation. There was no question about it, Charlie just didn't have the energy to deal with one more new development in her life.

Fifteen

Everything was a mess. Charlie was supposed to start her new job in just under two weeks and she was never going to have her replacement, Liana, trained sufficiently so the girl could take over her duties at the store. Roger had not taken the news that she was leaving his employ very well at all. He seemed to feel it was some kind of personal betrayal. Of course he didn't say that. He just made the training of her replacement very difficult. Besides watching them darkly and muttering under his breath whenever she tried to teach the girl anything, he often contradicted her. The instructions she issued were not complicated. She taught Liana how to use the ancient cash register, just as she'd been taught, and Roger told the girl it would be a while before she'd be ringing up sales. Charlie told her to keep the shelves neat and that that would help her to keep track of the inventory, but while she was at lunch, Roger told his newest hire that she didn't need to worry about inventory because he'd take care of it.

Charlie wanted to tell him that she wasn't too happy about leaving the store, either. She was very excited about working at the bookstore, but she was also very nervous. She had never before had a job that might turn into a career. She was afraid she wouldn't measure up next to her coworkers, or that they wouldn't like her, or that the company would decide to downsize its staff a week after she started work.

Things weren't going any better on the home front. Arthur and Deon talked to each other only through her, and she was growing a little bit tired of it. She laid most of the blame for this sad state of affairs at Arthur's door. He was the adult after all. But he still didn't seem to realize that there was anything seriously wrong. Charlie kept hoping he would come to his senses, but she couldn't wait forever.

When she started the new job at the beginning of March, she found that it took her mind off of the situation some of the time. It was such a relief not to spend twenty-four hours a day thinking about her son and his father. And she liked the work. Everything about the job was interesting; reading the catalogues, opening and unpacking boxes of books and putting them on the shelves, even dusting them gave her a thrill. Rose wasn't there all the time, but Mary Ann generally was, and the rapport they'd established at the interview grew with each passing day. The store manager appreciated her willingness to pitch in, her enthusiasm for working the cash register, helping the customers, answering the phones, and straightening up. It was a pleasure to handle the books, a nice change from juggling cans of food and making deli sandwiches. She liked the smell of this store, and couldn't believe she'd spent so many years breathing gas fumes now that she was away from the other. They sometimes let her read to the children who came in every day for story hour at noon, and Charlie couldn't imagine being happier.

She felt challenged, and exhilarated, and stimulated, and, most of all, fulfilled. Her family continued to be a challenge as well, but despite the problems with her home life, or perhaps in part because of them, it was very satisfying to look forward to going to work in the mornings.

In the evenings, Charlie concentrated on her college applications. They were coming along, slowly but surely, but the essay they required that she write about herself wasn't nearly good enough. She was sure they would take one look at the story of her life and burst into laughter, or tears. Either way, she knew she wasn't selling herself at all well. Bruce came over to the house one afternoon to work with her, but Arthur made such a fuss about that that she couldn't ask him again. It wouldn't help the situation with their son if he and she were to start arguing as well.

Arthur had started to drop by more often, when he had time off, mainly because Charlie wasn't able to work around his schedule lately, between the new job and the work she needed to do on her essay. His visits were welcome, because they showed he cared, and, more importantly, because they showed he could relax at her place, now. That seemed like a sign that they might have a future together after all, but Deon was clearly less than thrilled about Arthur's visits. He didn't say anything outright, but Charlie knew he was holding in a lot of frustration. She wished she could help him, but she just didn't know what to do besides making it clear that she was willing to speak with him about it whenever he was ready.

She suspected that was why Steve was so helpful with Deon. Her son was sleeping at the Parker house two, sometimes even three nights a week these days. She would have put a stop to it, but when she spoke to Steve he said, "Hey, it's only temporary. Finish your college applications; then things will calm down, and you can help Deon with the adjustment. If you still want to.'' She couldn't argue with his reasoning. She had finally started to try to improve her life and, by extension, Deon's life as well.

It turned out that Arthur's return home had been just the catalyst that she needed to get out of the rut she'd been in for years. Their new relationship seemed to have given her the courage to take some chances, to try and change her luck. She refused to allow his presence in her life to become a reason to quit. Not now that she was so close. She'd fulfilled two of the three dreams she had put on hold when he left. All she had left to do was to get into college.

He proposed on a Monday night, a month after Valentine's Day. ''Sit down and talk to me,'' he said. ''Deon's in bed, the dishes are washed, relax for a minute, will you?''

''Yeah, yeah,'' Charlie answered, distracted. ''I'm sorry I've been such a crazy person. Work is—''

''If you marry me you won't have to work,'' Arthur announced, out of the blue.

Charlie smiled, shaking her head at him. ''If you'd said that a couple of years ago, I'd have been ecstatic. Now that I've got a chance at a real career, I'm not sure I want to stop working,'' she said. ''Maybe it will be too hard to work full-time and go to school, but I want to try at least.''

''Did you hear what I said?'' he asked. He pulled a small velvet jewelry box out of his pocket as Charlie watched, dumbfounded. She looked from it to him, unable to believe her eyes. He opened it, revealing the diamond ring inside. ''I'm asking you to marry me, Charlie.'' She sat, staring at him, amazed. She was speechless. He picked up her hand from her side, and put the box on her palm. ''You look surprised,'' he said, sounding pleased with himself. ''I was sure you had guessed what I was planning.''

He waited, staring at her eyes, her mouth, her hand, and the small black box upon it. "Charlie, aren't you going to say something?"

She nodded. "I—I—" she stuttered. "I can't believe it."

He smiled. Then he picked her up and spun her around in the air. When he put her down on her feet again and she'd gained her balance he stooped to look her in the eye, his hands on her shoulders. "Aren't you happy?"

"This is just . . . such a shock," she said, faltering. "I wasn't expecting it." It had gone completely over her head, she realized. Charlie hadn't even heard the words *marry me,* only the reference to her work. She couldn't believe she was so involved in planning her future that she'd missed out on the one factor that might well be the most important part of it. Marriage to Arthur.

Again.

She could have the life she'd dreamed of since she was sixteen years old. She could have it all . . . college, career, Arthur, Deon! So why didn't she feel ecstatic? Why did she have to work so hard just to smile back at the man she had loved since she was eight years old? The man who loved her. He was clearly delighted, and just as clearly sure of her answer.

"I'm going to have to think about it, Arthur," Charlie said gently.

His smile faded for a moment, but only for a moment. He recovered quickly from the lapse. "What is there to think about, babe? We've been planning this for as long as I can remember."

"We didn't only plan it," she reminded him, "we did it. And it didn't turn out exactly as we planned."

"I know, but . . ." He was obviously confused. "I thought that was all behind us. In the past. Ancient history, remember?"

"It's the past, yes. It's our past. It's a part of me, a part of us. I told you I would try not to let it get in the way, but I didn't say I would forget. I can't forget, Arthur. Don't you see?" He seemed to be unable to digest this information, so Charlie didn't bother to mention that they had other problems, too. New complications.

Charlie didn't know what to do. She wanted to say yes, or rather she wished that her heart shouted, "Yes!" It didn't. Her head counseled that she think this out, and her heart was silent. She loved Arthur. She had always loved him. But she wasn't sure she wanted to marry him again.

He had hurt her. And Deon. He left her and then stayed away when she needed him. He put himself before the two of them. She might have been able to forget all that, maybe, if she wasn't so afraid that he had really been showing his true colors when he abandoned her and their son. Maybe he really was selfish and self-centered as Brenda had insisted ever since she had first heard about him—until he dazzled her friend from New York with his skillful hands. Charlie just didn't feel sure of Arthur. He didn't seem to her to care about her or Deon the way she had expected.

That Friday night, she got a call from Steve. "Your son tells me that you're thinking of getting remarried," he said.

"Damn!" Charlie whispered. She had asked Arthur not to mention his proposal to Deon until they could all sit down and discuss it together. "How is he?" she asked.

"Not so great," he answered. "I put him to bed with Michael. They're finally asleep."

"I wasn't keeping it a secret from you," she explained. "I didn't mean to tell anyone yet. Arthur proposed and I told him I had to think about it and we'd talk to Deon about it together."

"Well, he slipped up. It seems he told Deon that you guys were going to be together forever from now on."

''Why did he do that?'' she wondered aloud. ''Doesn't he realize he's only reinforcing the barrier between Deon and himself by making an announcement like that?''

''He doesn't respect you, that's why,'' Steve said harshly. ''That's become more and more clear to me.''

''He asked me to marry him. That isn't exactly an insult,'' she responded.

''He tries to undermine you every chance he gets,'' he asserted. ''It was bad enough when he asked you to dress in another woman's clothes, but now he's really pushing it. He acts as if he's doing you a favor when he spends time with his family in your house.''

''What has Deon told you?'' Charlie asked.

''Not Deon. Or not just him. I've seen how you are about Arthur. You were driving yourself crazy worrying whether he would deign to come over a couple of weeks ago. You may not be dropping dishes and spilling things around him anymore, but he's still got you tied up in knots.''

''That's not his fault,'' she replied.

''I hear his voice coming out of your mouth every time you talk about that essay you're writing for the college applications.'' It was clear from his tone that Steve considered that the ultimate betrayal. ''Your life is not boring and unacceptable. You have accomplished a lot. You are a strong, vital woman, who has created an amazing home for yourself and your son on that little farm of yours, but you don't see that. Arthur should *make* you see it, but instead of building you up, he's tearing you down.''

''He is not,'' she responded automatically. ''That doesn't make any sense. He loves me.''

''Maybe it's not intentional. Maybe he wants to believe that he can rescue you and undo the damage that he did. I don't know. I *can* say that he is underestimating your spirit.

One of these days he's going to go too far and you're going to start fighting back. I hope I'm there to see it."

He had to be wrong. Arthur wasn't like that. But as she watched her ex and listened to him, over the next week, Charlie had to admit there was a grain of truth in what Steve had said. Arthur didn't respect the life she had created for Deon and herself. He believed she had done her best, but in his eyes, her best was not good enough. He blamed himself, and her grandmother's ill health, and a screwed-up social welfare system, and a host of other factors but, in the end, she heard him saying that he didn't think much of what she had managed to achieve.

Charlie was far from conceited. If anything, she was the opposite. She certainly didn't toot her own horn, but she was reasonably proud of the fact that she had overcome most of the curves that life had thrown her way. She was doing all right before Arthur ever came back into her life, and she'd be doing even better now that she'd gotten herself together and started to dream again. She had him to thank for that. But, as for the rest, he had a lot to learn.

She tried, gently, to make him understand. When Friday rolled around again, she invited him over to her place, to talk. Deon was spending the night at Steve's house, as usual, so they had the place to themselves. Charlie was determined to make it count. She didn't plan to yell at him for telling Deon that he had proposed, or that she would eventually accept his offer. She wanted to speak to him calmly and rationally about what she did and did not expect or want from him, and find out if that was going to be enough for him.

He arrived at nine, after work, with flowers for her and a pint of her favorite ice cream, almost as if he knew that he was in trouble.

"Hey, Charlie," he said, kissing her cheek. "I brought

a video for us to watch. Grown-up stuff,'' he said, wriggling his eyebrows at her suggestively. He walked into the family room and inserted the videocassette in the recorder, then took her hand and led her to the couch, pulling her onto his lap as he sat down to nuzzle her neck. It was clear to her that he had no idea that she'd invited him over for anything other than a laid-back evening of necking on the couch.

She stood up and he looked up at her with a quizzical expression in his eyes. When she didn't say anything, his attention was caught by the action on the television screen. She stood looking down at him for a moment as he watched the movie, then sat down on the couch next to him, unsure of how to begin. He reached out to take her hand in his and she looked up at his face, but he didn't even glance at her. It was harder than she expected to start the conversation. Finally, she got up the nerve to press the stop button on the remote.

He looked at her again, then at the blank TV screen. ''Didn't you want to see this flick?'' he asked.

''We have to talk,'' she announced.

''Sure,'' he acquiesced. ''What about?''

''If what you want is a wife who shops, you're not going to enjoy being married to me. I hate shopping.''

''I don't care if you shop or not,'' he said, shrugging.

''I don't like to golf, either. Or to throw lawn parties. Most importantly, I don't really care much for your friends,'' she confessed.

''I told you. They're not close friends,'' he said, looking at her curiously. ''What's this all about?'' He put his hand on her thigh and she picked it up and held it in her own.

''I love these hands,'' she said. ''They've got magic in them. The power to heal.''

''Thanks,'' he said, lifting her fingers to his lips and kissing them. ''I love you.''

"I'm not sure you know me well enough to love me," she retorted.

"I've known you all my life," he replied. "And I want you to be a part of the rest of it."

"I'm not sure I'd make such a great doctor's wife," she continued. "I've met some of them at these get-togethers you've taken me to, and I just can't understand their priorities. They have nannies and housekeepers to raise their children, and they don't seem to spend any time with them. They seem to think that raising their kids isn't as important as, say, investing their money wisely."

"Not all doctors are like that," he answered. "I'm not. My family is the most important thing in the world to me."

"More important than getting a position on the staff at Boston General?" she asked. "Because you said—"

"I know what I said," he said, smiling. "Look, maybe I haven't explained this right, but if it came down to a choice between you and Deon or the most prestigious post in the country, I know which one I'd choose. I choose you, Charlie. You have to know that, too."

She was so happy to hear those words that she leaned forward and kissed him. "Thank you for saying that."

"So is that a yes?" he asked.

"Don't press your luck," she warned. "We still have a lot to work out. Between my insecurity, and your arrogance—"

"Arrogant? Me?" he said in mock horror.

"Between the two of us, we've made a real mess of things so far," she said, laughing.

"That's why I want to marry you and make us a real family," he declared. He might be a little impatient, but at least he seemed, finally, to understand. It was going to be okay, Charlie thought, snuggling up to him.

"Let's not jump the gun," she advised. "We have plenty of time."

"Maybe *you* do," he said, smiling. "I'm getting older every minute."

She turned the movie back on and gave him the remote control. "Now that's true love," she told him. "Nobody touches my remote control but me."

During the movie, Arthur fell asleep on the couch next to her. She woke him when the credits started to roll across the screen.

"Hey," she said. "It's time to go."

"Ummph," he grunted slightly as she helped him up from the sofa. "There, see that, that's what I mean. I never used to make that noise when I stood up. Gandy makes that noise. I told you I was getting old."

"Don't be ridiculous," she scolded. "We're the same age and I'm not getting old, so you can't be getting old. You . . . are tired."

"Come 'ere," he ordered, reeling her into him like a ship pulling up anchor.

"No," she protested, laughing and trying to twist away, but Arthur pulled her slowly closer, inch by inch.

Despite her worries about their future, when she went into his arms, Charlie raised her face to his. He brought his mouth down to hers. His lips were warm and firm as they settled on hers. They'd done a lot of necking over these last two months—recreating their teenage years—and she'd finally grown familiar with his touch again. This was a long, deep, passionate kiss that left her feeling reassured, which was much better than feeling all stirred up, she thought.

He raised his head only to put his hands on either side of her face and look into her eyes. "Feel better now?" he asked. "I don't ever want you to worry about us. We're going to make it work this time." He tenderly kissed the tip of her nose. "I'm not a boy anymore. I can take care of you and Deon now." Charlie's heart sank at his words. She didn't need him to take care of them. She could do that herself. She needed him to love Deon and to love her. She honestly believed that, when it came to love, there was no such thing as too much.

Charlie was making a big mistake. Steve had seen it coming for some time, but there wasn't a thing he could do about it. It was partly his fault. He admitted that. When he made an error in judgment, he owned up to it. Too bad other people were too stubborn to do the same. If Charlie could just admit she was in over her head, maybe he could help. But she didn't want his help anymore. All because he was the one who told her to give Doc a second chance. He'd go back and change it if he could.

Doc had not turned out to be the man Steve had hoped. He wasn't a bad guy, but he wasn't right for Charlie or for Deon. He treated his ex-wife as if she weren't good enough for him. It was his attitude toward his son, though, that really annoyed Steve. Charlie was an adult. She could fight back. The way the man behaved with Deon was unpardonable. The kid had been through hell because of that jerk, and now he was having his heart broken all over again. Arthur Ross was a fool.

He could have had it all. A great woman, a great kid, and a great life. Instead, he was obsessed with the kind of people Steve couldn't stand. Country gentry. Why compete over power and money and social standing in the city that boasted more millionaires per capita than any other in the U.S.A.? Who wanted to be one of those rich folks that came down from D.C. and New York in order to *pretend* they were real, normal folks?

Charlie knew better. He knew she knew it deep down. He'd seen her hesitate, and look down at herself, and then go out the door in Brenda's expensive, ridiculous New York outfits despite her better judgment. But she was not going to be able to keep playing against herself. He knew her. One of these days she was going to get disgusted with the whole thing and then she'd regret wasting her time this way. Until then, he planned to stay on her. He kept whispering in her ear, reminding her of what was really important to her. Her future, her self-respect, her real life. Not this image of a woman she created to impress Doc.

Her son kept her somewhat real. She was hurting for him already. Steve knew she couldn't live with herself if Deon was damaged by this game she was playing. She was too good a mother to let it go that far. But he couldn't help wondering where she was going to draw the line. That move that Doc pulled, telling Deon about his proposal when Charlie told him not to ... *that* should have been the end of it. She was holding out though—trying to believe in the man. Steve couldn't blame her for that. He had wanted to believe in Doc so badly at first that he hadn't even taken a good look at the guy. If he had, he would have seen what a fool the man was right from the beginning. Steve let himself believe in the fairy tale because he wanted it so badly to come true for someone, even if it couldn't be him.

Doc was an idiot. He'd worked hard and it had paid off. He made good. He was a heart surgeon. He was a man who could support his wife and child. All he had to do was reach out and take the love his family offered him. But he couldn't do it. Steve didn't know what was ailing the man, but he'd lost out. He had a second chance with the love of his life, and he blew it. Steve would have given anything if it could have brought his wife back. But God didn't grant those kinds of miracles. Instead he brought a woman like Charlie into his life.

She was an amazing woman. Gorgeous, sweet, and smart.

He'd always known that, but he hadn't truly taken it in. That was the one good thing about Doc coming home and screwing things up. It gave Steve the chance to see his best friend differently. He had thought of her as untouchable. What a waste! She spent ten years pining for her long-lost love, and he'd been comfortable with that because it had made them compatible. He thought they were the perfect couple, both of them in mourning. In his mind that was what drew them close. It drew them close all right. Too close for him to notice that she was one beautiful, incredible, *available* woman. Who loved him. As a friend.

She was coming over to get Deon pretty soon. He couldn't wait to see her. Every time they got together he noticed little details about her that he'd never picked up on before. When she came to breakfast Sunday mornings, she left her hair down, still wet from the shower. It was a riotous mass of soft-looking curls. He had never had the urge to touch it before, but these days he could barely restrain himself. He couldn't believe he hadn't realized how sexy she was before now. And her body, in a T-shirt and shorts, was a work of art. Just thinking about it sent him into a tailspin.

Steve forced himself to concentrate on the hot skillet in front of him. He ladled dollops of pancake batter onto it. They sizzled and swelled up and then bubbled so he knew to turn the perfect rounds over and tan their other sides. He had to feed the boys and tell Deon that Charlie had said no to his request to go with Steve and Michael to Richmond where the high school basketball team had a game. She was planning to have a real heart-to-heart with her son. It was past time, he thought.

The pancakes ready, he called the boys. "Come into the dining room for breakfast."

They shuffled in, still in their pajamas, tousled from their early morning pillow fight. "Hey, coach," Deon said.

"Morning, guys. Hope you're hungry."

"I am," Michael answered him. "I could eat ten pancakes."

"I could eat all of them," Deon said, not to be outdone.

"Let's just start with two each," Steve suggested. At ten, the boys could already eat almost as much as he could, but they tended to overdo it in their attempts to outdo each other.

"Did you talk to Mom about me going to the game with you guys?" Deon asked as he poured syrup liberally over his hotcakes.

"I called her last night. She said she'd be by this morning to get you. I think she wants to talk."

"Can we talk here?" he asked.

Steve hesitated. He didn't want to step on Charlie's toes, but Deon sounded so hopeful, so needful. "I guess so," he agreed finally.

"I knew that butthole was lying," Michael told his friend. "Your mom wouldn't marry someone like him."

"Language, Mike," Steve said automatically. "Charlie is a smart woman. She wouldn't do anything she didn't want to do. Or anything that wouldn't be right for you." He couldn't give Deon any firmer assurance than that. He didn't know what Charlie was going to tell her son.

"Why do parents always think they know what's right for kids?" Deon asked.

"Listen, wise guy, we made you, we fed you, and we kept you alive when you didn't know the difference between a sharp knife and a teddy bear. That gives us the right to try and protect you for the rest of your lives."

"If she was just going to do whatever Arthur wanted, I don't see why she didn't get rid of me before I was born. He didn't want me."

"I don't know about that. I do know *she* wanted you. Charlie chose to have you. And I know for a fact that she's really glad she did. She told me so many times. She loves you to death, Deon.''

''I know, I know,'' he said, waving a hand in the air, carelessly. ''She tells me that all the time.'' Michael looked at his friend enviously, and Steve realized his son felt as strongly about Charlie's remarriage as Deon did. He loved Charlie. She was the closest thing to a mother he'd ever had. Maybe, if things worked out the way Steve hoped they would, they'd be a family.

Charlie arrived at ten. Steve met her at the door. ''Deon asked me if you guys could talk here,'' he said in a low voice. ''I told him you could. I hope that's okay.'' She nodded. ''We can make ourselves scarce,'' he added.

''If he's more comfortable with you there, maybe it will make this easier for him,'' she answered.

''What about you?'' Steve asked, sympathy in his eyes.

''It's okay,'' she said.

He called the boys into the dining room and they all sat around the table. It took Charlie a moment to get started. ''Deon, what did your father tell you?'' she asked.

''He said that he asked you to marry him, and if things worked out we'd be a family again.''

''That's all?'' she pressed. Deon nodded. It was enough, Steve thought, but Charlie sat back, looking relieved. ''You weren't too happy about that, huh?'' Deon sat staring at her, his expression mulish. ''But you know I would never make an important decision like that without discussing it with you first, don't you?''

''Maybe,'' he conceded.

''We've always been a team, right?'' she continued. ''You've got my back and I've got yours?''

''Yeah,'' he said, starting to soften. ''I'm sorry I let *him* on the team.''

''He's Dad to you,'' she corrected.

"He never cared about being my dad before."

"He always cared about you, and loved you. He just . . . wasn't too good at showing it. So we have to teach him," she said.

"I don't want to," Deon objected.

"He wants to be a good father to you, D. Cut him a little slack. He needs a chance to prove he's learned his lesson."

"He's too old to teach him anything," he declared.

"Hey!" Charlie protested. "Your father and I are the same age. Be careful with those kinds of remarks, please."

"Wow, Charlie, you look lots younger than him," Michael exclaimed.

"Thank you, Michael. You are good for my ego," she said, flattered. "Come here and give me a kiss. Both of you."

The boys didn't hesitate. They went straight to her and she gave them both big wet smacks on their cheeks. They made faces, but it was plain they both loved it. When they stepped back, Steve got up from his place at one end of the table and moved toward her chair on the other end. Charlie looked up at him, curiously.

"What about me?" he asked. "Do I get a kiss, too?"

"Hmm, sure," she said nervously. He leaned down and her lips brushed lightly over his cheek. It felt good. It felt right. He would have followed up on it right then and there, but there were two pairs of round brown eyes boring a hole in the back of his neck.

"Thanks," Steve said, straightening up. "I love these little family meetings."

He looked around at the boys, then back at Charlie and smiled. She smiled back, but her eyes didn't contain their usual sparkle. They held questions. He held her gaze for a while, but he was careful to keep his expression neutral. He couldn't let her see what he was feeling. He didn't want to give himself away before he was ready to go for the gold. Steve didn't want Charlie to think that his dislike for Arthur was the product of jealousy. He might be a little envious of the doctor, but that had absolutely nothing to do with the fact that she didn't belong with the guy.

Even if he hadn't decided that he and Charlie belonged together, he still would have advised her to dump the geek. Arthur Ross was not right for her. Anyone could see that.

Part Three

Sixteen

It was video night—a tradition that had begun when Michael and Deon were in the second grade and their teacher, Selena, had given them one night a week off from doing homework. Steve and Michael came over with a video that the boys had chosen, and the two families had dinner together. Now that Deon spent at least one night a week with his father, and often another with Michael, and now that Charlie sometimes worked late, they hadn't been able to uphold the tradition too well and Michael and Deon both complained about it. So Steve and she had arranged to get the two families together one Thursday night late in March.

Charlie had decided to make her famous macaroni and cheese, and when Steve and Michael arrived she sent Deon out to show them in.

"Tonight's selection is *The Iron Giant*," Steve announced as he came into the kitchen. "How long till dinner?"

"About fifteen minutes, I think," Charlie replied. She

reached for the pot without thinking and burned her hand on the broken section of his handle. "Darn it!" she yelped.

"What did you do?" Steve asked, coming over to her to take a look.

"It's nothing. I forgot to use the mitten." She nodded toward the large glove in the shape of a cow that lay on the stove next to the pan. "I just singed myself," Charlie told him, sucking on her finger.

He went to the sink and turned on the water. "Come here," he said. "This will make it feel better."

Charlie obediently put her hand under the stream of cold water for a minute. Steve stood, leaning against the counter, watching. When she pulled her hand back, he took it in his and said, "There. All fixed." She was surprised at the sudden jolt she felt when he touched her. She was even more surprised when he lifted her finger to his lips and kissed it.

"Nice hands," he said, letting her go and reaching to turn the spigot off.

The spot that she'd burned still smarted a little, but it was the tingle she felt in the rest of her hand that made her rub it against her pant leg as she walked back to the oven. She was just in time to grab the pan off the stove and stop the butter from scalding. "Rats!" she cursed softly, under her breath. She turned the gas off under the pan. She was going to have to wait for the pot to cool a little before she could add the milk. She took a sidelong glance at Steve. He was still standing by the sink, watching her. "You want to grate some cheese?" she asked.

"Sure, anything to help," he answered.

"It's on the table, with the grater there."

Now that he was occupied with something besides staring at her, she could concentrate on the job at hand. She took inventory. The green beans were ready and waiting, cooling in the steamer. The macaroni was in the strainer next to the stove. All she had to do was make the cheese sauce, and dinner would be ready.

"Guys, go wash your hands, okay?" she called out to the boys in the living room, as she tested the side of the pot, very carefully, to see if it had cooled enough. It had. She started to pour the milk.

"What should I do with this?" Steve asked, from right behind her.

Charlie jumped, spilling some of the milk on the stove top. "Uh, just, wait a second." She stirred the milk and butter together. "Put it right here, where I can reach it," she told him, continuing to stir the mixture as she added flour to thicken the sauce.

"I'll hold it for you, okay?" He stood so close that she could feel him next to her.

"Fine, but this needs to simmer for a minute."

He leaned a hip against the counter. "Fine."

Charlie added the seasonings to the mixture, then looked at the mess she'd made on the stove. She needed a paper towel to wipe it up. The paper towel dispenser was affixed to the wall between the sink and the stove, right behind him. She couldn't get one without reaching past him. She didn't want to do it.

This is ridiculous, Charlie told herself. Steve and Michael had come over once a week to watch videos for the last three years. What was the matter with her?

"Umm, I just need to get . . ." She leaned over to rip off a paper towel from the roll. She tried not to touch the large, male body standing directly in her path, but it was impossible. He was too big, and the space was too small. Her hip bumped his, then her shoulder.

"Sorry," she mumbled, as she started to wipe up the spilt milk.

"What for?" Steve asked. She was saved from having to answer him when the boys appeared at the door.

"Get yourselves a drink and take it into the living room," she told them. With the two ten-year-olds bustling from the table to the refrigerator and back, the tension she had felt seemed to dissipate. "We're ready for the cheese. Pour it in," she ordered. In a minute the cheese had melted and the sauce was bubbling gently. Charlie tasted it. "Perfect. If I do say so myself," she said. Then she poured the noodles into the mix, and turned off the gas while Steve washed the grater and the mixing bowl.

When the boys came back from the family room, she had their plates ready. "Be careful," she commanded as they walked out of her kitchen, their hands full. "Wouldn't it be great if we could get so excited by the idea of dinner in front of the television?" she babbled as she prepared plates for Steve and herself.

"You are acting very strange tonight," he commented as he stood aside to let her precede him out of the kitchen door.

"Tell me about it," she muttered to herself, as she walked ahead of him into the safety of her living room, where her child and his would be able to chaperone them for the rest of the night.

When Arthur came over to have dinner with Gandy, Deon, and her on Sunday night, she asked him to proofread her essays afterward. "This is important to me," she said. "I want you to be a part of it." What she really wanted was to prove Steve was wrong about her ex.

Arthur agreed to help her, but when she pulled out her files after getting Deon to bed, he seemed more interested in nibbling on her neck than on getting any work done. "This is serious," Charlie said, growing impatient with him.

"I've driven myself nuts trying to finish these things, and I think they're done." She paused, expecting him to congratulate her, but when he didn't say anything, she continued doggedly on. "You can help me with them. You went to college, and med school, so you should be able to give me some idea of what they want to hear."

Grumbling good-naturedly, he took a look at the pages she had written so far. "I think you're angling this wrong," he said. "You don't want to include this note here about job number fifteen, for example. You don't want to look like a flake. Concentrate on your high school experience, and your work with the PTA, and choose one or two jobs that you've had—like this one where they gave you the computer training—to show that you haven't just been sitting around since you finished school."

Charlie looked the essay over, trying to keep in mind what he said. "I think the fact that I've had over twenty jobs in the last ten years might interest them," she said. "And without that, this could be very boring. The joke might make them laugh, at least."

"They're academics," he said lightly. "They don't have a sense of humor."

She didn't have time to get back to work on her applications until Thursday. She had plans with Arthur on Friday night, so she was determined to write a final, final draft of each essay. She had finished filling out the application forms, and hoped that when she put everything all together, and saw all the paperwork in its pristine, finished state, it would provide the impetus she needed to actually mail them.

After she got Deon to bed, though, she couldn't find them. Anywhere. She looked all over the house, even in Deon's room, and finally admitted to herself that they weren't there. She couldn't have lost them, so someone must have taken them. And she could think of only one person who would have the nerve to do that. She sat down by the telephone, and made herself count to one hundred before she dialed Steve's number.

"Steven Edison Parker, what have you done with my applications?" she demanded as soon as he picked up the phone.

"I mailed them," he said blithely.

"You what!" She hadn't expected that. She thought he might have been "helping" her out again by working on them when she didn't have time, but Charlie had never imagined that he might have done anything so arrogant.

"I mailed them," he said clearly and concisely. "You owe me two hundred and thirty-five dollars." She spluttered inarticulately for ten full seconds. He let her stumble to a halt; then he said in his most soothing tone, "Charlie, calm down. They were ready."

She found her voice at last. "That was my decision to make, not yours. I wanted to go over them one more time."

"You sweated over every word on those essays, and it was time to move on to the next step."

"I was going to mail them myself on Saturday." She was so angry at him, she couldn't see straight.

"Sure you were," he said sarcastically.

"I could strangle you," she threatened.

"I'm sorry." He didn't sound contrite.

"You think all you have to do is say I'm sorry and this will be over?" she raged.

"Look, I'll pay the application fees. Will that make up for it?" He tried to placate her.

She hung up on him.

It took all of Brenda's powers of persuasion—and they were quite extensive—to get her to speak to Steve again. It was only because Charlie knew that he truly meant well that she even agreed to see him. And then that was only because

Brenda promised to be there, to keep Charlie from physically attacking him, she said.

Brenda arranged the meeting for Sunday morning at their usual restaurant. Charlie had had enough time to calm down somewhat, but she was still furious with Steve for doing this to her.

"I want to hear what you can possibly say to excuse what you did," she said as soon as he sat at the table.

He launched right into his explanation. "I love you, Charlie," he proclaimed. "I couldn't stand watching you torture yourself anymore. That's the only reason I did it, I swear to you. It wasn't because I didn't think you were capable of handling this on your own, or anything like that. I didn't mean to hurt or insult you or to be patronizing. You're my closest friend in the world, and I just wanted to do something for you."

She sat gaping at him, her outrage dissolving in the face of his honesty. "Next time, buy me a food processor," she finally said.

"There, you see?" Brenda said, pleased with herself. "I knew you couldn't stay mad at him. Not if you gave him a chance to explain. Good work, Steve."

"Thank you."

"I'm not quite over this yet, so will you two please stop patting each other on the back and let me say something?" Charlie interjected.

"Of course," Steve said.

"Anything you want," Brenda agreed.

"Don't *ever* do anything like that again," she told Steve.

"I won't. I promise," he swore.

She turned to Brenda. "And don't *you* think that all you have to do to get around me is tell me how much you love me. I know you both love me. I know you want to help me. But I'm a grown woman."

"Amen to that," Steve said with feeling.

She quelled him with a glance. "Listen. I'm serious. Don't treat me like a child."

"Never again," Brenda vowed very solemnly. She couldn't keep up the serious facade for long, though. "I will never do anything for you again as long as I live," she said, smiling.

After breakfast, Charlie went to visit Nana at the cemetery. Here was someone whose advice she really could have used. She didn't regret telling Brenda and Steve what she had told them, but now that she couldn't expect their help, she couldn't help thinking that she was all alone on this. Charlie wished the wise old woman who had guided her through her first relationship with Arthur Ross could give her a hint as to what she should do now. Things were just not working out as she planned.

"Arthur isn't . . . what I thought he would be," she started. "I mean, he is and he isn't. It's me, with him, that isn't what I expected. Us. You know?" If she had been asked to predict what would happen when Arthur Ross came home, she would have said she was worried about making a complete fool of herself, one way or the other. She had told Nana that she was scared. Had even run to this graveyard to confess, first that she didn't want him back, then that she was jealous of his relationship with her son, and then that it seemed that they were going to work things out after all. She hadn't been back, though, since Christmas—they started dating.

"I should be happy as a lark. He's a good man. Did I say that before? I know I did. I keep saying it. Having to say it. Because he's trying so hard and he just keeps . . . messing up. That was one thing she never would have predicted—Arthur being the one who didn't measure up. "Deon is no longer in love. I can tell you that." She hated to tell her grandmother how badly Arthur was handling his relationship with his son. "He just doesn't seem to see him. I don't know what he's thinking. When he looks at Deon, he just . . . looks through him. To me, maybe. I don't know if he sees Deon as an extension of me, or of himself, or what, but Valentine's Day was a disaster, I swear. I know you thought I was silly about it, but it is a special day— at least it is to me. Arthur proposed on Valentine's Day, remember? I know that didn't work out, but when we got back together again, I thought it would be like it was in the beginning." She stopped speaking, and listened to the wind whistling through the leaves, hoping they might whisper something she could understand—some message from beyond—anything she could use.

Charlie didn't want to admit, even to the solid marble headstone, that Arthur's kisses barely seemed to affect her at all. When she made dinner for her family, she could imagine that they had never been apart, but when he kissed her, she didn't get weak at the knees anymore. The man who used to make her heart flutter with a simple smile barely moved her. He frustrated her, and confused her. He did the wrong thing at the wrong time, and he so obviously did it with the right intentions that she couldn't get angry at him. Not when he was only trying to put things right between them.

She could, however, yell at him in Deon's behalf, worried and alarmed about what was between the two of them. "He's blowing it with Deon, Nana. I try to tell him but . . . he won't listen to me. And if I can't get through to him about my son, how can I possibly explain about myself?" Charlie couldn't bring herself to say the words—to say that she was afraid that the magic between them was gone. It had taken all this time—and a visit to her dead grandmother—just to think it.

"Maybe I'm like you, Nana. You were only married to Gramps for a couple of years before you lost him and you never seemed to miss having a man in your life."

She thought that her no-sex rule would be as hard on her as on him, but actually it was no trouble at all. When the evening was over she was ready to say good night and go to bed. Alone. Charlie remembered perfectly what it was like when they were young—how she couldn't wait to see him, couldn't stand not to touch him. That, she was pretty sure, was how she should feel now. Or something akin to it at least. She wasn't seventeen anymore, but she had desires. They hadn't decreased. But she had more than enough self-restraint when it came to anything intimate between Arthur and herself. Charlie didn't feel a single pang of regret or longing when she said good night to him at the front door and she was pretty sure she should have. She *was* considering marriage to the man.

"At least Arthur and I were together for longer than you were, all those years before we were married. My whole childhood. Maybe that was all we were supposed to have. Maybe I'm supposed to carry on the family tradition—stay here, raise my son, and pass it along to him or his children."

She liked holding hands with a man again, though, and kissing him. Steve had done a very good job of reminding her of that when he kissed her. Since then, too, she had thought of *him* often . . . thought of him kissing her again, and thought of the feel of his skin. At first Charlie could easily explain it away. Steve's kiss had moved her because she had a man in her life again—and not just any man—but the man she had given herself to so long ago. Her senses had come back to life. She lusted for the man she had loved with all her heart. Her heightened sensuality was completely understandable. But since then, Arthur's repeated sexual overtures had not had a similar effect. If anything, Charlie found him easier to resist him now than she had then, while she grew more and more aware of every move that Steve made.

"It's crazy, Nana. The other night, when Steve came over for dinner, I was so edgy, I nearly jumped a foot when he kissed my hand." Charlie felt her whole body heat up just remembering the incident. "It's like . . . it's like my body's got them reversed. Steve is just a friend." Charlie had never even considered dating him, let alone envisioned anything physical occurring between them, but ever since Steve had kissed her, and told her to pretend he was Arthur, she found herself wondering what it would have been like if he'd been kissing her as himself. She couldn't tell her grandmother that, though.

"I love Arthur. I have always loved him. For ten years I fantasized about Arthur when I kissed other men. Now when I kiss Arthur . . . there's something missing." It was Steve she thought about, Steve she imagined touching her. "Nana, I could really use your help here." Again she stopped speaking to listen. But there was no reply. Of course. "I'm sure it's just . . . just the stress. I'm under a lot of pressure, with the new job, and Arthur . . ." Charlie sighed. This hadn't been helpful. Her grandmother couldn't give her any answers anymore. The old woman probably wouldn't have been able to help her even if she'd been alive. It was time to go home.

Steve showed up at her place on Wednesday night, after Arthur had picked Deon up for their regular weekly visit. "I come bearing gifts," he said, as she let him in the front door, holding up a T-shirt bearing the legend *So many books, so little time*.

"You didn't have to do this," she said, but Charlie couldn't help smiling when she saw that he had also brought pizza and a bottle of wine.

"Okay, don't bite my head off. But we never did celebrate you finishing your college applications," he said.

"That's because I didn't finish them," she said mulishly.

He ignored the remark and walked ahead of her into the living room. "Did you tape *Seventh Heaven* last night?" he asked.

"Yes, but you don't even like that show," she reminded him.

"Come on. Pop the tape in and we'll watch it. It'll be my penance for being such a putz."

They ate the pizza and watched the television program together. Steve groaned at the sappy parts, and she told him to shut up.

"Penance, remember?" she said. "That includes suffering in silence."

"Yeah, yeah," he agreed, and was quiet. When Charlie's eyes filled with tears, he handed her a box of tissues. "I can't believe you do that every time," he said, smiling, when the tape came to an end.

"I admit, when you guys are around I do feel a little bit stupid for getting all emotional about a ridiculously perfect, fictional family, but I happen to believe it's good for me," Charlie said. "They say crying is good for you. Like laughing. It's a release."

"Okay," he said, clearly unconvinced.

"Releasing your pent-up emotions is good for your soul. Really," she tried to persuade him. "I feel much better now." She blew her nose. "You should try it."

"Hey, I can believe in television-as-therapy. You should see me watch the news. I yell and scream and curse at the anchormen."

"I don't think that's the same thing. After I watch the news, I think my blood pressure goes up ten points."

"That's because you don't talk to the TV," he joked.

"And, anyway, you have seen me get very emotional watching the games. It depends on the team, and the sport, but I've even been known to cry a few times."

"Very funny." Charlie stood up, determined not to let Steve have the last word. "Why do you think women live longer than men?" she challenged.

"I have a theory about that," he answered. "It's hormones."

Charlie sat back down again, smiling. "I've got to hear this," she said.

"The main difference between men and women is hormones, right? My guess is testosterone is toxic at certain levels," he postulated. "It'll kill ya."

"There's only one problem with that theory," she said, laughing. "How do you explain all those horny old guys that we see all around?"

"That's all part of it," he explained. "As we grow older, the testosterone affects certain men like ... a drug. The hornier they get, the better they feel. But they don't actually die from it, it just ... saps their strength, their life force, if you will."

"Yeah, sure," she said cynically. "I think it might be sex that's the drug."

"Doesn't work," he replied, shaking his head. "If that were true, then women would get addicted, too. You never hear people talk about horny old women, do you?" She almost interrupted him then, to argue the point, but she decided to humor him instead. "Estrogen is like the opposite of testosterone. That's why women have so much more self-control than men."

"We do?" she couldn't resist asking.

"It makes sense, don't you think? Toxic testosterone kills men off, and estrogen keeps women alive. It explains why even men in happy marriages, who we can assume have the exact same amount of sex hormones in their blood as their wives, still die sooner than the women do.''

She couldn't resist turning this lecture into a debate. It was just such a juicy subject. ''So let me take this analogy one step further. Testosterone is a drug, like heroine, which men crave more and more when they use more of it, and which saps the life out of them. So according to your theory, the hornier they get, the sooner they'll die. Have you got any actual statistics to back this up?'' she asked facetiously.

''Nah. I figure the doctors will figure it out one of these days.''

''If they do, I'm guessing that will be the best-kept secret in medical history,'' she said. ''No one's going to tell men they need to reduce their testosterone levels and take estrogen. They'd be lynched.''

''I never thought of that. You're right. The medical establishment may already know.''

''I sure as hell wouldn't want to be the one to release that information to the media. Can you imagine the reaction from men around the world? They'd rather die young!''

''I wouldn't,'' he said.

''You lie,'' she accused him.

''Well, maybe I wouldn't,'' he said, shrugging.

''Damn straight.'' Charlie laughed. ''Anyway, I'm not sure I'd like you so much with long hair. Or breasts.''

''Me either,'' he agreed, his expression serious.

Charlie couldn't stop smiling. She hadn't had such a good time in weeks. She felt a twinge of guilt as she realized she never had this much fun with Arthur, but she refused to let that ruin her mood. It was, however, time to put an end to the evening. ''Time to go,'' she announced, picking his hand up from the couch and pulling him to his feet.

''Already?'' he whined.

"It's Michael's bedtime," she said, leading him toward the door. "Where is your son tonight anyway?"

"At a sleep-over," he answered, lengthening his stride to beat her to the door and turning to face her. "So I don't have to get home before midnight."

"On a weeknight?" she inquired.

"I broke the rule. After all, this is a special occasion. I wanted to make up with you." He took her hands in his.

"That's sweet," she said dryly. "But what you really wanted to do was gloat over getting those applications in the mail despite me."

"I wouldn't use the word gloat," he said, gloating.

"Just go ahead and say it," she dared him.

"Say what?" he asked innocently.

"I told you so," she prompted.

But instead of repeating her words as she expected, he leaned forward and kissed her on the forehead. "I wouldn't say that. I know how much you hate it when people say I told you so."

Flustered, Charlie took a moment to think of a comeback. "I notice you still managed to say it."

He leaned forward again, but this time he kissed the corner of her mouth. "I really shouldn't do this," he said, as if to himself, right before his lips came down gently on hers.

Charlie put her hands on his shoulders to push him away, but that was as far as she got. She left them lying there as she lost herself in the sensations he evoked. His lips were warm and dry, slightly tinged with the flavor of the red wine they drank with their pizza. He coaxed her lips open with his tongue and then explored within, hungrily, searchingly, surprising her with the force of this sudden assault. It was seductive and exciting, and she was tempted to do some exploration of her own, but she held back, afraid.

She had already gone too far—just by standing there and

letting herself feel the heat of his body and his mouth. Tremors shook her limbs and torso, and within her chest she felt an answering flutter, a vibration that traveled to the pit of her stomach and made it reel. She concentrated on that quivering sensation. It reminded her of the mild shock she received when she touched an exposed electrical wire once, but this tingled more. She suspected it was much more dangerous. Charlie felt as if she had split into two women at once. One was a sensual being—reveling in the sensation he aroused. The other was pure thought—curious about every detail of the kisses she received. The conscious Charlie catalogued each movement of his tongue and mouth, his hands as they grasped her waist and pulled her close into his chest, his fingers as they dug into her waist, his long hard legs against hers. The other Charlie was unrestrained, and lewd, overwhelmed by the physical sensations she was experiencing, and eager to get even closer, to remove the cloth between them and feel his flesh against hers.

She didn't know how long it would have gone on, if the phone had not rung. She quickly broke away from Steve and almost ran to the extension. It was Deon calling her from Arthur's place.

"Mom, can I come home?" he asked, sounding as if he was on the verge of tears. It was just the dose of reality she needed.

"Where's your father?" she asked, watching Steve warily as he prowled around the room.

"He's in his room, watching TV," her son answered.

"Did you guys have a fight?"

"No, but . . . I guess we're sort of mad at each other," he said.

"What happened, baby?" she asked.

"Is he okay?" Steve whispered. She covered the mouthpiece as Deon rambled on about his afternoon and evening with his father. It sounded like a long, convoluted story.

"Yeah, I think so," she said softly. "He's upset, though."

"We can talk later," said Steve, the coward, backing out of the room.

Charlie nodded her agreement. She didn't want to discuss that kiss with him, either. They were going to have to talk it out sometime, but at the moment she had the perfect excuse to let him go.

"I'll call you," he mouthed at her.

Deon was winding down. "He took me to see *Dinosaur Park Four*," he concluded, unhappily.

"I thought you wanted to see that," she said, confused. "Isn't that the movie you and Michael were talking about going to?"

"Yeah, it is," he answered. "We've been planning to see it on Saturday afternoon. It opens Friday night. But Dad got these tickets to the preview from some doctor who knows the director or something, so he asked me if I wanted to go." He sniffled, but Charlie still couldn't figure out why he was so upset about this.

"And you said yes," she prompted, when he paused.

"Yeah," he confessed. "And it was fun and all, but I told him I promised to go with Michael."

And that was the crux of the problem, Charlie realized. Deon felt bad about breaking a promise to his best friend, even though Arthur had tempted him beyond bearing with the opportunity to see the movie before it opened. "I'm sure Mikey will understand," she said soothingly.

"I think so," Deon said anxiously. "Anyway, I knew it wasn't Dad's fault, so I didn't say anything to him. We went to the preview and it was really cool. So afterward I told him I really liked the movie and I was glad because I had to see it again with Michael, and he s-said . . ."

"Calm down. It's all right, kiddo," she soothed him.

Charlie heard him draw in a deep breath. "Dad said he didn't think I should see it again so soon, and it was a waste of money, and I should do something else with Michael. I tried to explain that I couldn't just blow off my b-best friend, but he w-wouldn't listen." The ten-year-old was on the verge of tears. Charlie could hear him trying to hold them in.

"Look, your dad doesn't mean to exclude Michael, he just doesn't understand that you *like* to see movies more than once. You and I have had the same argument, a couple of times. I never want to go to the same movie twice, either."

"Yeah," he said. "But you wouldn't ask me to go see a movie I wanted to see with Michael."

"I probably wouldn't, but if I got to take you to a preview, I might."

"Come on, Mom, you know you wouldn't take me without Michael," he said.

"Your dad doesn't know about making these kinds of arrangements yet," she said, trying to excuse Arthur.

"I thought he was supposed to be . . . like a genius or something."

"He hasn't hung out with ten-year-olds in about twenty years," she explained.

She knew that the real reason Deon was upset was that he tried to be a good sport and thought his father should have given him kudos for that and been pleased, and proud of him. Arthur didn't even notice.

"Deon, you are a nice kid. I'm sorry about your dad. I'm sure he didn't mean to be mean."

"What's the point in trying to be nice to a guy like that?" he asked.

"The point is, he's your dad," she retorted. "He loves

you, and you have to learn to get along with each other. He's the only father you have.''

"That's good,'' Deon said nastily.

"You've got to give him a chance,'' Charlie persisted. "He may not be going about it right, but he's trying hard to show you how much he cares about you.''

"Why?'' he wanted to know. "Why is he so interested in being friends all of a sudden?''

"It's been six months, Deon. I wouldn't call that sudden.''

"But he never cared about us that way before he moved back here. Why now? Did you ever think about that?''

"I—'' She faltered as she realized it was a really good question, especially given the source. Arthur had suddenly reappeared after a decade's absence and spent six months trying to take up where they left off, as if the intervening years hadn't changed anything. But that decade was Deon's entire life span. Why should he trust Arthur's motives? "I think that's a question you should ask your father, Deon,'' Charlie said. "He can explain it better than I can.''

That was certainly true. Charlie believed Arthur's intentions were good, though his motives, as he himself had admitted, were selfish. He wanted his family together. Charlie was convinced that could be a good thing, for all of them. Deon needed persuading, though.

"Ask him, okay?'' she urged.

"I'll think about it,'' he said doubtfully.

Charlie hoped that Arthur would handle the upcoming interrogation with more finesse than he had used tonight. It could be an opportunity for him to really connect with Deon, to explain himself and why he had done what he had done. He was good at selling himself. He would be a great father— she knew he would. All he had to do was convince his son that he was the best man for the job.

Seventeen

Arthur Ross was caught off guard when his ex-wife didn't exactly jump at his offer of marriage. After all, he wasn't a man to be tossed aside like a used bandage. Some women might even see him as a catch. He was tolerably good looking, had all his hair and nice, even, white teeth, and, best of all, he knew where he was going.

He was a successful doctor. True, he didn't make a lot of money yet, but he would. It wouldn't be too long now, either. The bottom line was he knew his own worth. He thought Charlie knew it, too. It had seemed she had, but lately it appeared her priorities had changed. Changing jobs and going to college was a bad idea at this juncture. The timing was all wrong.

He firmly believed that Charlie was making a mistake. She needed to concentrate on Deon. The kid was going nuts. He had been so fantastic when Arthur first arrived. He was the son Arthur had always dreamed of having. Now, however, they were growing apart, right when they should have been growing closer together. Right when his mother was finally coming around and beginning to accept that Arthur was destined to be in her future.

The kid knew he had proposed. Arthur told him. At first, he thought Deon was going to try and get in the way, but after his initial negative reaction, Deon actually became more cooperative than he had been in some time. That boded well for the future. But it wasn't enough. Deon had to get on board. Arthur was sure it was just a matter of time before he and his son were close again.

Charlie talked to the boy. She told Arthur that. And she encouraged him to open the lines of communication. It was a good suggestion and he had taken it. But for every one step forward that he and his son managed to take, it seemed they took two steps back. Like tonight.

Arthur had planned the evening carefully, and for his son's pleasure. It had gone well, too. Until that little argument they had in the car on the way home from the movie. He certainly didn't intend to get into a fight when he told Deon that Michael and he shouldn't go to see the same movie that week. All he did was point out that it was a waste of money. It wasn't his fault that the kid was so sensitive. He couldn't believe that Deon ran to the phone to cry to his mother. If that was how Charlie encouraged him to behave, it was a good thing his father had come home. The boy needed a male role model who was strong, and who could demonstrate that a real man dealt with his own problems without running to Mommy or anyone else. He could teach Deon that.

He was going to need Charlie's help though. She and the boy were so dependent on each other, she would have to work with him or they would never be a real family. Deon wouldn't be able to accept his father's guidance unless his mother made it clear that she was one hundred percent behind him, and that meant she would need to give them, their family, her full attention. He needed her to concentrate on Deon, and himself, and their family. That was going to require all of her energy. She wouldn't have enough time to devote herself to her new job, or to building a new career, or going to college full-time. Or for her men friends.

Her new boyfriend was going to have to be phased out. That shouldn't be too difficult since she barely knew the guy. Steven Parker was a different story. He and his son, Michael, were a part of the family. Separating them was going to take a lot of work. Luckily, Arthur was not afraid to face the problem head-on. He had always enjoyed a challenge. The only real difficulty would be getting Charlie to agree it was necessary to distance herself and Deon from the Parkers. But Arthur had faith in his ability to steer her in the right direction. He knew just where this was all going, and he couldn't wait to get there. He was so close to getting every single thing he'd ever wanted that he could taste it.

He had to try to talk to Deon again, before he took him home. Charlie kept saying that they had to resolve their differences, and he knew that she meant she wouldn't say yes to his proposal until he and his son started to get along better.

He brought him a dish of ice cream and sat opposite him at the dining room table where Deon was doing his homework. Arthur waited for Deon to look up at him, but he didn't. He ignored the ice cream as well, which was unusual. The kid had his father's sweet tooth. Luckily, he also had his metabolism. They said the apple didn't fall far from the tree. Physically, the resemblance between them was uncanny. Unfortunately, it seemed it didn't go any deeper. Arthur couldn't believe he'd ever been this sensitive. Everything he said seemed to hit a nerve with this kid. He didn't even know what he'd done to upset him.

Arthur apologized anyway. "I'm sorry, I didn't mean to hurt your feelings."

"You didn't," Deon replied, still working determinedly on his math.

"I don't know where you got the idea that I don't like your friend Michael. He's a great kid. I'm glad he's your friend." When Deon still didn't respond, he added, "I want to be your friend, too."

"She cried over you," Deon said quietly, swiping away tears on his own cheeks that Arthur hadn't seen falling. "I used to hear her at night. When Gandy came to dinner he always told us stuff about you, what you were doing and all. Then, at night, I'd hear her crying. When you came back, she stopped. But now she's worried all the time."

"I didn't come back to make things worse," he assured the boy.

"You haven't made things better," Deon said.

"I'm trying. Your mother and I are both trying to work out our problems. It may not seem like it right now, but things are going to get better." Arthur told him.

"I don't think so. She doesn't laugh hardly at all anymore. Never around you."

"Your mom and I laugh together," Arthur said.

"You shouldn't have come back."

"Deon, I'm sorry I messed up. I didn't mean to hurt you, or Charlie. I wasn't ignoring you, I just never felt I deserved to be a part of your lives and every year that went by it was worse. How could I come see you with nothing to make up for all the time we missed? But I'm going to fix that now, if you'll give me the chance. One of these days, I'll make both of you laugh so hard, you won't be able to breathe. I promise."

When he drove Deon home, he thought they had come to an understanding with each other. Charlie would be pleased, and he'd be one step closer to marrying the woman he loved.

Charlie didn't know what she was going to do about Steve Parker. She was not supposed to feel this way about him. If she had to become, all of a sudden, a wanton slut who craved the touch of a man's hands all over her body, it should be Arthur's touch she craved. She was ashamed of her inability to control her animal urges. Not that she would ever act on them, but, still, it was disconcerting.

Talking to Nana hadn't improved her situation. She couldn't very well hash it out with Steve, as she usually would when faced with a serious problem. She was too embarrassed to tell anyone about her dilemma, even Brenda. Charlie worried about it all week and then decided she was having these feelings only because the sexual fantasies, inappropriate as they were, offered a welcome distraction from her confusing feelings about her ex-husband. It was such a relief to finally think of a reason for her odd behavior that she felt almost giddy.

If this was so hard for her, she could understand why her ten-year-old son was having such a difficult time with all the changes that were happening in his life. She wondered if she told Deon that she really was thinking about saying yes to Arthur's proposal if it might be easier for him to accept his father's presence in his life. Once the decision was made, the words said, she thought it might make it easier for *her* to deal with it. It wouldn't be a nebulous possibility anymore then. It would be a fact, a choice she had already made. She wouldn't have any more doubts. Once she actually said the words *I'm going to marry your father,* she would have to live up to them. Right?

Charlie really wanted things to work out with Arthur. She

was willing to do just about anything to put her family together again, the way she'd always dreamed it would be. So she decided to accept Arthur's proposal.

Before she could tell Arthur, however, she had to tell Deon. Her son deserved to know before anyone else. Thursday night, at dinner, she announced, "I want to call your father and tell him yes."

"Yes?" he repeated. "Yes, what?"

"What do you think?" she said sardonically.

"You're joking, right?" he asked. When she didn't laugh, his young eyes searched her face. "You're not joking?" he said, in disbelief.

"It could be a good thing for us, Deon. Your father loves us, and he wants to take care of us."

"You take care of us," he argued. "We don't need him."

"Maybe I do," she said gently.

"No!" he yelled. "I can't believe this!" He jumped up from the kitchen table, and ran out of the room.

Charlie followed him up to his bedroom, where he lay sprawled facedown on the bed. She hovered in the doorway. "Deon, we should talk. I know this has been a shock for you, but I really want to know why you are so against it," she said, starting slowly toward him. "You always wanted to live with your father." At that, he turned his face toward her, and shook his head.

"I wanted him to come live with us here," he exclaimed. His cheeks were wet. "I don't want to move."

"Who said anything about moving?" Charlie asked, bewildered.

"He said when we got married we'd move to his house in town. He asked me what color I wanted my room to be. I told him I wasn't going anywhere, but he said we'd have to come live with him."

She sat on the edge of his bed and laid her hand on his

shoulder. "Deon, I promise we don't have to move. We might decide to move later, after we get used to the idea, but there's no law that says we have to live at your father's house. I kind of like our house." He grew quieter after that. His skinny little body shook as he let out a few wet hiccups, but he stopped crying.

"Okay?" she asked, rubbing his back.

"I miss Nana," Deon said.

Charlie hadn't expected that. "Me, too," she said. Especially now, when she was trying to make some of the biggest decisions of her life. She'd have liked to talk to the wise old woman who raised her. "I go talk to her sometimes, at the graveyard. Do you want to come with me next time?"

"You talk to dead people?" he asked. Then he added in a whisper, "Do you see dead people?" She was glad he'd recovered his sense of humor, even if it was a little morbid.

"Ha, ha," she responded. She stood up. "If you go wash your face, you'll feel better."

He pulled up a corner of his T-shirt and dried his face with it. "Ahhh," he said. "Much better."

She left him alone. If he was making jokes, things couldn't be that bad. She'd been shocked when he mentioned his great-grandmother in the middle of that very emotional conversation, but as she thought about it, Charlie realized that it did make sense. Nana had helped to raise Deon. She'd been like a parent to her great grandson. And she died only a year and a half ago. The wound was still pretty fresh. Charlie knew she hadn't healed yet. She missed the old woman every day of her life. Why should Deon feel it any less? Children were resilient, but they still felt things just as deeply as any adult. He'd suffered a loss. And on top of that, she and his father were putting him through this trauma as well.

He was probably afraid that he was going to lose her. He had certainly believed he was going to lose his home.

"I can't believe you would say something like that to him," she told Arthur the next night as they drove into Charlottesville to have dinner. "You should have known you couldn't make an announcement like he might have to move without upsetting Deon terribly."

"I was just saying that after you married me, that room would be his all the time, not just on weekends." He said it so calmly, so rationally, Charlie wanted to shake him.

"We don't even know that yet. We haven't even talked about where we're going to live, *if* we get married. Don't you realize how frightening something like that is for a ten-year-old? He already has to deal with getting to know his father."

"I thought it would make him feel good to know that I was making a room for him. He seemed to like it when it was done." He was starting to sound as frustrated as she felt. The difference was he was put out not because Deon was upset, but because he himself was.

Charlie didn't know how to make him understand that she didn't mean to irritate him, she only wanted to make him see how important it was that he stopped alienating his son. "Of course he's happy that he's got a room of his own in your house. He wants to be a part of your life. But he's still getting to know you. And in case you hadn't noticed, Arthur, you are no longer da bomb."

"I noticed, but there doesn't seem to be anything I can do about it. Everything I say or do is wrong."

"That's because he had built up this image of you in his mind over all these years, and that image just isn't possible to live up to. You were his idol. But that's easy enough to do when you're never around to make mistakes."

"So getting to know my son and letting him get to know me means I lose his respect and his love."

"You didn't lose anything. He gave you his love because you're his father. You didn't do anything to earn it." Arthur was shaking his head, frowning. Charlie knew he didn't like what she was saying, but it had to be said. "I know you've tried, but I think you took a lot for granted, and now you've got to stop doing that. You've got to do more than pretend you're interested in him. You're going to have to *prove* you care about him—who he is—for himself."

"I do. He must know that. We have spent almost every other weekend together for the past six months."

"Because you're here!" she interjected. "When you moved back here he was so excited, so sure that you would be everything he ever dreamed of in a father. But of course you couldn't fulfill his dreams. No one could."

He was nodding now. Charlie thought maybe he was finally hearing her. "It's hard to find out your hero has feet of clay," he said thoughtfully.

"You don't have feet of clay," she told him. "You're just an ordinary man, with flaws, and weaknesses. But he will love you in spite of the fact that you are not perfect. Give him a chance. He's got a big heart. There's room for you in there."

She would have told him more, told him that he had hurt Deon's feelings time and time again—by preferring her company to his, and by trying to buy his love at Christmas with all that junk, instead of offering his love, which was the only gift his son really wanted. It would have been returned. But Charlie didn't think it would help to point out his mistakes. They were in the past. The recent past, it was true, but Charlie had only recently learned that letting go of the past was the first step in rebuilding her life. Arthur had to figure out where to go from here.

''I'd just like to know what I have done that's so terrible. I love him. I love his mother. I want us to be a family.''

''You and I have known each other forever, but you're new to Deon. Maybe it would have been easier if he hadn't idolized you since he was a little boy, I don't know. Anyway, there's nothing we can do about that now. We have to start fresh.''

''What does that mean?'' he asked.

''You remember how he was so happy to see you when you first arrived.''

''And you weren't,'' he added.

''Well, that was because he didn't know you.''

''Thanks,'' he said sardonically.

''No, I mean he didn't know you were a flesh-and-blood person, who made mistakes, who wasn't perfect. He knows that now. That shouldn't make you feel bad. It's something he had to learn. But the important thing is he has to learn to accept you for who you are.''

''I feel like I've been on trial for the last six months. First it was you, and now, when we've almost gotten everything settled, Deon turns on me. When will it end?'' he asked, baffled.

''Deon isn't turning on you. He's just a confused kid, and he thinks you're taking his mother away. You have to show him that that's not true.''

''You mean *we* have to show him, don't you?''

That brought her up short. ''What?''

''We. Not me alone, the two of us together.'' He paused, waiting. ''Right?'' he prompted.

Charlie didn't know what he expected her to say. ''Sure,'' she agreed, but she could tell he'd hoped for more of a response.

Charlie could tell he wasn't satisfied, but he let it go, for the moment. He didn't leave it alone for long. They spent the weekend with Deon, and Arthur was great company, then and during the following week. On Tuesday, Deon had a half day because of some teachers' conferences. It was the perfect time to go to Monticello, the estate of Thomas Jefferson, which was nearby but was nearly always too hard to get into on the weekends. It was a very popular tourist sight, for locals, as well as out-of-towners, and the wait to get in was often over an hour long. Charlie had been there four or five times, but after the second time she only went during the week when she wouldn't have to wait in the parking lot for a long stretch of time. She hadn't brought Deon here since he was five or so and he didn't remember that visit at all, but he enjoyed exploring the place.

Monticello was beautiful, and the tour included something for everyone to enjoy. Deon liked the underground passage from the kitchen to the dining room, and the eight-day clock, which still kept time. Arthur was intrigued by Jefferson's invention of a copying machine, a complicated gizmo that connected two pens so that when he wrote with one, the other made an exact duplicate. Charlie had always been intrigued by the man. Looking at his beautiful home over a hundred years after he died, she felt she got a glimpse of the man himself. He obviously had taste, and style, and she just couldn't understand the apparent contradictions in his personality.

How could one of the most impressive of the country's founding fathers keep a young slave as his mistress, and keep their children in slavery until they reached the age of twenty-one? The Hemmings name was all over the estate—slaves from that family had worked in all different areas, the house, the kitchen, the stables, the vineyard. And some of the plaques made it clear that he acknowledged some of the family as his blood.

"I've always wondered how he could justify his affair

with Sally Hemmings to himself. He was obviously a very intelligent man.''

''Intelligent people can be hypocrites, too. In fact, they can probably justify their hypocrisy more easily,'' Arthur said cynically.

''What's hypocrisy?'' Deon asked.

''Saying one thing and doing another,'' his father explained.

''Lying?''

''Sort of. It's like if you say that you don't think people should be allowed to watch a lot of TV, and then you watch hours and hours yourself,'' Charlie said, smiling.

''Oh. So why was he a hypocrisy?''

''Hypocrite. He was what they call a hypocrite,'' Arthur said. ''Because he said it was wrong for black people and white people to have babies together, and then he slept with Sally Hemmings, who was black, and they had babies together.''

''And because Sally was a slave, and he knew slavery was wrong, but he kept her as a slave and slept with her, and kept their babies as slaves, too,'' Charlie told her son. If he was old enough to ask what a hypocrite was, he was old enough to know the facts.

''White people slept with their slaves?'' Deon asked.

''Yeah, like the man who owned our ancestor, Sophie Brown,'' Charlie reminded him. ''I told you about that.''

''Oh, yeah. But that guy was a jerk.'' Deon dismissed the slave owners whose blood probably ran in his young veins. ''Thomas Jefferson wrote the Declaration of Independence and he built this place, and made that clock and copier and stuff. Why did he do it?'' he asked, confused.

''Sally Hemmings's family was owned by his wife's family, and she came to live here when his wife came here to live with him after they were married. Some historians say she was probably Abigail's half sister. So she probably looked a lot like his wife. Some people think he fell in love with her because she looked like his wife who died.''

"His wife died and he slept with her sister. That's gross. Like sleeping with a dead person.''

"I think it was more gross that she was his slave. He had all the power, and she didn't have any.''

"Why didn't she kill him, then?'' he asked.

"It's not so easy to kill someone, you know. And anyway, she might have been in love with him. He was very smart, and very important and she was very young. Younger than his own daughter.''

"How could you fall in love with someone who owned you?'' Deon asked.

"We don't know. We don't really know her side of the story. Mostly we know what he wrote and what people wrote about him.''

Arthur added, "Jefferson even tried to make slavery illegal when he wrote the original Declaration of Independence. You know that part that says 'All men are created equal'? Well, he said that if all men were created equal, then no men could be slaves. But he kept slaves his whole life.''

"That sucks,'' Deon said succinctly.

"Yup,'' Arthur agreed.

They had ice cream sundaes on the way home, and Arthur kept looking at her with a question in his eyes—a question that Charlie didn't have the answer to. He must have sensed the change in her feelings toward him—her reluctance to go any further until the situation with Deon was resolved— because he didn't push it. He spent the whole time talking to his son, who responded more cheerfully to his father than he had in the last two months

When he arrived home from their outing, Deon jumped

out of car. "See ya," he called over his shoulder as he ran up to the house.

Charlie watched her son bound up the stairs onto the front porch and knew he was feeling better.

"I'll walk you to the door," Arthur said, when she would have climbed out of the car, too.

"Okay," Charlie said. They had had a good day, and a good weekend, and she was feeling very contented.

She didn't expect Arthur to stop her at the door and take her hands in his. "Charlie, what's going on?" he asked.

"What do you mean?"

"Are you trying to make me jealous? Because if you are, it's working," he said baldly.

"What?" she asked, confused.

"First, it was that adjunct professor and now it seems like you spend all your free time with Steve and his son. You're not purposely trying to keep me off balance, by any chance?"

She remembered how important it had been to her to do exactly that when he first came home, but that was a long time ago, before they became friends again. "No, of course I'm not," Charlie replied. "I wouldn't do that."

He looked relieved. "I guess I should know better, but you're making me feel a little paranoid, you know. Every time I think you're about to accept my proposal, something happens that makes me wonder if you're ever going to say yes. Like this latest problem with Deon." Charlie would have said something, tried to explain, but he stopped her with a shake of his head. "Just let me say this, okay? Then I'll leave it alone." She nodded. "I don't know where I stand with you and that makes me act a little bit crazy. The only excuse I can offer is that I love you, Charlie, and I can't wait to start our lives together." His impatience was flattering. And his request was only fair.

"I understand what you're saying, but . . . I need a little more time. It's a big deal, you know." Charlie knew she needed to accept the changes in her life and move on. She just didn't know what direction to move in.

"I know. I don't mean to pressure you. Just tell me I'm not going to have to wait forever," he said.

"Definitely not that long," she promised. "I've got to get used to all this. Deon and I have been on our own for a long time, and we had a . . . a routine, and now you want us to change tracks, which is fine. I'm not complaining, but it is going to take a little getting used to."

"Okay, okay. I'm sorry," Arthur said. "I just . . . I'm impatient. I can't wait to start our lives together, that's all." He kissed her.

"I know," Charlie said apologetically.

"I read somewhere that, when I say the L word, you're supposed to say it back. Or something."

Like what? Charlie thought, but she didn't say it aloud. She didn't want to hurt him. Instead she smiled at his feeble attempt at humor. "I promise. The minute I know anything, you'll be the first person I'll call."

"Fine," he said, clearly trying hard to be patient with her.

That was what she had said she wanted, after all. Patience, consideration, generosity, Arthur had it all. So why couldn't she get Steve out of her head? Charlie just didn't know. She wrestled with the question for a while, and didn't come close to finding an answer, so she finally forced it to the back of her mind. Once she and Arthur were on their way up the aisle, she was sure her relationship with Steve would go back to the way it had been before.

Meanwhile, she had a little planning to do. She needed a good scheme for surprising Arthur with her answer, and she knew the perfect person to call for help with that.

"So what are we celebrating?" Brenda asked when they met for drinks that night.

"Everything!" Charlie said. "Rose told me that she's going to make me assistant manager at the bookstore. After only two months!"

"That's great! Here's to you." Brenda raised her glass.

"And I think I'm finally ready to say yes to Arthur's proposal," Charlie announced.

"I thought you already decided to do that, a while ago," Brenda replied, puzzled.

"Yeah, but then there was that whole thing with Deon about where we were going to live," she explained.

"That's settled now? Brenda asked, as if she didn't believe it. Charlie looked at her, surprised at the sardonic tone.

"Well, we haven't talked about it much, but we're going to have to live here for now at least. I don't think Deon could handle moving—changing schools, leaving his friends, and all that—on top of me getting married. It's going to be a major adjustment for him to live with Arthur."

"For you, too," Brenda commented.

"Yeah, sure, but I was married to Arthur before. It won't be so new to me. Deon never had to share our house with another man before. It may take a while before he sees the advantages. I'm already looking forward to having another man around the house."

"Well, congratulations," Brenda said, but she still didn't sound as excited as Charlie had expected.

"Deon and he are doing much better," she said earnestly, thinking that that was what was holding her back. "Actually, I'm pretty proud of both of them. Deon has been trying his best to give his dad a chance, and Arthur is trying hard to be a friend to his son, as well as his father. We had a really nice time Tuesday. It was a half day at school—so we all went to Monticello together."

"I'm glad to hear it."

"Everything is finally falling into place," Charlie said, wanting her friend to rejoice with her. Between getting the promotion and finally feeling sure that she and Arthur should set a date, Charlie felt she was really making progress. She finally felt she was going somewhere. "It had to be hard for him to wait all this time. I want to do something special when I accept, to make up for it. I can't believe it took me so long to finally do it. It's obvious we were meant to be together. After all these years, he came back to be with me. That's pretty romantic, don't you think?"

"Sure," Brenda said, smiling. "A fairy tale come true."

Charlie knew there was something she wasn't saying. "What is it?" she demanded. "Spit it out."

"Do you really think you'll be able to forget? He left you, Char."

"That's all in the past. This is my future we're talking about. It will be just like he never left," she assured the other woman.

"Really?" Brenda asked doubtfully.

"Well, not exactly, but we can make up for lost time. It'll be great." Even to her own ears, she sounded less than convincing. "I'm going to do all the things I thought I missed out on the last time around. College. Marriage— the till-death-do-you-part kind this time—words that end in 'idge.' "

"You're still planning to go back to college?" Brenda asked, sounding surprised.

"Sure, why not?"

"I just thought that you and Arthur would probably want to have another baby soon, because of the age difference with Deon."

"We haven't discussed having more children," Charlie said slowly, as she thought about it. "But you're right."

She rallied. "I'm sure he wants more. He always did, and I always did, since we were both the only child in our families. We wanted a big family. I guess we probably will get started on that right away. But I can still get my college degree. I'm not giving that up. Not this time," she vowed. "I won't have to, right?" She laughed. "It will be easier now that I won't be a single parent anymore."

"I don't know about that," her friend commented.

They had gotten off the subject Charlie had come to discuss. "So? How do you think I should do it?" she asked. "Say yes."

"Let me think about it," Brenda said.

"Take your time. I've already kept Arthur waiting so long, I think he's just about to go around the bend. The other day, he asked me if I was trying to make him jealous with Bruce, and Steve—"

"Steve?" Brenda interrupted.

"Yeah," Charlie said, looking at her curiously. "It's sort of ironic, isn't it? I mean, I did ask Bruce out to make him jealous, but I gave up on that a long time ago. I told him no, of course."

"Why did he ask about Steve?" Brenda asked.

"Because I spend so much time with him, I guess," Charlie answered. "His birthday barbecue is coming up next weekend, and so we've been planning that—"

"What made you suddenly take the plunge?"

"What are you talking about?" Charlie asked, mystified.

"You haven't talked about kids, or where you're going to live. What have you two been talking about all this time?"

"I don't know. Deon, mostly, I guess."

"I'm not surprised that you kept Arthur waiting. I don't think you want to marry him."

"Of course I do," Charlie insisted.

"I think the real reason you haven't said yes up till now is Steve Parker."

"What? But—?" Charlie spluttered. "Steve is, I mean he isn't . . . Steve has nothing to do with my relationship with Arthur."

"Oh really?" Brenda said, in a very dry tone. "You haven't noticed anything different about him lately?"

Charlie stared at her, confounded. Had Steven told Brenda that he kissed her. She couldn't believe that. "Yes, well, he's been acting a little bit strangely, but—"

"He has done a complete one-hundred-and-eighty-degree turn. He's gone from thinking that you and Arthur are some kind of star-crossed young lovers, to thinking that your ex-husband is some kind of monster."

"He'll get over it when we're married," Charlie asserted.

"I don't know," Brenda said, shaking her head. "I wasn't going to say anything, but I think he's in love with you. And you have feelings for him, too. Don't bother trying to deny it, either," she added, as Charlie was about to protest. "You don't want to give him up and that's why you kept Arthur waiting all this time."

Charlie sighed, relieved. Brenda had figured out much of what was going on with her, but not everything. "I'm not going to give him up. Why should I? We're just friends."

"Uh-huh," Brenda said cynically. "I'll think about how you can say yes in some unique and special way, but I think you should resolve things with Steve before you do."

"Umm, sure," Charlie agreed. Brenda was probably right, but she had no idea how to do as her friend advised.

Eighteen

That Saturday afternoon when Charlie went to Steve's place to pick Deon up, she still didn't have a clue as to how she could resolve the situation with her best friend. As always, when she asked if Deon was ready to come home, the boys pleaded with her to let them spend more time together. Deon was never ready to leave Michael at the end of their dates.

"Come to lunch with us, instead," Steve urged. "We can go to the County Café." He winked. "I know the place holds a lot of happy memories for you."

"Ha, ha, ha." She pretended to laugh, but Charlie was tempted. It would be fun to eat with the boys, and Steve.

"Come on, Mom," Deon urged. "It will be so much better than sitting around at home eating tuna fish sandwiches and fruit rollups." She let herself be persuaded. She had the afternoon off, and even though it might not be the smartest idea she couldn't resist the lure of a pleasant hour with the boys.

"That's true," she agreed. "Okay, I'm in." She had always enjoyed spending time with these three.

Charlie let the three boys carry the conversation in the car on the way to the little restaurant and spoke only when she was addressed directly. She didn't want Steve to get the wrong idea about why she was there. She wasn't in that car because she wanted to continue, or even to finish, what they had started a few nights ago. Far from it. Charlie couldn't take the tension that came along with the new development that seemed to have tainted their friendship. She figured that, since the boys would be with them, nothing could happen. She could pretend nothing *had* happened. This might be the best way to get their relationship back on track.

Despite all her rationalizations, she knew she shouldn't be going to lunch with Steve Parker. She just missed their old, uncomplicated interaction too much to give it up without a fight. Besides, Steve's birthday was coming up the next day, and she really wanted them to have a nice time at the birthday barbecue that Michael and Deon and she had arranged to have at her house as usual. She decided to use this little interlude as a practice session for the next day.

The diner wasn't too busy. They were seated right away at a table by the window, and the waitress gave them their menus.

"So, are you doing grilled cheese and tomato today?" Steve asked, teasingly. It was her usual choice. It was cheap, and it was the meal her Nana made her when she was a girl. Comfort food masquerading as a nutritious vegetarian meal.

"Yeah, but I'm going to splurge today." She didn't care at the moment if she appeared mature, sensible, or sophisticated. "I'll have a chocolate shake, too."

"That sounds good." The three of them ordered chocolate shakes with their hamburgers and fries.

"So what's happening at school, guys?" she asked them.

"Nothing new," Deon said, taking a huge sips of his water.

"Is there any good gossip?" she questioned Michael as they waited for their food. "Give me the lowdown."

"In the fifth grade? The lowdown-est you get is Carrie Ettinger barfing on Paul Stamler in the cafeteria."

"Nice luncheon conversation, Mikey," his father scolded.

"No, no, I asked," Charlie said, defending the boy.

He beamed at her. "It was gross. She had just eaten lunch and it still looked pretty much like spaghetti," he elaborated.

Deon, unaffected, took a huge bite of his burger.

Charlie grimaced. "Why did she toss her cookies? Was she sick?"

"Take human bites, please," she requested, then turned her gaze back to Michael.

"Sick of Paul," Deon answered her. "He's been bugging her for weeks. Following her around. He's in *love* with her." He made kissing noises. "I almost barfed myself."

"Poor guy," Steve said. "No one deserves *that*, just for liking a girl."

"Paul did," Michael said, and Deon, his mouth full, nodded his agreement. "He was, like, stalking her."

"Oh, come on. The kid is nine years old. He can't be a stalker."

"Things have changed since you were in the fifth grade, Dad. Kids grow up a lot faster these days. We know all about this stuff."

"Oh, you do?" Charlie replied. "Well, just remember that we are old-fashioned parents and don't grow up too fast. That means I don't want to hear you've been stalking any girls."

"Aw, Mom," Deon moaned, embarrassed.

"Don't worry about it," Michael said, offhand. "Stamler is a doofus. You wouldn't catch me following some girl around like a puppy dog."

"You never know what you might do to get a girl's attention when you're in love," Steve said. "Some women like their men to beg."

"Stay away from them," Charlie warned.

Charlie left her car at Steve's place when they went to lunch, so he drove her back to it afterward. But when they arrived at his house, he asked her to come inside with him.

"Boys, you stay out here and shoot hoops," he commanded. They were overjoyed. Charlie looked wistfully back at them as she walked to the front door, which Steve was holding open for her. She wanted to stay out here. But she didn't want him to say anything about what had happened between them in front of her son. Deon was confused enough already.

Apparently Steve was aware of that. "Deon's upset, you know," he said, walking next to her through the entry hall.

"Yes?" she said warily.

"About you and the ex. Why are you still trying to make it work with Arthur?" he asked, turning to face her as they got into the living room.

"Because I always knew we were meant to be together. You said it yourself. Your first love is special. You never forget it."

"He was an idiot to let you go. And from what I've seen, he hasn't improved with age."

"He's trying."

"Great, give him an A for effort and tell him he's too late."

"Why? Because I let you kiss me?"

"Yes, and because you enjoyed it."

"I've been kissed before. That doesn't prove anything."

"You don't want him anymore," he said. "It's got to be clear to you by now that you don't belong with him." He reached out, cupped her cheek in his hand, and turned her face up to his.

"Stop it," she ordered, but the words came out less forcefully than she intended. Charlie started to tremble, expecting him to kiss her again, but he didn't move any closer.

His thumb brushed across her lips and she gasped at the subtle intimacy. "Does he make you feel like this?"

"No, but ... I—" She stepped back and his hand fell away but he stepped toward her and reached for her again, and Charlie found herself retreating, with him slowly following—until her back hit the wall. "He loves me, " she said desperately.

"You care about me, too," he said definitely, as he closed the small remaining space between them until he was only inches away. "Isn't it obvious to you that we could have something amazing together?"

"No, that's not obvious to me," she denied. "Not at all. There's never been anything but friendship between us."

"I think that's changing," he said, lowering his head slowly. Charlie waited, holding her breath, unable to protest, or to look away from the glint in his coffee-colored eyes. His hands came up to her waist and he held her, gently, as his lips met hers.

She couldn't move, and she didn't want to. He sucked her top lip between his own, and gently urged her mouth open beneath his, an unspoken invitation. Charlie tentatively touched the tip of her tongue to his, and he twined his tongue around hers, beckoning her to explore his warm, wet mouth. Her body melted into his, and her hands went up, around his neck. She held on for dear life as her blood coursed more swiftly through her veins, her heart thundering, the quivering back in her stomach. She hadn't thought he could do this to her again.

"Why now?" she asked breathlessly when his mouth left hers to trail kisses across her cheek to her ear. He didn't seem to hear her at first. He was very intent on the ear he was nuzzling. Then his lips moved down, under her chin, following an erratic path to the spot below her ear where her jaw met her neck.

"Because you are so . . . sweet," he answered, nuzzling her neck, then running the tip of his tongue down to the hollow between her collarbones. He kissed the slight indentation there. "And beautiful." As he traced the top of her chest with his chin, his long fingers slid up from her waist to the top of her rib cage, the top of his hands coming to rest just below her breasts. His grasp tightened as he molded her even closer to him. "And strong." His breath brushed over her neck and the moist spots he'd left there and sent a shiver through her. If he hadn't been holding her so tightly, Charlie wasn't sure she could have remained standing. "And loyal," he said.

Her eyes flew open and she found herself looking straight into his deep, dark eyes, alight with a heat she knew was mirrored in her own. "I don't feel very loyal." She lowered her eyelids, unable to meet that searching gaze after his unintentional reminder that she had forgotten Arthur for the past few seconds.

"Why? Because you're kissing me instead of him? You and I are much better suited to each other than the two of you ever will be," he insisted.

He slid one of his hands up to cup her breast and Charlie tried to twist away, shocked and yet not surprised by the intimacy.

"Stop. Please."

He took his hands off her body, but he placed them on the

wall beside her head, boxing her in. "We're not finished," he said.

"What in the world do you think you're doing?" she asked her old friend.

"I'm trying to show you how I feel about you," he said.

"Horny?" she asked. He let her go immediately and stepped back, looking at her as if she had pointed a loaded gun at him.

"You know that isn't—" he started to protest angrily.

She held up a hand to stop him. "I'm sorry. I didn't mean that." He kissed her fingertips. She quickly pulled her hand away. "I'm just ... embarrassed ... about letting this go so far. I should have stopped it long ago. I don't know how I ... why I ... but this is wrong."

"It feels right to me." His voice was silky soft.

"It ... I don't think you're thinking straight." As he shook his head, she added, "I *know* I'm all mixed up." He placed a soft kiss on her cheek. "You've got to stop doing that. I can't believe we already—"

"You can't help who you're attracted to," he said, excusing their behavior. "We just picked a bad time to discover there's some powerful chemistry between us."

"Maybe," she said diffidently. "I admit I'm attracted to you, but I don't want to feel this way." The last part came out better than the first. More emphatic.

"Why not?"

"Look, Steve, I don't want to screw up our friendship, and that's all that could happen here."

"I don't care about our friendship and I don't think that's what's holding you back either." He brushed her cheek with his hand. "It's just too bad that we waited this long."

Charlie was irritated at the suggestion that she might have been secretly lusting after him all these years. "I wasn't waiting for anything," she denied. "I never thought of you that way and I don't want you now. Not like this. I'm in love with Arthur.''

''I don't believe that. You just can't admit that you wasted your entire adult life waiting for him and it turns out he's not the one you want.''

''Please let's drop this. I don't want to hurt your feelings, but this really does have to stop.''

''What? This?'' He leaned forward and kissed her eyes closed.

''Yes, this,'' she said. With her eyes closed, she became acutely conscious of his large hand, splayed across her abdomen. She pried his fingers away with her hands and opened her eyes as he lowered his head, his intention clear in his flame-hot eyes. ''Stop. This,'' she said firmly.

He paused, his lips so close to hers that she felt their warmth. ''You don't want me to stop,'' he said.

''Yes, I do.'' Charlie swallowed nervously, but she met his questioning gaze squarely. ''I'm with Arthur,'' she said. ''For better or worse,'' she added deliberately.

''You can't be serious about marrying him.''

''Of course I am.'' At the moment, she thought it was by far the most sensible thing she could do. She had always loved Arthur. That hadn't changed. She wasn't as in love with him as she had been at seventeen, but she had measured every man she met in the last ten years against him. And none had stood up to the comparison with the man she still thought of as her true husband. No one was as brilliant, as driven, as handsome, as sexy, as the Arthur Ross she fell in love with as a girl. That was why she had never come close to marrying again.

She continued to love him when he left her to go to college in Boston. Now he had achieved every goal he set for himself when they were together. And he had come back for her. Charlie believed he truly loved her still. That should be more than enough to build a marriage on. Why shouldn't she say yes to his proposal? As Steve himself had said, it wasn't her fault that she was physically attracted to someone else. She wasn't about to upset all her plans just because she finally noticed what a great body her best friend had. Charlie was pretty sure the only reason this had happened was that Arthur's return had stirred everything up, including her hormones. Steve saw her ex and, like Deon, he became jealous.

It was one thing to believe in true love and fate and destiny in theory. It was a different thing entirely to see it in practice. Steve was all for it, until he saw Arthur and her together. It was only then that he realized that her true love was not, after all, a fairy tale prince but a man, with flaws and weaknesses. Once again, he was trying to save her from herself, but this time, her knight in shining armor couldn't save the day. It was up to her.

"I always wanted to have a June wedding," she said.

He flinched.

"I'm sorry," Charlie said.

"Stop saying that. You don't have to apologize to me," he said, his shining eyes shuttered now. "Look, you may find this hard to believe, but I didn't bring you in here for . . . this. I know you don't want to hear this from me, but somewhere, deep down, you know that marrying Arthur would be a mistake. Even Deon knows that you and Arthur don't belong together."

"Deon?"

"I overheard Michael and him talking about it last night. He was saying that you never laugh with him. You don't cry anymore, but you never really laugh either, he said— like you do with me." He repeated that last line with relish.

"His words, not mine," he added, when she shot him a sour look.

"That's all?" she asked. "I don't laugh enough?"

Steve answered her question with a question. "What did he mean, you don't cry anymore?"

"I don't know," Charlie said, distracted. She was thinking furiously about how she could allay her son's fears about his father and herself. "If that's all he's worried about—" she started.

Steve stopped her. "That's not all he's worried about. He's worried because he says you're always worried these days. He can see that you're not happy. He doesn't think you should marry Arthur because he doesn't like the things you like, he doesn't like the things about you that Deon—and I, by the way—like best."

"My son said that?"

"More or less. I'm paraphrasing, but he's a very perceptive kid."

"He's ten years old. He doesn't understand," she whispered.

"What? That you are turning his whole world upside down because of some ridiculous notion about how you and Arthur are destined to be together?"

"That was your ridiculous notion," she said. "Not mine. Arthur and I belong together because we've been in love since we were Deon's age, and because we still love each other. Most of all, we belong together because of *Deon*."

"*Deon* doesn't think so," he retorted dryly. "He thinks you'll be very unhappy with Arthur, and I agree. That's why I told him I would talk to you."

"Why would you say that to him?"

"Because he asked me why I wasn't helping you, and I thought it was a very good question. What kind of example would I be to him and Michael if I just stood back and let my best friend make the biggest mistake of her life?"

"It's *my* life. Deon may have something to say about it, but you certainly don't," she said furiously. "Why didn't you tell him to talk to me?"

"I did. But I guess he thought he needed reinforcement. He wanted me to talk to you, too. In fact, before he knew I was listening, he called me a butthead for not doing anything."

"Well, he's right about the butthead part," she shot at him, as she twisted away from him. She nearly ran out of the house into the yard where the boys were playing. Charlie couldn't take any more.

Steve followed her but he didn't try to continue the conversation right then. He called her that evening, but she just told him she'd see him at the barbecue the next day. She didn't know what to say to him yet.

On Sunday morning, Charlie puttered around the house all morning, trying not to wake Deon up until she could figure out how to tell him she did plan to accept Arthur's proposal of marriage. After her conversation with Steve the day before, she was pretty sure he knew it was coming. And it wasn't like the last time. During the last week, he and his father had been getting along really well.

Still, after Steve's revelations, Charlie was nervous about what exactly she would say to her baby. She decided to take him with her to visit Nana before the party. She could tell him at the graveyard. She had promised to bring him the next time she went, and it just seemed like the right place to resolve the issue of the wedding. It was so peaceful there.

"Hi, Nana," he said, placing a rose he had bought for this purpose on the ground in front of the gravestone.

"Hi," Charlie echoed. Although she usually didn't address her grandmother as if she were actually in her presence, it couldn't hurt to be civil, she thought.

"Nana, I told Deon that I'm planning to marry Arthur, and he can't seem to figure that out."

Deon bristled. "I figured it out, I just don't think it's a good idea, Mom. Dad's okay, but I don't think you, or I, would like living with him. Remember, I spend the night with him lots of times, and I know what he's like better than you."

"So what's he like?" Charlie asked.

"He's a little bit strange. He brushes his teeth weird, and he's obsessed with getting to work on time. I don't think you'll get along very well."

"I spoke to Arthur about what he said about us moving," she told him gently. "And he agreed that I should tell you we wouldn't make any major decisions without you."

"But you are making one right now," he argued.

"And I'm trying to get your opinion," she said.

"You know my opinion," Deon said scornfully. "You just want me to change it!"

"There's some truth in that," Charlie admitted. "But I hereby solemnly swear that I won't make any major choices that affect you without at least discussing them with you first, okay?"

"Does that include Michael and the coach?" he asked, turning away from her and staring at his great-grandmother's grave.

"They're our best friends, so anything that we do has to affect them, too," she said consideringly. "I guess I'd have to say yes."

"Dad isn't going to like that," he warned.

"What do you mean?" Charlie asked.

"He wants to be our best friend," he said, with all the wisdom of the ages.

"You may have a point," his mother conceded. "In fact, I think you're exactly right. But you know what?" She waited for him to look up at her. "Whatever happens with your father, Michael will always be your best friend."

"Coach, too?" he asked.

"Both of them will always be a part of the family. A lot of things will be different, and we're all going to have to get used to it, but nothing can change that," she assured him.

Eventually, Steve would come around, she was sure. And, once she married him, Arthur wouldn't be so insecure about the gym teacher. She might not be able to be quite as friendly with her old buddy, but he would still be one of her best friends. After the last five years, she couldn't imagine her life without Steve Parker in it. They—Arthur, and Steve, and she—would figure out how to make it work.

"Speaking of the coach, Steve and I had a little chat yesterday," she said. "Can you guess what it was about?"

Deon looked at her guiltily. "Sorry, Mom. I thought maybe he could help."

"Help what?" she asked.

"Help you. If you and Dad get married, you will be just like some of my friends' divorced parents. They can't even stand each other. I don't want you to start hating each other, and fighting all the time." He looked so sincere, and concerned, that she almost surrendered right then and there. But Charlie quickly regained her senses.

"I don't want you to worry about this stuff. I promise that everything will be all right. Okay?"

"Uh-huh," he mumbled.

"Don't you believe me?" she asked. He didn't answer. "You know you can trust me, right? To always do what I think is best for us?"

"Yeah," he said hesitantly.

"So I promise I will take care of you. Just like always."

"Okay," he said finally. She kissed him on the cheek. "I'm just trying to take care of you, Mom," he said into her ear.

"I know. Thanks, Deon," Charlie answered.

Nineteen

Charlie would have loved to cancel Steve's birthday barbecue, but Deon and she had celebrated the date with the Parkers for the past two years and it would have been very strange of her not to let the boys throw their annual birthday bash. She couldn't think how she would explain it to either one of them, Deon or Michael. On top of that, it was sure to make Arthur wonder if she were to call the party off without an explanation. There was no way around it, she was committed.

She baked a cake and prepared Steve's favorite snack food and, of course, she had to help Deon decorate the living room. It wasn't long before she found she wasn't only going through the motions, she was caught up in the spirit of the thing. It was fun working side by side with her son, whose enthusiasm was contagious.

It felt strange to greet Steve at her door that afternoon with Arthur by her side, but he insisted on acting the host.

Arthur came to the party, not out of any desire to celebrate Steve's birthday, but because he was jealous of the phys ed teacher. Whether it was Deon's relationship with Steve, or her own, as Brenda suggested, Charlie didn't know, but he got tense lately whenever she and Deon spent time with Steve and Michael.

He hovered, anxiously, as she greeted the arriving guests, including Brenda, Calvin, the bridge moms, and their families of course, as well as the neighbors, half of Charlie's graduating class from high school and their husbands, wives, and children. Then there were Steve's colleagues from school, Mary Ann from the bookstore, and most of the children from Deon's and Michael's class in school. Soon, there was a large crowd milling around her backyard, and delicious odors were seeping out of the barbecue grill.

Her backyard looked lush and green in the golden glow of the afternoon sun. It was a perfect day, and the farm seemed to Charlie to be welcoming her friends and neighbors. Laughter echoed back from the trees that adorned the lower slopes of her mountains.

Not long after the party got under way, Steve leaned over to whisper in her ear, "Charlie, we've got to talk."

"There's nothing to discuss."

"I think there is."

She glanced over at Arthur, but he wasn't looking at her. He and Calvin were manning the grill, cooking and serving up burgers, dogs, corn, and chicken and vegetable shish kabobs.

She headed into the kitchen and motioned for Steve to follow her. "Steve, there really isn't anything more for us to talk about," she said for his ears only as soon as they reached the other room.

"You know what I want for my birthday?" he asked.

"I got you a gift certificate from the bookstore," she answered.

"Nope. Not even close." He kissed her.

Charlie was so surprised, it took a few seconds before she pulled away. "Are you out of your mind!" she hissed.

Arthur chose that moment to appear at the kitchen door. "Everything okay, Char?"

"Yeah. Sure."

He hovered in the doorway for a moment waiting for her. He reminded her of a tall, thin, praying mantis. The thought flitted through her mind that the female praying mantis devours her mate after sex. "Deon and Michael planned this birthday party for Steve and he knows they're planning some big surprise, but he doesn't know whether it's animal, vegetable, or mineral. We're trying to figure out what it could be. Could you go watch the kids and make sure they don't come in here?"

He left, reluctantly, and she turned back to Steve. "I can't believe I just lied to him," she said desperately.

"I can't believe how *well* you did it," Steve said admiringly, reaching for her again.

"Whoa! Are you drunk or something? You've really got to stop this."

He did not look repentant. "Why?"

"You know why. We already talked about this."

"Say it again. Tell me you're in love with Doc and you want to marry him."

"I do," she said.

"Charlie, Charlie, Charlie, what am I going to do with you?"

"You're not going to do anything with me, you're going to get a grip on yourself and forget all this nonsense."

"It's too late for that," he said, grinning. "I already made my birthday wish."

She didn't find him amusing. "Grow up already," she admonished.

"What was that?" he cried, looking toward the door.

"What!" Charlie exclaimed, and spun around quickly, but the doorway was empty. She listened, and heard the boys talking excitedly in the living room, their voices interspersed with the sound of Arthur's deeper one. "We should go," she said, her heart pounding.

He was smiling. "Are you sure? I'd rather hide out in here." Steve pulled her to him, and gave her one more deep, surprising kiss. "Sorry, I couldn't resist," he said.

"Try harder!" Charlie ordered and marched out of the room ahead of him.

After everyone had eaten, Charlie sat at the picnic table next to Arthur. She saw Steve and Deon looking at her.

Charlie leaned over and said softly so that only Arthur could hear her, "I think it's time." The doctor smiled. Steve looked sour at the whispered exchange, which was exactly what she had hoped for.

Arthur stood up and tapped his glass with a spoon. "I have an announcement to make," he proclaimed. Neither Deon nor Steve looked happy but since Charlie wasn't too pleased with either of them at the moment, she didn't bother to reassure them that this wasn't the announcement they feared.

"Both Charlie and I have been promoted. Charlie is now the assistant manager at the Book Nook and I am now the fellow of pediatric cardiology at the UVa Heart Center."

Steve and Deon cheered and applauded loudly. Arthur looked surprised and gratified, and she almost told him that they were just happy because his announcement had not been about their engagement, which both Steve and Deon were praying would never occur.

She heard Deon let out his breath. "Phew," he exclaimed, smiling. "I thought that was it."

"Don't worry, sport," Steve said, looking equally relieved. "I'm sure Charlie will come to her senses soon. Anyway, however long it takes, at least you don't have to worry that she'll do anything she'll regret later. Your mother isn't that kind of woman."

Charlie didn't appreciate the compliment. In fact, she was more than a little bit irritated by the nerve of the man, presuming to judge her. He had no right. Already on edge, Charlie snapped. In a fit of pique, she grabbed Arthur's hand and called out, "I have another announcement to make."

Steve looked at her, surprised, and she glared back at him, calling loudly, "May I have your attention, everybody!" His expression turned to one of alarm.

Steve started toward her. "Charlie!" he warned her.

"Mom!" Deon cried at the same time.

"You're all invited to my wedding," she announced.

Deon groaned and Charlie thought she heard Steve moan. She didn't even have time to look his way to see if her bombshell had had the desired effect because Arthur grabbed her up off the floor and twirled her around in his arms.

"I was starting to get worried," he said softly, in her ear. Putting her down, he yelled, "Yes! She said yes!" And people started to gather around to congratulate them.

"Thank you, thank you," she kept repeating to the well-wishers who crowded around her, kissing and hugging her and making strange, inane comments such as "We had no idea you were thinking about remarrying when we saw you at the Christmas festival," and "When did you ask her, you sly devil?"

Her husband-to-be-again was as thrilled by all the attention as he was by the reason for it, she assumed, since he seemed to come alive amidst the throng of neighbors and friends who crowded about them. He was either laughing or grinning from ear to ear as he shook hands with one person after another, hugging her to his side with one arm and telling anyone who would listen, "I don't mind telling you I was as surprised as you all are. I asked her weeks ago, and she didn't give me a clue that she was going to do this today."

Charlie's eyes kept going to Steve and Michael and Deon, who wore halfhearted smiles, but were obviously unhappy with this turn of events. Her son slid behind Steve every time anyone looked his way. She felt bad for him. This wasn't the way she'd planned to handle this. Steve's patronizing attitude had made her so angry that she lost control.

Arthur was clearly overjoyed by the manner in which she had accepted him, Brenda pointed out when she worked her way to Charlie's side, after the main onslaught had passed. "You didn't need my devious mind to help you with this. You made it really special all by yourself."

"Don't start," Charlie admonished.

"What is going on with you and Steve?" Brenda asked, looking at her speculatively.

"What?" Charlie asked, blankly.

"He's over there glaring at you, and you know it. I thought you were going to talk to him."

"I tried. It didn't do any good," she told her friend.

"Why not?"

"I don't know. He's got some strange ideas about Arthur and me, and him and me. I couldn't get him to see sense."

"So you announced your engagement at his birthday party. That seems unnecessarily cruel to me."

"I'm worried about Deon," she said. Her son had disappeared again.

"Poor kid." She listened to Brenda with only half her

attention. The other half was on Arthur, who was hugging Gandy again, for what must have been the fourth or fifth time. The old man held the younger one for quite a while. When he let Arthur go, he pulled a large handkerchief out of a pocket, swiped at his eyes, and blew his nose. He and his grandson exchanged meaningful glances; then he walked away, toward Deon.

"Oh no," Charlie muttered. She raced over to intercept him before he could reach his great-grandson.

"Charlie!" he greeted her happily. "You and Arthur, together again. It's going to be wonderful. When's the wedding?"

"We haven't discussed any specific dates yet, Gandy."

He nodded. "Plenty of time for that. I'm so happy for you, Charlotte."

She saw Deon walk toward Steve and Michael, looking dejected, and she watched as Steve sent both boys off together.

"Have some cake, Gandy," she said, and steered him toward a picnic table laden with all kinds of desserts that had been brought here today by all her friends and neighbors, including the cake she had baked in the center.

She wandered toward Steve, who was standing alone, watching Arthur. He looked over and noticed her a moment before she reached him, and smiled, wryly.

"Congratulations!" His ironic tone was not lost on her, though to those around them he probably sounded sincere. "You did it."

Despite all of the people around them, she couldn't bring herself to say a simple thank-you. She thought the words might choke her. She was damned if she would accept his insincere congratulations just for form's sake.

"Yes," she finally said.

"Arthur looked surprised," he said.

"Yes, I hadn't told him that I made my decision. There wasn't time to talk to him before I made the announcement," she said, glaring at him.

"Now you have plenty of time to talk to him. The rest of your life."

A shiver ran down her spine. "Yeah," Charlie said. "I will, won't I?"

"So? Are you planning on a long engagement? A big wedding?" he taunted her.

"I don't know yet," she replied, wishing with all her heart that she could let loose and tell him what she really thought of him.

"You should ask Deon what he suggests," Steve said. "He's going to be involved—in the ceremony—right?"

"Of, of course," Charlie stuttered, looking around for her son. He and Michael had not yet reappeared.

"This is really going to be exciting for him. Being at his own parents' wedding. That's a story he can tell his own children someday." That little dig was one too many. Since Steve was well aware how Deon felt about his father, and their remarriage, he clearly meant to hurt her with that last comment.

"He'll be fine," Charlie said stiffly. "I'll see you later."

She walked away from him and went directly to Arthur, reaching his side just in time to hear Jeanine Donner's interrogation.

"So I guess this means you'll be sticking around for a while, huh?" she asked, beaming up at him.

"I should be at the next reunion," Arthur said.

"Will you be living here or in Charlottesville?" she pressed.

"Here," Charlie said, just as Arthur started to say, "I love my apar—"

He paused, then finished the sentence. ". . . my apartment, but I'll have to discuss that with Charlie."

She looked at Arthur, really looked at him, for the first time in a long time, and saw a six-foot, 170-pound man. Not a god, or even a fallen idol, but an ordinary-looking twenty-eight-year-old black man who carried himself well and had intelligent eyes. A good man, whom she knew to have skillful, gentle hands, but who did not look especially like a successful heart surgeon. He was just her Arthur, the boy she loved so deeply and so long that she couldn't imagine loving anyone else. But whether she ever fell in love again or not, she couldn't marry him. He deserved someone who loved him the way that she used to.

She found Brenda. "I've done an awful thing," she said, ashamed.

"What?"

"You were right. I only made that announcement because I was angry at Steven. I wanted to make him stop."

"Stop what?" her friend asked.

"When I tried to talk to him, he told me he loved me."

"I told you," Brenda said. "Didn't I tell you he was in love with you?"

"Yes, you did," Charlie answered. "So what do you recommend I do now?"

"It's a little late to ask me now, isn't it? You just announced your engagement to your ex-husband—while I was busy trying to think of a really cool way of doing it, by the way, at your request."

"I said I was sorry."

"No, you didn't. But I accept your apology anyway." She grew pensive. "Mmm. This is a tough one. You can't exactly just go up to him and tell him, 'Sorry, honey, I made a mistake. I think I'm in love with someone else.' Not ten minutes after you accepted his proposal."

"Me? I'm not in love. There's nothing like that between Steve and me."

"Sure there isn't," Brenda said skeptically. "Tell me you don't want to rip his clothes off and drag him into the closest bedroom every time you see him," she demanded.

"Steve and I don't have that kind of relationship," Charlie insisted.

"If you don't already, you will soon," Brenda predicted. "It's in his eyes, and yours, whenever you look at each other. Unless, of course, you get married."

Twenty

Later that evening, Charlie visited the graveyard. She needed to commune with nature, or the spirits, anyone or anything wiser than herself. "I realized almost as soon as the words were out of my mouth that I made a big mistake," she told her grandmother. "I couldn't take it back, though. Arthur was running around like a fool, kissing and hugging everyone in sight."

She didn't want him after all. She'd outgrown her old dreams, and she had started to chase some great new ones. She didn't want to give all that up for Arthur. And that's exactly what she'd have to do, she realized, if she went through with this marriage.

A year ago, even a few months ago, she could have called Steve and asked for his help with the strange dilemma in which she found herself. But it seemed like it had been a long time since she could call on him. He used to be her rock. Now he was a big part of the reason that she was in this predicament in the first place.

Tired of going round and round with her own thoughts, Charlie called Brenda at midnight. Luckily her friend wasn't asleep. "Ten years I spent, waiting for Arthur to come home and beg me for a second chance, and now here he is, ring in hand, and I don't want him," she said wistfully. "Why does it have to be like that?"

"I don't know, girl. Things are the way they are."

"He doesn't really want me, you know. He just thinks he does."

"Like you just thought you did?" her unsympathetic friend pointed out.

"So what do I do? How do I get him to understand?" Charlie asked.

"Hey, you keep forgetting. I'm not supposed to help you anymore, remember?" Brenda mocked her.

"I'm lifting the ban. This is an emergency."

"Well then . . . do you know any women you might pass him on to?" she asked.

"Pass him on to? You're kidding, right? He's not a—"

"It's the perfect solution. He's happy. She's happy. You're happy." She laid it out neatly.

"But . . . well, maybe I know one woman. Deirdre Cox. She's a doctor who works with him in the hospital and she seems nice, and driven. She's single," Charlie offered.

"Perfect. Now how can we get them together?" Brenda mused.

"We can't. Don't be ridiculous. I can't fix my fiancé up with another woman," Charlie protested.

"I'm not saying it's a foolproof plan, but this is an emergency, right? That's why you're calling in the middle of the night?"

"Yeah," Charlie said doubtfully.

"So? Have you got a better idea?"

"I'm just going to have to tell him the truth."

"Which is what?" Brenda inquired. "What are you going to tell him?"

"Well, that I spoke too soon. I'm not ready for that kind of commitment yet." Said aloud, it sounded lame, even to her own ears.

"Girl, you married the man when you were sixteen years old. He knows perfectly well that you've *been* ready for years. You just don't want to marry him again, now."

"Well, I can't tell him that."

"He's going to need an explanation. An honest explanation. Or you're going to need a plan."

"I don't have either. I can't explain why I can't marry him, at least not in any way that he'd like. I just know I'd be miserable."

"I admit I didn't think much of the man, or his chances, at first, but now that I've gotten to know him, I think he deserves to know the truth."

Charlie wished she could cry; she could have used the release. But she was too miserable. "So those are your only suggestions? Give him an honest explanation or another woman?"

"Or both," Brenda said. "Actually, that would probably be your best course of action."

"Even if I did agree to this insane idea, how would I ever make it work?"

"What do they like to do in their free time?" Brenda asked. "Arthur and the lady doctor?"

"Surgery?" Charlie said hopelessly.

"Come on, there must be something Arthur enjoys in his free time."

"Me, and Deon, and work. As far as I know, that's it. That's his life."

"Hmm," Brenda mused. "So, he's a workaholic. Maybe he could do something that's related to his work. There is that medical writers' conference coming up that you told me about. Arthur and Deirdre could be on a panel about surgical stuff together."

"I don't know, Brenda, I'm not sure that lying and tricking him is really the way I want to end this relationship."

"Oh, so you prefer brutal honesty. That's going to hurt him a lot more than this. You're trying to fix him up with a woman who might be perfect for him, *because you're not*. Do him a favor. Do yourself a favor. Just try it!"

"I could invite Gordon Watts and Deirdre Cox to dinner. Arthur would like that. He wants me to get to know his friends better."

"Perfect. A dinner party. You'll get Arthur and Deirdre together and if sparks fly then . . . voila! You've introduced him to the future love of his life. If not, well . . . no harm's been done. You share a pleasant meal with some nice people, and you come home."

"You always make these things sound so harmless, but you are really an evil woman," Charlie whined.

"Does that mean you're going to do it?" Brenda asked, slyly.

"I guess it's worth a try."

"Absolutely," her devious friend asserted.

"I want to go on record right now by saying that I do not think this is going to work."

"Fine, your objection is noted. Now, get to work," Brenda urged.

It took Charlie a full twenty-four hours to realize that Brenda's plan was her only acceptable option, crazy as it was. She didn't have anything better. She didn't want to hurt Arthur, and if she told him that she really thought they were wrong for each other, he'd just waste a lot of time and energy trying to prove her wrong. She didn't want to end their short engagement without any explanation, and she didn't want to hurt him by telling him there might be another man in the picture. The next morning she called Arthur's boss, Gordon Watts, and invited him to dinner the following week. He said he was thrilled to hear from her, and accepted. The game was afoot.

Charlie wasn't sure what Deirdre would think when she called the woman out of the blue, but if she was going to do this, she wanted to do it all at once, quickly, before she lost her nerve.

She had to remind Deirdre Cox who she was when she telephoned. "We're having a small dinner party next week, and we were hoping you could join us," she jumped in, as soon as she'd reintroduced herself. "Gordon Watts will be joining Arthur and me, and I'd like a second woman to round out the numbers."

"Thanks," the woman said, sounding if not eager, at least intrigued. Charlie reckoned that she was a tad surprised, but she said, "I'd be happy to come."

The stage was set. Charlie only had to make a few more phone calls. She and Brenda spoke to the people who were organizing the writers' conference, and volunteered Arthur and Deirdre to speak on the subject of their work.

There was only one detail remaining to complete phase one of the harebrained matchmaking scheme. She called Gordon again. She had to enlist the help of the medical director if she wanted to make this work. She couldn't tell the old gentleman what she was really planning; if she said she was trying to set Arthur up with another woman in order to get out of her engagement, he would think she was either incredibly stupid or completely insane. She had to lie to him. "I've done something I'm not proud of," she said. Charlie had heard that the best way to lie was to stick as close to the truth as possible. "I volunteered Arthur, and Deirdre Cox, to speak at a writers' conference on a panel."

"Interesting," Gordon said with his customary sangfroid. "Why did you do that?"

"I thought it would be good for Arthur to do something outside the hospital, and Deirdre told me she loves to read, so I thought she could meet a few authors and keep him company ... so he wouldn't be the only doctor there." Desperate for his approval and afraid that he might see through her thinly disguised plot, Charlie added, "I thought they might make a good team." At least that last was true. They definitely complemented each other. Both Arthur and Deirdre were heart surgeons, and both were also very driven, and dedicated to their work. They even looked well together. *Could it be that simple?* she wondered.

"I like it," Gordon announced.

"Good, because I could use your help," she said. Here came the tricky part. "It would be much easier for Arthur to accept the challenge if he thought it came from you. Do you think you could possibly say that you volunteered them, when I mentioned the conference? Arthur isn't a big fan of medical fiction, and on top of that, he thinks writers are flakes. If I suggest he speak on a panel to novelists, he'll think I'm nuts. You, on the other hand ..."

"No problem, Charlie, leave it to me," Gordon said cheerfully. "I'll have him begging for the chance to help you out."

"Thanks, Gordon. So I'll see you next Tuesday then?"

"I'm looking forward to it. I'm so glad Arthur brought you into our dreary little circle. It's always interesting talking to you, Charlie Brown." He chuckled. "Bye-bye, honey."

She felt a pang of guilt as she realized that if her plan worked, he would actually be helping her to extricate herself from that dreary little circle—and under false pretenses—

but she was able to justify her deception by promising herself that she would still remain his friend, whether she married Arthur or not. She wasn't going to use him and then dump him. She liked him too much. No matter what happened, they would remain friends.

All that was left was to inform Arthur that his presence was required at the dinner party she'd arranged. She brought the subject up with a little trepidation. "I've invited Gordon Watts and your friend Deirdre Cox to dinner on Tuesday."

His reaction was even more dramatic than she expected. He froze, his fork halfway between his plate and his mouth. "You did?" he asked, sounding astonished.

"You always say you want me to get to know your friends better," she said in explication. "A small dinner party seems like a good way to do that."

"Wow, Charlie!" A smile slowly formed on his lips. "I wasn't expecting anything like this." He looked gratified and flattered, and not at all suspicious. "Commencing with your wifely duties already?"

She felt another small pang of guilt at his obvious appreciation, but it was all for a good cause, as Brenda would say, so Charlie steeled herself and barreled on.

"I already like Gordon, so I thought he was a safe bet, and Deirdre ..." She watched his face closely for any reaction to the attractive surgeon's name, but his expression didn't change. "I'd say she seems to have ... potential." When he just continued eating, she tried probing a little. "She's nice, don't you think? Unusually good looking for a doctor."

"Um, sure," Arthur said, distracted. "Maybe we could invite a few more people, make this into some sort of engagement dinner," he suggested.

"No!" Charlie exclaimed with more force than she intended. When he looked at her in surprise, she explained,

"I told Gordon it was going to be a small, intimate dinner. I think he prefers them to big parties. I know I do." He nodded. "Let me do this my own way, okay, Arthur?" she added, for good measure. She didn't want him inviting some nice couple to their party and ruining the ambience she planned to create.

"You're right. This is your affair, and I'm sure you've got your own ideas about how you want it to work out," he said.

If you only knew, Charlie thought, but she just smiled and nodded, relieved.

"So. Wow!" he said again. He dug into his pasta with gusto. "See, I told you you would be a great wife for an up-and-coming young surgeon."

"I wouldn't be so sure of that," she retorted.

The last thing she wanted was for him to fall even more in love with the idea of Charlotte Ann Brown-Ross, perfect wife. "It's more like a test to see if your notion of our married life and mine are compatible."

"A test, huh?" he said. He was so pleased and excited, Charlie almost wished Brenda never came up with the stupid plan. She hadn't realized how easily it could backfire on her. Arthur was so enthusiastic about the silly dinner, she was afraid he was going to want to elope any minute now. She had already told him she wanted to wait until she was accepted in college before she set the date, in the hope that he'd be rooting for her to get into school as soon as possible. She had to maintain a delicate balance here, between appearing to try to make the relationship work and, ultimately, helping him realize that it never could. Maybe she would spill her soup in her lap, she thought, but just as quickly nixed the idea. She didn't want to sabotage the whole evening, she only wanted to show Arthur that there might be a more suitable mate out there for him. She hoped this might give him an opportunity to really notice Deirdre. Charlie thought she just might be the perfect woman for him.

Charlie chose to have the dinner party at Arthur's apartment for a number of reasons, not least of which was the dazzling newness of his furniture. She loved her little house with its eclectic decor, but she just couldn't picture the impeccable Ms. Cox making herself comfortable on her worn-out old sofa. Also Arthur's place was located in Charlottesville and neither of their guests, Deirdre and Gordon, would have as far to travel. Lastly, she didn't have to clean up either before or after the party, since Arthur employed a cleaning service at his place.

She might have guessed that Deirdre Cox would arrive early. "Please excuse the way I look. I just came from surgery," she said as she entered. At first, Charlie thought she might be kidding, since she didn't have a hair out of place, but she didn't crack a smile.

"You look great," Arthur said politely, but without enthusiasm. "We're glad to have you here."

Gordon Watts arrived a few minutes later, promptly at seven. After sitting across the coffee table from Deirdre for five whole minutes making inane conversation, Charlie greeted him with relief. "Thanks so much for coming."

"Thank *you* for inviting me, missy," he said cheerfully.

The conversation grew more lively once he was esconced on the couch next to Deirdre, who seemed to unbend a little in his presence. Arthur, who had been a bit uptight, became positively expansive in the presence of his idol. Neither of the surgeons seemed able to think of anything to talk about besides the hospital.

"Dinner will be ready in a few minutes," Charlie told them. "I've just got to pop into the kitchen for a second."

She rushed out to take the Cornish game hen stuffed with wild rice out of the oven, and melt the butter for the lemon sauce she planned to drizzle over the asparagus.

"Let's alternate: boy, girl, boy, girl," Charlie suggested as she ushered them into the dining area.

The table looked lovely when they all sat down to eat, and Gordon said so. Deirdre, on the other hand, looked a bit taken aback.

"Is anything the matter?" Charlie asked, when Arthur had helped the doctor into her seat.

"I, umm, can't eat anything with citrus fruit. The acid," Deirdre said apologetically. "And I'm allergic to garlic," she added in a rush.

Charlie looked down at her plate in dismay. The asparagus had lemon on it, the wild rice had been cooked in broth with garlic in it, and the salad was prepared with Italian dressing. She had even made garlic bread rather than her usual dinner rolls. There wasn't a single thing on the table that Deirdre Cox could safely eat.

"I'm so sorry," Charlie said. "I didn't know."

"Usually I tell people. I must have forgotten. It's my fault," Deirdre said. "I'm the one who's sorry."

"Don't apologize," Charlie insisted. "We can fix this easily enough. I'll make you some nice pasta with broccoli. I have some nice fresh capellini in the fridge. It'll only take a minute." She started to rise, but Deirdre stopped her.

"I can't eat wheat either, I should have told you. My dietary requirements are complicated," Deirdre said.

"Well, at least I can make you a salad without garlic in the dressing," Charlie said, quickly jumping up from the table before anyone could stop her. She nearly ran to the kitchen. The kitchen didn't have a door, so she could still hear Arthur and their guests as they chatted and ate.

A cell phone beeped. It had to be Deirdre's, she thought.

Sure enough. "I've got to take this," Deirdre said apologetically. "Of course," Gordon said graciously. Arthur didn't say anything.

The salad prepared, Charlie went back out into the living room, where Deirdre was putting on her coat.

"I've got to go. Complications in a post-op case," she explained. "I'm so sorry," she said again.

After Gordon left, and the table was cleared, they collapsed on the couch, each of them much more exhausted than they should have been after a small dinner party. She suspected Arthur was tired because he had been wound up so tightly at the thought of entertaining Dr. Watts, while she herself was very disappointed with the results of her matchmaking.

"Well, that went well," she said ironically.

Arthur took her words at face value. "It went pretty well, except for Deirdre. Why did you invite her?"

"You don't like her? I thought she was a friend of yours."

"We work together, but she isn't an easy person to get to know. She's a real stickler in her work and she reads every medical journal and review."

"You're jealous," Charlie exclaimed, surprised.

"I am not," Arthur denied.

"I have never seen this competitive side of you before," she told him.

"It was rude of her to answer the phone and worse to go on and on. She was just showing off for Gordon."

Charlie stopped listening halfway through his rant. "What the heck *does* she eat?" she wondered aloud.

"I've heard of people having a stick up their butt, but I think she's had one surgically implanted in her spine," Arthur was saying.

Charlie had to agree. "But it's understandable," she said. "I'd be uptight, too, if I never ate."

Twenty-one

She had been avoiding Steve, dropping Deon at school and at the Parker house and picking him up without getting out of the car. But one Saturday afternoon, two weeks after the barbecue, Deon didn't come out of the house when she honked the car horn.

"Hello-o!" she yelled as she let herself into the house. "Guys!" Charlie shouted again. But there was no answer. She went through the front room, into the dining room, and stopped dead. The table was set with Steve's finest china, his mother's silver candlesticks, and a centerpiece composed of a small bouquet of spring flowers. "Steve?" she called, but the house was still.

The doorbell rang, and she went slowly toward it. It seemed something was afoot, and Charlie wasn't sure how she was going to deal with it. A van from Milo's Restaurant was standing in the driveway, and a young man in jeans was standing at the front door with two large bags in his arms. Charlie breathed deep. The aroma issuing from those white paper bags was absolutely heavenly.

"I've got your delivery from Milo's Restaurant."

"There must be some mistake," Charlie told him.

He looked down at the slip of paper in his hand. "This is the right address."

"But I didn't order this," she explained.

"Well, it's paid for, and I can't take it back, so will you please sign for it? Otherwise, it's just going to go in the garbage."

"Okay," she reluctantly agreed. The young man winked at her and left. Charlie carried the food back into the house, tempted to check inside the bags to see what dishes they contained. She had eaten at Milo's only once. Arthur had recently taken her for a romantic dinner there, and she enjoyed it thoroughly. The restaurant really deserved its reputation for serving northern Italian cuisine rivaling that of Washington, D.C.'s finest restaurants.

She had thought Steve had gotten the message, since he hadn't pestered her lately, but it appeared he'd just been biding his time. The scene in his dining room was charming, and romantic, and she was tempted to tell him so, but Charlie definitely didn't want to give him the wrong idea. Or lead him on in any way. She didn't plan to go from mistakenly getting engaged to her ex-husband, to getting romantically involved with her misguided best friend. She would wait for some time to elapse and then she would try talking to him sensibly. She wanted Steve in her life, but only as a friend. This seduction stuff was not good for her equilibrium. She couldn't deal with the idea of her old buddy as a lover.

She was still checking through the bag from Milo's Restaurant when she heard the sound of a car engine outside. She looked out of the window and saw Steve's car pulling into the driveway. The kids were nowhere in sight.

He headed for the kitchen door. She brought the bag of Italian delicacies with her and went into the kitchen to meet him as he entered. "What are you doing here?" he asked, clearly surprised to see her.

"I was supposed to pick Deon up here. I thought. But when I got here, I found . . . this." She led him into the dining room.

"I had to coach an away game this morning. I arranged a sleep-over for Michael and Deon."

"Then what? Who?" All of a sudden, Charlie knew who had done this. "Deon," she blurted out.

"That makes sense," Steve said, calmly. He didn't seem the slightest bit surprised.

"You didn't . . ." she wondered aloud.

"Uh, no. It's not my style," he said. "You should know that by now."

"No, I mean yes, I do," she averred. "Sorry."

"No need to apologize," he assured her.

"When I get my hands on those little . . ." she threatened, balefully.

"Don't be too hard on them," he said. "Their hearts are in the right place."

"I don't suppose you plan to punish your son at all?" she said wryly.

He looked again at the bag she'd placed on the table. "Oh, he'll be punished. It's expensive to eat *in* Milo's restaurant, I can't imagine how much it cost to get it delivered."

"I wouldn't know." Milo's was completely out of her price range. That was why she had made such a fuss about it when Arthur took her there. Which was probably why Deon and Michael chose to order their dinner from the place. She didn't bother to inform Steve of all that. She just shook her head no in answer to his rhetorical question.

"I have the feeling that I'm going to find out exactly how expensive this is, when my credit card statement arrives. And then I'll decide how much Michael will suffer for this. When he gets home, I plan to let him know there will be consequences for this."

"Where are the boys, by the way?" she asked.

"Jahleel invited them to the movies and afterward his parents are taking them to McDonald's. Then they'll drop Michael and Deon back here."

"Why didn't you let me know?" Charlie asked, baffled. It wasn't like Steve to give her son over to someone else's care without telling her, unless it was to one of the baby-sitters they both occasionally employed.

He smiled wryly. "Deon said you gave your permission last night when he called and asked me if Michael could go."

"That sneak!" Charlie cried. "He's been planning this since last night?"

"At least," Steve confirmed. "Manipulative little buggers, aren't they?"

"I can't believe our sons managed to do all this," Charlie said, looking around at the romantic decor.

"Let's see what we've got here," Steve said happily. He opened the first bag. "Mmm. Shrimp."

Charlie started salivating. She couldn't help it. It smelled so good. She swallowed so hard she was sure he heard it.

"Hungry?" Steve asked.

"I don't think so," Charlie answered. "I had a really big breakfast." But she suddenly felt ravenous. It wouldn't be a smart move, though, to share the meal with him.

He started to carry the covered dishes into the living room. "You don't want half of this food to go to waste, do you?"

"Half?" Charlie asked.

"I'm sure going to eat," he said. "Since I'm going to

pay for it." He looked at her knowingly and added, "I promise I'll be good."

She wasn't sure it was wise, but Charlie sat down opposite him at the table. She figured she might as well. One of these days she and Steve were going to have to start sorting out this mess. It would be nice if that could happen today.

They ate and talked and she even found herself responding to his slightly flirtatious remarks. They had done stuff like this before Arthur ever came home, so Charlie knew there was no harm in it. Eventually, she relaxed her guard. They finished the wine and Steve joked, "No dessert? What were those kids thinking?"

"They were probably thinking that if we ate any more of this delicious dinner, we'd put on about twenty pounds each."

"What makes you think our sons have a clue about that kind of thing?"

"I don't know about Michael, but Dean monitors every bite I put in my mouth and he warns me at least once a day that if I keep eating junk food, I am going to get as fat as a rhinoceros."

"He doesn't really *say* that?" Steve said, laughing.

"Of course he does. Single moms have a very different relationship with their kids than single dads. From everything I've seen, you guys can get away with murder. You can eat whatever you want, get as big as a house, and still be a great catch. Guys can even beat each other up for no reason, whereas a woman who beats people up is not considered a fit person, let alone a fit mother. Your kid will spend the rest of his life saying what an amazing guy you were, not because you were a loving and devoted father, but solely because you raised him alone. No matter how hard I work to give my son a safe, comfortable home and no matter how much I love him, people will be convinced—and probably will convince Deon—that he will be scarred for life, and I will be blamed because I didn't provide him with a father."

"That's a pretty gruesome point of view you've got there, honey," Steve said cheerily.

"I'm not making this up. That's just the way it is."

"All except one thing," he disputed.

"Yeah? What?" Charlie asked, prepared to defend any and all of her hypotheses.

"I don't plan to raise my son alone," he said definitely.

That took the wind out of her sails. "Oh" was all Charlie managed to say after that pronouncement.

"Don't look so shocked. You know I've always hoped to marry again," Steve went on.

"I know, and I ... I'm glad you're looking," Charlie lied. She didn't want him herself, but that didn't mean she wanted some other woman to have him.

"So you have said many times," he retorted.

"I meant it," she said. *Then,* she thought. "It would be a shame if you were to end up alone," she told him, but she was thinking that it would be a shame if he did get married and she ended up alone. She wasn't sure which would be worse, Steve married to someone else, or still single and pursuing a romantic relationship with her. He was hers—her friend. She wanted him always to be there for her. If he were married, that would be the end of them. No woman in her right mind would allow her husband to maintain a close friendship with another woman. It would be too threatening. No matter how aboveboard and high-minded the man and the woman were, there was always the chance that something less than platonic might develop. It would be too simple for something to happen between them. The present situation was a perfect illustration. She thought that she and Steve were immune because he worshiped the memory of his late wife and she ... well, she had been fixated on her ex-husband since high school. They were two healthy consenting adults of the opposite sex, so Charlie had known that someday, somehow, they might be . . . drawn together, but she could never picture it actually happening. She still wasn't at all sure why it had.

She certainly wasn't going to ask him though, at least not tonight. The fragile truce they'd maintained throughout the evening was too new and too delicate for her to ask him questions about his feelings about her, or to bring up their attraction to each other. It was over and done. It was out of their systems. And if tonight was any indication, they'd be back on their old familiar footing in no time.

Charlie was waiting when Deon and Michael arrived at the house. They came through the front door quietly. She and Steve listened to them as they hung up their coats, their whispers unintelligible, but with the sound of an argument.

Steve, annoyingly enough, decided to make a joke out of it. "Lucy, you have some 'splainin' to do," he said to Michael and Deon as they came into the room.

Charlie didn't think this was funny, at all. "Why would you boys do such a thing?" she asked. She knew she sounded hurt and angry. She could not hide her feelings from them, and would not have wanted to, even though the boys were clearly embarrassed.

"We're waiting," Steve said.

Michael looked at Deon, who was looking at the floor. "We didn't know what else to do," he said, finally. "We didn't want you to marry Arthur."

"Did you really think that if I had dinner with your father, I would call off the wedding? That doesn't make any sense."

Deon burst out, "I used to think that if Dad came back and married you and we all lived together, then everything would be perfect. We wouldn't have to worry about money, or anything. You wouldn't have to work at Tom's, and you could read all the time, and do all the things you want to do. But nothing worked out like I expected. You like work, now. You're going to college, maybe. And Dad doesn't want you to do any of that stuff. He wants you to come live at his house, and have dinner parties, and maybe babies. It's like he doesn't even care what you want. You can't marry him. You would be happier, and he would be happier, and maybe I'd even be happier, if we lived in two different houses. You could do what you want, and he can do what he wants."

"Like I said, you've got a very perceptive kid there, Charlie." Steve commented.

She shot a look of annoyance at him, then turned to her son. "Come on, Deon, we're going home."

"Now?" he asked, looking from Michael to Steve for help.

"Yes, now," Charlie answered, through gritted teeth.

"Maybe you should calm down a little first," Steve suggested.

"I'm perfectly calm," she said, glaring at him. "My son and I have a few things to discuss with each other. So do you, right?"

"Umm, yeah," he agreed, slowly.

He shrugged at Deon and the ten-year-old preceded her out of the house, hanging his head.

"We were just trying to help," Michael called out of the door after them.

"I know, Michael," Charlie yelled back. She circled the car and looked back up at the porch where he stood, arms at his side, looking from her and Deon into the house, and then back again. He appeared to her to be poised for flight. "We'll be okay, honey. Thanks!" she called to him and was rewarded by the sudden appearance of a wide smile on the little boy's face.

As she drove away, Charlie looked back and watched as he put his hands in his pockets and, shoulders hunched, walked back into his house to his waiting father.

"Deon," she began.

"Yeah?" he said in a small voice.

"I'm not angry with you. Okay?"

"Hm-mm, sure," he answered uncertainly.

"We've already been through this."

"I know."

"I mean, we talked about my getting married," Charlie said.

"I *know*," he said emphatically.

"I thought you were getting used to the idea of Arthur and me remarrying. I mean, I know you're a little nervous, but you seemed happier about it. Why would you do this now?"

"I didn't think you were really going to do it, Mom. I still can't believe it."

"Why on earth not?" she asked, flabbergasted.

"Because Arthur's such a . . . a . . . doofus, I guess. Really. You can do better. That's why Michael and I thought this might be a good time for you to have a date with the coach. He's much cooler than Dad. We thought you might see what you'd be giving up."

"Even if I agreed with you about your dad being uncool, which I don't, how could you lie and cheat and steal like that? I didn't raise you to behave that way."

"But you and Brenda set Dad up with some chick," he argued.

"Don't call her a chick. It's rude," Charlie said automatically, while her brain worked furiously on a response to his accusation. He must have overheard one of her conversations with Brenda about their stupid plan. "What do you know about Deirdre?" she asked.

"I heard Brenda talking about Daddy and Deirdre last week, saying how they'd make a good couple, but you just laughed, so I figured she was joking. And then last night, I heard you on the phone. I wasn't really listening, but it didn't sound like a joke anymore when you said that the setup didn't work, so then I thought you didn't really want to marry Daddy after all. When you said, 'I guess I'll have to marry him then, because I'm not telling him that,' I thought you might need a little help, so I told Michael about it; then we got the idea to do the same thing to you and Steve. I didn't think we could really do it at first, but Michael said we would go to Jahleel's house and—"

Charlie only half listened as Deon continued to reveal the devious plot that he and his little friend had come up with, as she turned over various explanations and excuses for her own behavior in her mind. Her regrettable actions were no excuse for his and Michael's transgression—especially not their use of Steve's credit card. It did go a long way toward explaining why her innocent young son came up with such a nefarious scheme.

When Deon got to the end of his long, rambling story about how he and Michael managed to arrange the whole stunt, Charlie still didn't have any words of wisdom for him. At least none that didn't sound hypocritical. "This is not something to be proud of, young man," she began. "You *stole* Steve's money when you borrowed his credit card number, and you lied to him when you said I gave you permission to go to Jahleel's house. Worst of all, you lied to me. Not just about your sleep-over with Michael, but when you didn't tell me how you were really feeling about my marrying your dad."

"I tried—" he started to argue.

She cut him off. "Not hard enough." Charlie took a deep breath. "I shouldn't have done what I did—setting Arthur and Deirdre up on a date. It was a stupid idea, and it wasn't fair to your father or to Ms. Cox. If I had thought for one second how it might seem to you, or anyone else, I might even have figured that out a lot sooner. But, anyway, I've learned something from all of this, and that is that I have to be honest with Arthur, and tell him I don't want to marry him.''

''Really?'' Deon said, sounding very impressed. ''Because of me?'' He smiled.

''That doesn't mean that you are off the hook, my boy. What you did was wrong.'' His smile slowly disappeared. ''Don't try to tell me you didn't know it, either.''

He shrugged. ''I guess,'' he mumbled.

''You know that the first rule of our house is you have to let me know where you are every minute. And you also knew that ordering expensive food using someone else's money is stealing.''

''Michael and I didn't think he'd mind because he loves you, like we do, Mom. Michael and me think he *wants* to date you anyway. All the signs are there.''

''Deon!'' she said sharply. ''I can understand that you might have thought it was fun to trick me and Steve, but I think deep down you knew I wouldn't appreciate being manipulated by you guys. It was sneaky.''

''Sorry, Mom,'' he said. He sounded like he really meant it this time.

''We'll discuss your punishment tomorrow,'' Charlie said, and left it at that.

Twenty-two

There was no punishment that she could give her son that could be as bad as what she herself had to do now. He'd been grounded all week and, as further penance, Deon wasn't allowed to go to his father's that weekend, but had to stay home, doing his homework. "If you finish with that before I get home, clean your room," his mother ordered.

"But it's already clean," he protested.

"I don't mean make your bed, or pick up your toys. I mean vacuum, dust, wash the windows . . ."

"Aww, man," he groaned.

Brenda was baby-sitting under strict orders not to let him play any games, turn on the television, or speak on the telephone. That was Brenda's punishment for her part in the affair, although the woman didn't know it. Charlie derived a certain grim satisfaction from seeing the former Wall Street wiz sitting at her kitchen table, trying to help Deon with his math homework.

Charlie herself had to tell Arthur that she couldn't marry him. She dreaded it. When she left Brenda and Deon at her house, Charlie felt the two of them had gotten off easily, compared with what she was facing.

She had told Arthur that she wouldn't be dropping Deon off this morning, but she would be by to explain. Charlie tried to figure out what she was going to say to him on the drive to his place. She was still rehearsing her part of the conversation—acting out his possible responses as well—when she arrived at his building.

She turned the car off. "Arthur, I shouldn't have accepted your proposal. I can't marry you." She put her head down on the steering wheel. Charlie could imagine his hurt expression, the arguments he would make, his disbelief and anger as he realized that she was actually refusing his offer of marriage.

"I can't face this," she moaned.

When he let her into the apartment, he seemed distracted. He kissed the air near her left cheek and turned away. "Come on in, Charlie," he said, leading her into the living room, where Deirdre was sitting on the couch, a legal pad on her lap, papers and a laptop set on the coffeetable in front of her. "Deirdre and I have been working on an article on chest wall resection," Arthur said in explication. "I thought we'd be done by the time you arrived, but it's taking much longer than I expected to outline the material we want to cover in this piece. Would you like a cup of coffee?"

"Uh, sure," she said, stunned at finding the woman there. Charlie certainly couldn't tell him what she'd come to tell him in front of Deirdre.

"Me, too," Deirdre called as Arthur started toward the kitchen.

"I'll help," Charlie offered, following him. The kitchen wasn't big and homey like hers, but it sparkled. Shiny new appliances sat atop gleaming countertops. The coffeemaker was a far cry from her battered percolator.

Arthur put coffee beans in the grinder and then turned to her as it whirred behind him. "You wanted to talk to me about Deon?"

"Umm, he can't come to visit you this weekend, he's under house arrest."

"What did he do?" he asked curiously.

"It's a long, complicated story," she answered. *With luck*, she thought, *you will never hear it.* "I couldn't put off his punishment, I'm sorry."

"No problem. We'll switch, okay? I'll take him next weekend."

"Sure," Charlie agreed.

"So if it wasn't Deon you wanted to talk about, what was it?" He looked at her inquisitively as he poured the ground beans into his coffeemaker.

"Well, uh, I . . ." she said, faltering. "I think it would be better if we spoke alone. I mean, after Deirdre leaves."

"This sounds ominous," he said. "Give me a hint, so I can prepare myself."

"No, no. She's waiting for you out there. I don't want to be rude."

"Ha," he snorted. "The house could blow up and she wouldn't notice. She's got a one-track mind and right now she's focused on outlining the article. And when I say focused, I mean the girl has tunnel vision. Talk about concentration!" He said it derisively, but Charlie could hear an undertone of admiration in his voice.

"Finish up your article," Charlie instructed. "I can come by later. Or tomorrow."

When she arrived at home, Steve was waiting for her. "I sent Brenda home and Michael and Deon are upstairs doing their homework together," he said.

"Not much of a penalty, is it, if the two of them get to spend their afternoon goofing off together?" she pointed out.

"Don't worry, I'm watching and listening. At the first sound of fun, I will pop my head in and tell them to cut it out," he assured her. "I wanted to talk to you, so I called. Brenda told me you'd gone to speak with Arthur and left Deon here at home. How'd it go?" he asked eagerly.

"How'd what go?" she answered, turning from him to walk into the living room. Charlie collapsed onto the couch.

"Your little talk. How did he take it?" he demanded, facing her.

"I couldn't tell him," she reported.

"But you were going to tell him the wedding is off?" he asked. "Right?"

"Yes," she admitted. "That's why I went over there. But I *couldn't* tell him. He wasn't alone."

"Who was there?" he asked suspiciously.

"Deirdre," Charlie told him.

He didn't know about her matchmaking scheme and he didn't recognize the name, that was clear from his expression. "Another woman?" he asked incredulously. "That should have made it easier."

"No, it was nothing like that. Believe me," she added forcefully. "They're working on an article together. It's just, I wouldn't say anything in front of her and it wasn't clear how long she'd be there, so I had a cup of coffee with them while they talked about cardioenthrepomyology or whatever, and then I got out of there and left them to it."

"Oh," he said, deflated, sitting down next to her.

"Yeah," Charlie agreed.

"So, nothing's changed."

"He knows that I have something important to tell him,

in private, but I don't think he has a clue what it's all about,'' she said unhappily.

He sat silently, pondering this for a moment, then turned to her. ''You are going to tell him you don't want to marry him, aren't you? You're sure?''

''Yeah, I've got to tell him,'' she confirmed.

''Well, I didn't want to say anything until you were completely free, but I can't wait. I've got to tell you how I feel now, Charlie.''

She couldn't do this right now. She was tired, and thoroughly miserable, and at the end of her tether. She didn't want to argue with him.

''This isn't really a good time for us to talk.'' She tried to put him off. ''I know we have a few things to work out, but there's plenty of time for that later. Can't this wait until I'm feeling a little less like a basket case?'' she begged.

''I don't think so,'' Steve said. He turned to face her. ''You are waiting for all of this to blow over, but I don't want things to go back to the way they were. I don't want to be friends with you anymore, Charlie. I want you.''

''That's too bad,'' she said. ''Once things settle down—'' she started.

He interrupted her. ''I don't think so,'' he said. He reached out and slowly, inexorably, turned her body toward his. His massive hands wrapped around her upper arms, he shook her gently and held her until she looked up at him. ''I'm in love with you,'' he said simply.

''Steve—'' Charlie began, but that was as far as she got.

''I've been in love with you for years, but I couldn't admit it,'' he said. Charlie tried to pull out of his grasp, but he wouldn't let her go. ''You've got to hear me out. You owe me that.'' He didn't wait for her to respond, but went on quickly, ''For the past few years, I couldn't admit I loved you. It was easier to pretend we were just friends. I could care for you, spend all my free time with you and enjoy your company, celebrate the holidays and pretend to be a family . . . I could even say I loved you—as a friend.'' The words tumbled out of his mouth in a torrent, hammering at her, confusing her. ''I had to keep dating those women we have spent so much time talking about, so that I could keep this fantasy alive that—even though I wanted to be near you and couldn't stand the thought of losing you—I wasn't being disloyal to my wife's memory.'' Charlie pulled out of his grasp, finally, but she couldn't bring herself to move away; she was caught, bewildered by the sheer intensity of his painful confession. ''As long as I wasn't dating you, and I was dating other women, it wasn't—technically—a betrayal, I felt like Gloria wouldn't mind it.''

She wanted desperately to comfort him, but didn't know how to do that without touching him. And she couldn't touch him. She had to keep her hands to herself, to hold on to at least that much of herself.

''I know, Steve,'' she murmured.

''Gloria would have loved you, I'm sure of that,'' he said.

''I know all about it, Steve. I felt the same way,'' she said, forcing herself to hold his gaze.

''So you must know that things are different now. I can't keep pretending.''

''Steve—'' she started to protest, but he went on talking.

''It was Michael, and Deon, who woke me up. Thank God for our kids. They're much smarter than we are. They knew, instinctively, that we were headed in the wrong direction.'' He started to reach for her again, but she held up her hands and he stopped.

''Steve, our kids love us, and so they want us to be together,'' she said gently. ''And it's playing right into this fantasy of yours, that you're in love with me. We love each other. We're friends. We'll always be friends. We don't have to be a couple to stay together. I promise you," she vowed. "You don't have to do this."

"That's not why I'm telling you this, now," he claimed. "I don't know how many ways I can say this, so you can hear me, but I'm not going to give up until you do. *I am in love with you.*" He said it so urgently that, despite herself, Charlie felt herself leaning in toward him—giving in to his desperation. He kissed her, and she let him. His lips were soft, the kiss tender. "I want you, Charlie. I know you don't believe me, but I'm going to keep saying it and showing you, every way that I can, until you believe it."

"It's not that I don't believe you. I just think you're a little confused. You're afraid that you'll lose me. Like you lost your wife. But I'm not going anywhere. I can promise you I'm not leaving. I'm staying right here. For you."

He sat back, and she thought she had finally gotten through to him, but it wasn't comprehension she saw in his eyes, it was determination. "I'm not confusing you with Gloria. I couldn't do that. I know who you are, Charlie," he said with complete certainty. "Maybe you're getting me confused with Arthur, though. You think I can't really love you, or want you, because he didn't. But I'm not him, Charlie. We're not those kids."

Something clicked into place, and she suddenly understood what was really going on. He was right. In a way. He wasn't Arthur, and she wasn't seventeen anymore. She had just figured out that she'd been wrong about what was causing him to say this now. His timing had bothered her all along, but in a way it made sense. Finally.

"Steve, listen to me," she said. "I think I know what's happened to us. I thought that you were only interested in me because suddenly I was one of those sophisticated, independent, *unavailable* women you've been dating—

looking for Ms. Right. But it wasn't that. It was something else.''

"I know!" he shouted. "That's what I've been trying to tell you.''

"No, no! Let me finish. I've been your buddy, almost a mother to your son, and someone safe, someone you could love while staying faithful to your wife. That's what *you* just said. And you were right. That's what I was, and that's what I am, right now. But that's going to be taken away from you, and that's why you think you're in love with me.''

"You've got it wrong, Charlie. That's not what I was saying. It's not my feelings for Gloria that held me back. It was your feelings for Arthur. We've been building something all along. The thing with Arthur *wasn't* just an excuse I needed to act.''

"Right," she said cynically. "You just happened to fall in love with me when Arthur came back and I agreed to marry him.''

"No. That's what I've been trying to tell you. There was nothing sudden about my feelings for you. I wanted you for a long time. I have loved you for a long time.''

"Sure you did," she said, her voice dripping with sarcasm.

"I didn't act on it because I knew *you* didn't want me. You were still hung up on Doc. Or at least on your memories of him. And that was all right, because I still had you. Somewhere, deep down, I always thought you might want me, once you got over what Arthur did to you. And you've done that now. *That's* why this is happening now.''

But she was shaking her head. "We've been friends for years, completely platonic friends. We spent every almost every Sunday morning talking about the women you dated. Do you think we could have done that if we were in love all along?''

"Absolutely. That's why I didn't want any of those women. The reason we kept ruling them out as marriage material was that subconsciously I wanted to marry the best woman I knew. You."

"Now you want to *marry* me?" she asked incredulously.

"Yes, I do," he said solemnly. "Lately, I've been thinking about it a lot."

"This is ridiculous," Charlie said, somewhat angrily. "Steve, you can't be serious."

"I was never more serious about anything in my life," he said earnestly. "Charlie, you love me."

"Maybe I do, but . . . talk about jumping out of the frying pan and into the fire!" she exclaimed.

"I know you've been comparing me with Doc," he said knowingly.

She had certainly wondered how he would compare with Arthur as a lover. "Okay, but that was . . . I was . . ." She'd been fantasizing about him, his body, his hands, and the way he made her skin warm and her blood sing, and she couldn't tell him that. "I never considered marrying you instead of him."

"I did. When I thought you were going to marry him, I got a very clear image in my mind of you as a wife. Not his wife. My wife. It's obvious that we are very compatible—our lifestyles, our beliefs, our body chemistry—"

"All right!" Charlie cried. "I agree you and I have more in common than he and I did. We want more of the same things. That doesn't mean we should get married."

"What would?" he asked.

"What?" she blurted.

"What would it take to convince you?" he asked. "We're friends, we're attracted to each other, we want the same things, we love each other. If that isn't enough, what is it that would persuade you that we should get married?"

"It's not something you have to persuade yourself to do. Marriage is ... marriage is difficult enough without ... these kinds of complications."

"I didn't say it would be easy."

"I mean, it should feel natural. Not like this."

"It feels perfectly natural to me," he retorted.

"It's not just a solution to loneliness, or to make our kids happy. It's ... really ... hard."

"I was married, too, you know. I remember. I know it's tough. And I know it's scary. Terrifying even. But it's worth it. When it works, it's definitely worth it. And we could make it work, Charlie. If we try."

"I don't want to try," she said, exasperated. "I just want things to go back to the way they were. I was happy. Deon was happy. You were happy. Michael was happy. What's wrong with that?"

"This," he said. His arms were around her and his lips on hers before she could register his intention. This was nothing like the sweet, gentle kiss he'd given her a few minutes ago. His hands held her close against him, her chest crushed against his, her arms caught at her sides. His mouth was hot, hungry, and firm, as it pressed against her mouth, her cheek, her eyelids.

"Listen to me," he growled into her ear, sending a shiver right down her spine. "I can see right through you when we're this close together. I know how you feel right now. You can't hide it, Charlie."

She gave in. Pulling her arms free, she wrapped them around his neck. "Okay," she panted. "I believe you."

"So you'll tell Doc you're not going to marry him. You're going to marry me?" His breathing was as harsh as hers as he kissed her jaw, her chin, and then her lips again, deeply, triumphantly, desperately.

"Yes," Charlie said when she caught her breath. "I'll tell him."

"Good." He swung her body across his, so he could reach every inch of her, and then his hand traveled down her side, from her waist to her toes, as if he were branding her, marking her as his with his palm. His hand returned along the same path, stopping just below her breast, and she moaned softly, urgently, until he cupped the aching mound of flesh in his large hand. She'd been waiting for this for too long and could not wait any longer. She arched her back up into him, and he inhaled with a long rasping breath and buried his head in her shoulder. Charlie didn't know which of them was trembling more, or whose skin burned hotter, and she didn't care.

He raised his head for a moment to look down at her face. She opened her eyes and met his hot, ardent gaze. "Say it," he ordered. "You love me."

She did, so she said, "I love you," obediently. He lowered his head again, but she put her fingertips over his mouth. "Words are cheap," Charlie quipped. "I'll show you."

He lifted her off the couch into his arms and carried her toward the stairs to her bedroom. "Steve, Deon and Brenda are up there," she reminded him.

He halted where he stood. "Oh, right," he said. "I forgot."

"Are you going to put me down?" she asked breathlessly, as he stood thinking.

"Not if I don't have to." He swung around and started toward the front of the house.

"Where are we going?" Charlie laughed.

"My place," he answered.

He was strong. She felt safe in his arms. Still she had to ask, "Are you planning to carry me all that way?"

"No," he said. "We'll drive."

She couldn't argue with that. She couldn't wait to be alone with him. Charlie snuggled up against his broad chest and smiled to herself. She was engaged to the love of her life. Again. It was the second time in two weeks.

She felt a twinge of guilt as she thought of Arthur. "Maybe we should wait," she said aloud. "Till I talk to Arthur?"

"No chance," Steve said as they reached the car and he set her on her feet. He kissed her. Hard. "Ten years is long enough to save yourself for a guy who's too stupid to keep a woman like you. We're not waiting another minute for his sake. He doesn't deserve it."

"You're pretty hard on him."

"He's a jerk."

"I wasn't really thinking of him. He's happier not knowing. I thought it might be better for us if we did this with a clear conscience."

"Better for us. After five years of foreplay? I hate to tell ya, babe. But this is about as good as sex is gonna get."

"I don't know," she said, still unsure.

"Tell you what. You can tell him tomorrow and afterward we can do it again and see if it feels any different," Steve offered.

On Sunday, Arthur was on call, but Charlie couldn't wait any longer to end her engagement. It had gone on too long already. She went to see Arthur at the hospital and told him she had to speak with him about something important.

He looked at her speculatively, then said, "I can't get away for long. Can we talk over coffee in the cafeteria?"

She agreed, wishing it could be someplace more private, but unwilling to wait another minute to do what she had to do. "What do you see when you look at me, Arthur?" she asked when they were seated at the Formica table.

He thought about it for a moment, looking at her, but at the same time, she felt, looking inward. She could almost see herself as he did, in his mind's eye—preserved forever as a naive, loving, seventeen-year-old girl. "I see my future—someone to share everything I've worked for and help me build the life and the family I've always wanted."

"That's not me. That's who you want me to be. The woman you've described is . . . more like Deirdre. She could share your life and enjoy it. You and I would always be pulling in different directions."

"I don't believe that. Not for a minute. You're my Charlotte, my beautiful girl. You don't have a self-absorbed bone in your body. And that's not up for debate. That's a fact. The proof is in the fact that, even though I didn't deserve it, you kept on loving me after I left."

"I wanted you to see me that way. I convinced myself that that was what I really was. But I'm not. Not anymore. Can't you see that?"

"I see a wonderful woman who will always be there for me, no matter what comes, good or bad, and I want to spend the rest of my life proving that I'm worthy of that love."

"Why do you think I'll always be there? Just because I was still here when you decided to come home? Because I took you back?"

"Because you became the woman you became. No one, no one but you, can be the mother of my son. Deirdre could not, or would not, have raised him, loved him, like you did. No one else can be his family with me. I walked away from you once. It was the biggest mistake of my life."

Charlie sighed. "I always thought we should have stayed together, that maybe I should have gone with you, followed you, but maybe things happened the way they did for a reason. For ten years, I told myself that you made mistakes, and I made mistakes, and if we only got back together, we could correct them. Now, I think we did what we were meant to do.'' She kept her eyes locked on his, watching his face change as he listened to her, willing him to understand.

"No," he said emphatically. "No."

"Think about it, Arthur. If you had been different, you wouldn't have left, and if I had been different, I wouldn't have blamed myself. But we were who we were."

"I've changed," he insisted.

"You can't change. Not at that basic level. Neither can I. I always thought we wanted the same things. It turns out, I want what I've got and you want what you've got—not what you could have had."

"But I'm telling you, I know what I want. My family. Together. Finally. All of us in the same place at the same time."

"That's just it. We're not all in the same place. We don't even want to be. You said it when you left—Frementon wasn't where you wanted to end up. I do. I want to grow old here in my little house, with my family—past and present and future."

"I don't believe you," he replied. "This little hick town isn't enough for you. I know that."

"It's not everything I want. It's just a starting place. I still dream of visiting exotic lands. I want to travel, and see the world, and try new things. All I'm trying to say is that I wouldn't want to leave if I didn't have this farm to come home to. I believe I can do anything, go anywhere, live my dreams, and that's because I come from this place, this amazing place, where—for generations—my family has been. They started out and ended up *here*, don't you see?"

"We can plan to retire here, if that's what you really want—" he started to say, but Charlie shook her head, stopping him midsentence.

"It's no good, honey. I can't marry you because I don't love you and you don't love me."

"You can't speak for me. You don't know what I feel." She could tell that he didn't believe her. He was clinging to his illusions. He'd been so sure, for so long, that marriage to her was what he wanted, that he couldn't recognize the truth. She didn't blame him. She had done the same thing for long enough to know exactly what he was going through.

"All right then," she said wearily. "I don't know what you feel. I do know you want something I can't give you. You have made that very clear. As long as you want me the way I was, you can't want the person I am now. If we tried to force it, we'd only end up hurting each other and I don't want to hurt you."

"So don't hurt me," he said. "We can work this out."

"I can't marry you, Arthur," she repeated.

"You can't just end it like this," he protested.

"I have to." It had taken Deon's desperation, Michael's adoration, *and* Steven Parker's love to bring her around. Charlie wished she could help her ex-husband to come to the same realization that she had. There was no such thing as destiny when it came to love. It was something that had to be fed and nurtured and cherished, or it died. That was what had happened to them—their love had died for lack of real nourishment. It left behind fond memories, and, hopefully, a lifetime of friendly, warm feelings between them, as well as a child they would share for the rest of their days.

"I'm sorry." He was going to have to come to that understanding on his own. She couldn't teach it to him, or explain it to him. He'd have to sort it out for himself. "Goodbye, Arthur," she said sadly, and left him sitting there.

* * *

After work on Monday, Charlie was exhausted. She headed home feeling slightly depressed. Arthur hadn't returned her phone call from that morning, so she didn't know whether to plan on picking her son up after school on Tuesday, since his father usually did it. She didn't care about planning out the following evening, so much as she worried about how Arthur was handling their broken engagement. They hadn't spoken since she left him in the cafeteria Sunday afternoon.

Deon would cheer her up when she got home, she knew. He was absolutely thrilled about Steve and her, and he and Michael were busy congratulating themselves on the success of their machinations. He wasn't unsympathetic to his father's pain, but she was a little nervous about how he would act, and what he might say, when he saw Arthur again. He was a pretty sensitive boy, so she was hoping for the best. She had had a serious talk with him about showing that he was sympathetic, even if he did think everything had worked out for the best, but she hadn't been certain that he understood her until she saw him with Gandy, the previous night. The old man had come to Sunday dinner. It had been the first time since Arthur's return that he had been at the farm without his grandson, and he was clearly broken-hearted. Deon had consoled his great-grandfather, not with words, but with a casual pat on the old man's hand or his head, and a long hug when Gandy left.

When she arrived at the house, Deon wasn't alone. Steve and Michael were waiting there with him, and the three of them had prepared a spaghetti dinner.

"This was just what I needed," Charlie said as she sat down at the table. "Thanks, guys."

"And it's Monday night, so we can watch *Seventh Heaven* later," Steve said, winking at the boys.

"So you three can make fun of me," she said. "No way.

I'm going to tape it. I've already set the cassette recorder,'' Charlie told him.

"Oh.'' He looked taken aback.

After dinner, while the boys washed the dishes, they sat on the couch and he suggested again that they watch her favorite television program. "It's coming on in twenty minutes,'' he said. "I won't let the boys tease you, I promise. I'm sure they'd be happy to go up to Deon's room and do homework . . . and leave us alone.''

"You realize this spirit of acceptance and cooperation isn't going to last,'' she pointed out.

"I know. So let's take advantage while it does,'' he said.

"Mmm-hmmm,'' she said, eyeing him speculatively. "You're more devious than I thought.''

"Why, because I want to be alone with you?'' he asked, feigning innocence.

"Well, as long as we're going to be alone . . .'' she said, snuggling up against him.

"So you don't want to watch your show?'' he asked, waggling the remote control at her. "Got the tissues all ready for you, you know. And I promise I won't laugh.''

"I thought we could neck,'' she suggested, raising her eyebrows at him, suggestively.

"Sure,'' he said, putting the remote control on the closest end table. "I just thought . . .''

"What?'' she asked.

"Nothing.'' He sighed.

"Come on, tell me,'' she urged.

"I wanted to find out if Lucy said yes,'' he confessed.

Charlie couldn't help laughing. "I can't believe it. I got you hooked on *Seventh Heaven*,'' she cried triumphantly.

"At least it doesn't make me cry,'' Steve said, defensive.

"We can watch if you want,'' she offered.

"Okay,'' he said, happily. "Then we can neck.''

Epilogue

Arthur was feeling surprisingly good. He hadn't wanted to go to Charlie's wedding, and only agreed because Deon had mounted a campaign against him that had been as inexorable as Sherman's famous March on Atlanta. Arthur had been dreading the entire event, but now that he was here he didn't feel too bad at all. It was a beautiful summer day. The sun shone brightly, but not as brightly as his Charlie and her new husband, who were so clearly in love with each other it made his heart swell to look at them.

Deon bounded up to him. "Come on, Dad. There's tons to eat." His son grabbed his hand and pulled him toward the massive tables that had been laden with mountains of good country fare, for the enjoyment of the wedding guests, who were all partaking liberally. It seemed Charlie and Steve had invited most of the county to celebrate the day with them, and most of the county had accepted the invitation.

The ceremony was performed in his ex-wife's backyard,

under a canopy of white. The lush green grass beneath their feet, the pale blue sky above, and the pine woods beyond them, sloping upward into the hills, all combined to form a more inspiring setting than any church Arthur had ever seen. The sound of the stream that ran through the trees at the eastern edge of her property was a lovely complement to the small trio of local musicians who sat playing soft jazz beside an area under the canopy that had been cleared of chairs and tables to form a soft but quite adequate dance floor.

A few couples swayed back and forth to the music, but most of the guests were eating, seated at the small tables, draped with white linen and graced with small centerpieces composed of flowers and white ribbons and lace. Others were scattered about the lawn in small groups, talking and laughing, the indistinct murmur of their voices and the shouts of the children who ran about everywhere combining to make him feel oddly content. None of these people, many of whom he had known since childhood, had made Arthur feel the least bit out of place, despite his recent aborted engagement to the bride. That had been one of the things he'd feared the most about attending this event, along with the raised eyebrows, the whispers, the snickers of those who had been present for the announcement of that engagement. But everyone here had welcomed him without a hint of surprise or pity in their expressions. He was one of their own, and nothing could change that.

The seating arrangements were informal, but when Deon and he brought their plates back to the tables, Arthur found himself sitting at Gordon Watts's table, beside Deirdre Cox. He was somewhat surprised to see her there, but figured she had probably not wanted to miss an opportunity to schmooze with the big boss. It was typical of her to take advantage of any chance to further her career. Not that there was anything inherently wrong with trying to advance in your chosen profession. Arthur was all for that, himself. Gordon Watts was the medical director, in charge of the entire hospital, and you could have knocked Arthur over with a feather when the renowned old surgeon took an instant liking to Charlie at one of the hospital functions that Arthur had taken her to when they started dating. Arthur envied his ex-wife's friendly relationship with the hospital bigwig. He'd have bet any amount of money that Ms. Cox had attended the wedding purely for the chance to socialize with Gordon Watts. The old man and Charlie had become good friends in the short time they'd known each other. He had even taken part in the wedding. Charlie had asked him to "give her away," and he had agreed without hesitation.

Arthur guessed Deirdre was green with envy. "Hi, Deedee," he greeted her, knowing the nickname irritated her. She didn't respond.

He had spent a good deal of time with the annoying woman in the past month since they chaired a panel discussion at a local medical writers' conference, and collaborated on an article about multiple mass chest wall resection. Charlie, who had been one of the organizers of the writers' conference, and had been the one to volunteer both Arthur and Deirdre for the panel they were on together, had suggested that he and the surgeon come to the wedding together, but Arthur had declined. The woman was a barracuda. He watched her, for a moment, as she laid on the charm with the old man. Inwardly, Arthur had to admit, he admired her single-minded devotion to achieving her goals, but he felt sorry for her, too. It was a shame she didn't have anything else in her life besides work.

He turned his attention to Deon, who was shoveling his food into his mouth with speed and determination. "Slow down, son, there's no rush," he admonished.

"Dessert!" Deon said, around a mouthful of hot dog.

"It will still be there in ten minutes." Arthur tried to reason with him, without any noticeable effect. "Chew," he ordered.

"We haven't even cut the cake yet," said Charlie, from behind him, making Arthur jump. "You're going to make yourself sick."

"No, I'm not," Deon said, after swallowing half a glass of juice in one gulp. "The faster I eat, the more I can fit in my stomach." He tucked right back into his food.

Charlie laughed, looking at Arthur with a wry expression. "There's no arguing with that."

"I give up," he agreed ruefully. "It won't kill him."

There was a moment, as her smile faded and she looked into his eyes, when things could have been awkward. Just for a second. Then, she smiled again. "Thanks for coming. It really meant a lot to us."

He believed her. She and Steve and Deon had spent the last month trying to make him feel as comfortable as humanly possible in the odd situation they found themselves in.

"It was . . . great," he said, at a loss for words to say all that he felt. "Wonderful."

Charlie looked into his eyes again, searchingly, and then nodded. "Good," she said. "I thought so, too."

Gordon interrupted Deirdre to ask, "May I have this dance, Charlie, honey?"

"Of course," Charlie said, easily. She laid her hand on Arthur's shoulder for a moment, while she waited for Gordon to rise; then she took it away, to put it into the old man's proffered arm.

"Bye, guys. Deon, take it easy," she said, as she turned away.

Arthur watched her go, saddened again at the loss of the woman who had always meant so much to him. Everything, in fact. He had been an idiot to leave her. She was beautiful, charming, graceful as a swan on the dance floor. And she had been his. Once.

"Dad?" Deon's voice woke him out of his reverie.

"Yes, D?" he asked absently.

"Would you like to dance?" It wasn't Deon's voice, but Deirdre's that penetrated the haze of memory and might-have-beens that engulfed him. His son was pointing with his chin toward the woman on his other side. He glanced toward her, to find her gazing at him, half smiling.

"Uh, sure," he mumbled, awkwardly. He stood and helped her out of her chair, as his grandfather would have expected.

On the dance floor, she fit easily into his arms. He relaxed and swayed with her to the soft music, but Arthur still felt slightly dazed, as if he'd just awakened from a long sleep. It was a long time since he had danced with a woman like this—the first time that he hadn't had the thought, somewhere in the back of his mind, that this was just a diversion, that the woman in his arms was only a substitute for the one woman he was meant to dance with for the rest of his life, his Charlie.

"So, Artie?" Deirdre said teasingly. "What do you think?"

"Uh, what?" he asked, stupidly.

"Do you want to come home with me?"

"Huh?" Arthur almost came to a halt in the middle of the dance floor as he drew back a little to look down at her to see if she was kidding. He quickly recovered and drew her to him again, but one glimpse of her face had been enough to assure him that Deirdre Cox was, as always, completely serious. "Uh, well," he stuttered.

"It's a simple question. Do you want to? Or don't you?"

she asked, in her usual, straightforward, single-minded manner.

Arthur wondered briefly what it would be like to have that concentrated intensity directed at him. "Okay," he agreed. "Deirdre." It was the first time he had ever called her by her first name. Usually he called her Dr. Cox, or just plain Doctor, or something less respectful, but Deirdre was a nice name, it had a good feel to it.

She smiled. "Twenty minutes, okay?"

"Twenty minutes," he said and swallowed. "Sounds good."

DO YOU KNOW AN ARABESQUE MAN?

1st Arabesque Man HAROLD JACKSON
Featured on the cover of "Endless Love"
by Carmen Green / Published Sept 2000

92nd Arabesque Man EDMAN REID
Featured on the cover of "Love Lessons"
by Leslie Esdaile / Published Sept 2001

3rd Arabesque Man PAUL HANEY
Featured on the cover of "Holding Out For A Hero"
by Deirdre Savoy / Published Sept 2002

WILL YOUR "ARABESQUE" MAN BE NEXT?

One Grand Prize Winner Will Win:
- 2 Day Trip to New York City
- Professional NYC Photo Shoot
- Picture on the Cover of an Arabesque Romance Novel
- Prize Pack & Profile on Arabesque Website and Newsletter
- $250.00

You Win Too!
- The Nominator of the Grand Prize Winner receives a Prize Pack & profile on Arabesque Website
- $250.00

ARABESQUE
A PRODUCT OF
BET BOOKS